1̲ᵒ

To: Dad & Verne Pearson
Thanks for your talent
comments. Hope you enjoy
reading this as much as
I did writing it.

COUNTDOWN
TO
HELL

BY
GEORGE MEYER

Bloomington, IN Milton Keynes, UK

authorHOUSE®

AuthorHouse™
1663 Liberty Drive, Suite 200
Bloomington, IN 47403
www.authorhouse.com
Phone: 1-800-839-8640

AuthorHouse™ UK Ltd.
500 Avebury Boulevard
Central Milton Keynes, MK9 2BE
www.authorhouse.co.uk
Phone: 08001974150

First published by AuthorHouse 6/15/2007

ISBN: 978-1-4259-9779-3 (sc)

*Printed in the United States of America
Bloomington, Indiana*

This book is printed on acid-free paper.

*This story is a complete work of fiction. All persons and characters
are a product of my imagination and do not depict any person of any
kind. Any relationship to any person, living or deceased is purely
coincidental. Specific names of public places are fictitious and are
intended to instill a feeling of real places. Some locales are included
only to help depict realism to events that are fictitious. Any names or
places that are used are also coincidental and are not intended to refer
to actual situations, people, places or function. There is no intention
of presenting events, which may cause one to misinterpret that this is
anything but a story written to entertain. Which I hope it does!*

ACKNOWLEDGEMENTS

I WISH TO EXPRESS MY appreciation to my daughters, Sheila Breyer and Karen Buesing, who read this repeatedly both for entertainment value, and helping to edit my grammatical and punctuation errors. I am also indebted to my son-in-law Bill Breyer, for reading it over and over to help with some of the technical aspects of the story, for which I am grateful. I am also particularly grateful to Nancy Anderson, who proof read and edited many passages of this effort and provided solid editorial comments. There are others to which I am also indebted but who shall remain anonymous, be assured I owe my appreciation to a number of others.

Thank you each and every one,

George Meyer

CHAPTER 1

THE FLORIDA SUN WAS SETTING in its magnificent array of colors against the western sky as the baby blue Shelby Cobra sped southward on I-95. The driver's short curly brown hair fluttered in the wind as the speeding car wove in and out of the sparse traffic. The driver's face was partially obscured by the dark, reflective sunglasses protecting his intense blue eyes from the harsh rays of the sun. He was intent on his driving, concerned that he was behind schedule, a planned arrival time of early evening in the small coastal town of Cocoa Beach. He was cautious to not be caught in a speed trap, a delay he wanted to avoid. His eyes flicked back and forth between the dash-mounted rear view mirror and the unfolding highway before him. The speedometer hovered between eighty and eighty five miles per hour and produced a throaty growl from the Cobra's open dual exhaust pipes.

As he glanced once more at the mirror, his eyes caught sight of a late model Ford Mustang GT coming up behind him at a fast rate, it closed to within a few feet of the Cobra.

"Hm-mm, looks like somebody wants to play 'chicken'," he said aloud. He didn't increase his speed until the Mustang was almost touching his bumper.

"Looks like a couple of jackass rednecks," Walt Crawford the Cobra driver said to himself, as he saw the flushed, blotchy face of the driver when the passenger handed him another can of beer. Walt increased his speed and the Mustang doggedly hung on his tail.

"OK, that's it you assholes," he suddenly jammed his foot hard on the accelerator pedal. The Cobra abruptly jolted forward, its speed quickly rising to one hundred and thirty miles per hour. The Mustang faded back, completely out of sight and Walt slowed back to eighty. But it wasn't long before the Mustang came racing up, and he could see the men had turned ugly, as they pulled along side. The passenger, with an obscene gesture, screamed at him to pull over.

Not wanting a confrontation that would further delay his travel time, he kept going, ignoring the shouting. He could see they were drunk, as the Mustang weaved back and forth, almost banging into the Cobra.

"All right, guys," he said, easing the Cobra over to the side of the road. As he slowed to a stop he dialed 911 on his cell phone, and reported the harassment and his location according to the last mile marker he had passed. The Mustang slid to a gravel-throwing stop just in front of Walt's car. Both the men threw open their doors, staggering out toward him.

He got out, stepped to the front of his car, and in a deceptively soft voice asked, "You fellas got a problem?"

"Yo damn fuckin right," mouthed the driver, "You think you own thuh road, with yo piss-ant li'l ol' car,"

His bloodshot eyes rolled; his breath reeked of the rotgut they had been drinking, as he leaned against the back of the Mustang, to keep from falling flat

The other man shuffled to Walt's right, with the intention of getting Walt in between them. But with a quick step, Walt moved away, facing the two. For an instant they stared at him.

"Well, thas's OK," the one man said, "Me first, Bubba! I'll coldcock 'im." He swung a fist wildly at Walt, who sidestepped swiftly. The man was big, but he was ungainly and even if he hadn't been drunk, he couldn't touch Walt. Keeping an eye on the other one, Walt stepped close and rammed his right fist into his opponent's midsection. With a gasp, the big man went down, rolling on the ground, struggling to breathe again.

Walt saw the other man whip out a switchblade, the blade snapping out to its six inch length as he tried to slash him. Walt moved sideways, grabbing the man's arm and bent it back until he heard it snap. Bubba screamed in pain, all thought of attacking gone.

Walt admonished them both, "Be nice now, or I'll really have to hurt you." He walked back to his Cobra and sat on the hood to wait for the Highway Patrol. When the men started to rise, Walt stepped over to them and promptly kicked each of them in their ribs and again telling them to be nice and stay put.

A State Trooper arrived a few minutes later and laughingly said, "Well, at last somebody gave you guys what for!" He shook Walt's hand telling him these two had been getting away with attacking tourists up and down the highway. After completing his report they were placed in the rear of the Trooper's car in hand cuffs, albeit with much screaming on the part of the man whose arm Walt had broken.

The entire incident had taken less than 30 minutes, and Walt was permitted to go his way after he had provided the Trooper his location to be, in Cocoa Beach.

He was anxious to hear how operations were progressing and wondered if his late arrival would impact the schedule. He debated between an urge to use his cell phone and the concern for security. He decided that security should override time concerns. He resumed his trip, increasing his speed slightly in an attempt to shave a few minutes off his driving-time. It was after dark, nearly eight, when he finally crossed State Road 520, the Causeway to Cocoa Beach and checked into his motel

His first action after getting to his room was to call the Operations Center at Patrick Air Force Base to ask for Major General Billy Mayfair. The General responded after the first ring, and recognizing the voice of the caller he snapped, "Where in hell are you, Walt? I need you here now!"

He replied, "Sorry sir, but they held me a little longer in Washington than I thought they would. Got a late start and had a little incident on my way and was only able to make up less than an hour, pushing the speed limit at that."

"Well, get here as soon as you can. I want to update you on the situation," said the general, worry evident in his voice.

"I should be there in about twenty minutes or so," he replied.

The harried general merely grunted and hung up. He sighed audibly as he turned to the operations board to check the progress of the specially modified missile as it was being prepared to head out of the build-up area toward the brilliantly lit launch complex.

———————————

Just inside the launch complex razor wire-topped fence, was the interior perimeter road. On its shoulder was a series of massive searchlights, each about five feet in diameter, providing one million candle power of light each, turning the area into near-daylight. They were aimed at different elevations, so that the huge launch tower was completely bathed in light.

It was an immense structure, having twenty five different levels affording access to the missile during its preparation for launch. Each level was designed to allow technicians close accessibility to all parts of the vehicle during its pre-launch buildup. Entry was limited through controlled guard posts. Those who were permitted to enter were subjected to a higher level of background security check, requiring a special badge.

When the tower's huge doors were open, people on the various levels were cautioned to not look directly at the searchlights because of the risk to eyesight. Periodically, each searchlight was shut down to replace the carbon rods, but with some twenty in operation at a time, the down searchlight did not affect the overall degree of light still present. This level of illumination would be maintained until dawn, or until the operation in progress was completed.

———————————

The launch complex was designed to accommodate a very heavy-lift capability missile, able to use additional "strap-on" SRM's, relatively small Solid Rocket Motors, each about 30 inches in diameter and 15 feet long, plus the nozzle protruding another 24 inches. For propulsion the core vehicle first stage used a combination of hypergolic propellants, which ignite upon contact with one another. The second stage used cryogenic propellants, liquid oxygen and liquid hydrogen. The third stage was called a Transtage, it allowed launching an extremely large and heavy payload, within a special nose section that was actually larger in diameter than the core vehicle. It was referred to as the payload fairing, or nosecone, and completely enclosed the spacecraft at launch and during the early portion of flight.

This particular missile was special, modified to carry a super secret payload to an orbit that would allow it to move about in the reaches of space close to Mother Earth. Only highly qualified people were to work on it, necessitating hurried background checks, to be later examined more carefully to verify no mistakes had been made.

This payload could bring to an end all wars and conflicts, once placed in orbit.

Walt Crawford was one of the people selected to participate in this launch. He had brought his Team of specially qualified people together, to be called upon to help military personnel doing the actual launch. Each had been exposed to dangers that had threatened life and limb. They were devoted to Walt in a way seldom understood, unless they had seen the horrors of war in its worst form. They would lay down their lives without question for Walt. Their current task was to support the launch of this 'miracle missile'.

The launch complex was quite large, several hundred feet across, having facilities to handle the commodities necessary for launch. There were separate tank "farms" for the propellants, fuels and oxydizers, always kept separate until loaded aboard the missile itself. Super cold cryogenic liquids required vacuum insulated storage tanks because of their need to be maintained at very low temperatures, thus preserving its liquid state. Liquid hydrogen requires a temperature of minus 423 degrees Fahrenheit, while liquid oxygen needs minus 297.4 degrees. Maintaining these super-cold temperatures was a major task in itself.

Altogether, the complex presented an extremely hazardous condition when readied for launch. With propellants present, restricted access was necessary. Special training was required in order to be present when any of the propellants were being transferred from cross-country trucks to the complex storage tanks or from the tanks to the missile itself. Walt was genuinely attentive for this aspect of his indoctrination training. He became aware of the extreme complexity of each operation and the care needed to ready this missile for launch.

Since liquid hydrogen only weighs about one half pound per gallon, the transport trucks were huge and required special insulation to maintain the hydrogen in a liquid state. It is sometimes seemingly ridiculous to see one of these monstrous cross-country trucks halted at a roadside stop, being lurched back and forth. After being hauled cross-country in the heat of the day some of the liquid hydrogen would gas off and build unwanted pressure inside its tank. It was necessary to make the hydrogen slosh back and forth, causing the gaseous hydrogen torecombine and return to a liquid state.

The Solid Rocket Motors, SRM's, attached to the first stage of the missile provided significant extra power at launch and were then jettisoned in stages after they burn out. There are nine of the SRM's, which burn out in groups of three, equidistantly spaced around the first stage. When the first three approach burnout and are jettisoned, a second group of three ignite as the first three drop away, then the process repeats for the final three, providing continuous thrust augmentation through the early portion of flight.. The burned out casings fall into the ocean and sink.

The squat tractor pulling the missile first stage along the access road stopped at the south entrance to the launch complex. Darkness and scrub brush along the special roadway obscured vision to a certain degree. Night gave a modicum of cover to the operation at hand. Paradoxically, the brightly lighted complex was an obvious give-away that an operation was underway.

As it sat just outside the gate to the launch complex, the covered missile stage was surrounded by orange-clad technicians carefully observing the immediate area. Their attention was heightened to an elevated degree not normally seen when bringing a launch vehicle to the complex. The indoctrination given before the missile left the prep facility had warned them of the special concerns necessary to assure a safe arrival at the launch facility. All were impressed by the importance given this operation and the consequences of being careless.

The cost alone of this launch effort was enough to stagger the mind. It was part of the reason for the strict security measures. The government had invested close to a billion dollars in the design and construction of this missile, with its three stages, plus strap-on SRM's and secretive payload. It was imperative that no foreign nation be allowed to know details pertaining to this launch, or of the stupendous capabilities of the payload.

Each of the specially qualified people having access to any part of the operation had been subjected to an intensive background check before being permitted to come near the missile or payload. Those having access to the payload proper were even more carefully checked. It had been a backbreaking effort to bring this team together in time to meet the designated launch date. So many special skills were involved that some people were taken from other program efforts, causing delays to less important launches. Managers of these less important programs were summarily told to comply with transfer orders of specially qualified technicians without question, causing major disruption to ongoing preparations leading to other launches. More than one senior manager was told, "comply or take a hike."

Consternation was evident in several places, especially among the uninformed. A great deal of gossip was generated before orders were issued to cease and desist all such gossip at once. Failure to comply resulted in immediate dismissal of a handful of lower echelon people, causing all to realize the significance of careless noncompliance.

———————

As the first stage of the missile was halted at the launch complex south gate, the technicians were lined up and their badges carefully examined by first a guard and then by the guard duty supervisor. In spite of the inward pointed searchlights, and the abundance of illumination, each technician was required to face the supervisor and have a bright flashlight shone full upon his face causing minor grumbling. Only after the supervisor was satisfied that every person present had been checked twice, and accounted for on the approved access roster, was the launch complex gate swung wide to permit the tug and missile first stage on its trailer to slowly move into the complex. The hour was approaching midnight as the tug maneuvered its seemingly precious cargo into position for erecting on the launch pedestal.

The pedestal itself was a massively built structure, designed to withstand the tremendous blast from the departing missile engines and SRM's. Even though huge amounts of water were deluged onto the pedestal, it seldom escaped at least some minor damage at launch.

———————

The tower, normally capable of enclosing the missile, with its huge doors, was open to permit the stages to be erected on the launch pedestal. A special cradle was fastened around the first stage, and cables from the overhanging tower hoist were attached, allowing the first stage to be brought to the vertical and smoothly moved into position for attachment to the pedestal. The first stage engines and SRM nozzles projected into the opening in the pedestal above the 'flame bucket'. At liftoff the massive blast of fire from the missile engines and SRM's was directed down this flame bucket, a giant deflector, and away from the missile above. A pump station not far distant, provided tremendous amounts of water through strategically placed nozzles in the flame bucket, the pedestal and on the umbilical tower. This edifice remained next to the missile at launch and retracted cable connections as the vehicle lifted off.

As the first stage was being erected, the second stage trailer with its tug and personnel went through the same operation as was done for the first stage. Both erecting operations went smoothly, the crews having done this many times before for much less sensitive operations. As soon as the second stage had been brought to the vertical, and centered over the first stage. The mobile launch tower doors were closed around the two stages of the partially erected vehicle, blocking any possible view of further operations. Within the closed confines of the tower the two stages were mated and preparations made for arrival of the Transtage and the highly secretive payload. The SRM's would be attached later, after the second stage mating was complete.

It was difficult to maintain security attendant to the Top Secret label given this operation. The security measures alone were sufficient to alert the most naive that something unusual was taking place. Those not involved expressed considerable curiosity about what was happening, to no avail. Senior officers and every lower grade military person, as well as civilian technicians, were closemouthed to all questions.

Several miles away from the launch complex, in a luxury condominium, a Russian officer, Major Sergei Vostov pulled back from the high powered optical device through which he had followed the erecting of the launch vehicle stages at the distant complex. A splendid view was available from the condo's balcony. Just inside the balcony glass doors the special optics of his instrument permitted him to clearly see both stages being brought into launch position. As he observed, his instrument recorded each action when he triggered the recorder. In truth, his recording revealed nothing new; the far away operation had been seen and recorded many times before. Sergei and his assistant, Lieutenant First Class Valeri Shadosevil, realized they would be hard put to report something new to their superiors. The daily report was mandatory and failure to transmit a report would result in harsh disciplinary action. It was to be avoided at all costs.

Sergei and Valeri had worked together on clandestine operations before and each was in tune with the other's unspoken word during critical events, such as this one. They made an efficient team and were often selected for highly sensitive operations. Sergei was a nervous person, and a brilliant aerospace engineer. Conversely, Valeri was easy going and inclined to take things as they came. He saw to it that the equipment selected was on hand and appropriate for the operation, and that all the interminable small things often forgotten by less qualified agents, were adequately addressed. It was he who seemed to have an eye for willing female companionship. He was ruggedly good looking and spoke flawless English. Sergei, on the other hand, was a diminutive person with thinning light hair and dark, brooding eyes that seemed to mesmerize women. He also spoke English fluently. They did not suffer from a lack of female attention. Both were agents of long standing, and high caliber, and both knew better than to shirk their duties at this particular moment. Women could come later.

The Russian Office of Information, located in a suburb of Washington, was headed by an uncompromising man with a very short temper, Colonel Mikael Dantilev. He expected a daily report from the on-site monitors, though there was little for them to report. He already knew that the Americans had developed a new satellite of extraordinarycapability. Colonel Dantilev was cognizant his life would be made miserable if he could not pass something new to the supposedly defunct KGB in Moscow. He was counting on Major Vostov being able to detect the differences of the vehicle being erected and readied for launch, from a standard missile. He was impatient to hear from Vostov.

Sergei had consumed several small glasses of chilled vodka during his stint at the telescope, which had not improved his disposition. He snapped at Valeri, "This stuff the Americans drink as 'vodka' is nothing but swill. Why can't they send us something decent to drink?"

Valeri did not respond.

Vostov's report to Colonel Dantilev was due in three hours, and was expected to be of some value. He knew the Colonel would be annoyed at the hour and the paucity of new data. The report he would have to give would not earn him anything with his superior. He took a final look through the scope as the launch tower doors were being closed around the two erected stages.

He thought, 'Well, at least I can tell him they have started the process of erecting. That means the launch is probably only six or eight weeks away. I can report the erecting process seemed to go without problems, and we should expect to see the Americans start attaching the SRM's by tomorrow. Perhaps we can see something of interest during the process of attaching those solid motors'.

At 8 AM he reluctantly prepared to call Colonel Dantilev at the Russian Office of Information, to pass on about the successful erecting and mating of the first two stages. He was hesitant to mention his plan to use a sharpshooter to derail the launch. He wanted to keep this little tidbit for a later report when he might need to mollify the Colonel. He would report it in due time, but at a time of his own choosing.

Little did he know that the Colonel would forbid him to use a sharpshooter to damage the missile, the resultant furor would not be politically acceptable.

———————

Air Force Major Bill Holloway had supervised the erecting and mating of the two stages and was feeling the effects of too long without rest.

Dawn was rapidly approaching, as evidenced by lightening of the Eastern sky. As soon as the stage mating process was completed the Major verified the closed up tower was secure and the armed guards were at their posts. As he prepared to sign out, he reminded the civilian Security Officer in charge, of the critical importance of this launch.

The Security Officer was grim-faced and responded, "I really don't need further reminding that this is a special launch. You can be sure nothing is going to happen to her, or the launch complex, during my shift. All our launches are important and we can handle this one in our normal manner."

The Major stiffened and said, "Your normal manner is not good enough, and you damn well better understand that. I expect the very best you have. You had best remember that old adage about Murphy's Law, 'If something can go wrong, it will!' And if it happens on your watch, your ass is mine. Do you understand me?"

The Guard Supervisor was taken aback at the Major's vehemence, and formally replied, "Yes, sir!"

He immediately went out to check each guard post and emphasized to each sentinel the need for strict attention to duty. After having been told repeatedly of the importance of this launch, the guards were very much aware that if they shirked their duties there would be "hell to pay" for sure.

Security was vital, and was paramount in the minds of everyone associated with this launch. The adequacy of the security was carefully reviewed by several echelons of responsibility. In retrospect, it appeared to be well thought out and all areas were subjected to several careful reviews. The plan was finally approved by the Air Force Commander of the local Wing, and implemented by the senior civilian Security Officer. Though there was a frequent turnover of military personnel, the permanently assigned civilian guard contingent was relatively stable. Each had been subjected to background investigations and approved for Secret clearance. Select personnel had been further checked and approved for Top Secret clearance.

Guard posts were established at the entrance to each of the two complex gates, at the launch pedestal area, and every third level of the launch tower. Posts were established for guards to patrol the inner perimeter of the launch complex fence. An outer control area was established at each access road to the complex and lists of personnel approved for entry to the complex provided to each guard post. A civilian Security Sergeant was assigned to check each guard post on a rotating basis, thus ensuring that the entire area was under strict surveillance. Later, when the spacecraft was to be brought to the launch complex, the guards with Top Secret clearance would be used for its protection.

There was not much likelihood that an intruder could get near the launch complex without being discovered. There was little thought given that the entire operation was about to be subjected to an attempt to sabotage the launch. Safeguards seemed to be adequate, but the attempt would be so simple, that plans had not considered it. Responsible planners slept soundly that night. Little did they know, the security plan could be negated by enemy senior management. Their sleep was indeed sound, though through no efforts of their own.

The Russian sharpshooter lay on a slight rise just outside the cleared area adjacent to the perimeter fence surrounding the large expanse of the Cape. He carefully calibrated his powerful scope to accommodate the distance from his position to the lighted launch complex just under 7,000 meters away. He had been honored for his prowess at sniper shots taken from even greater distances.

He thought to himself, 'This will be like shooting fish in a barrel. The large expanse of either of the distant missile stages will be an easy target and with the new explosive bullets I should make one helluva big explosion.'

His concentration was complete, he anticipated he could punch a hole in both of the stages and still have adequate time to pack up and disappear, all he needed was approval to shoot. It seemed strange to him that the possibility of rifle fire had not occurred to the arrogant Americans. With his use of the special flash suppressor, they would never know from where the shots would come.

His concentration was interrupted by the approach of a routine security patrol making its way along the inside of the Cape perimeter fence. He had been too confident of lax security patrols. Scrambling quickly, he rapidly returned his prized sniper rifle, with its beautiful scope and bipod, to its special padded case. He then carefully retreated back through the scrub to his cross country

SUV, reasonably sure he had not been seen. After waiting until the patrol had passed he started the engine and made his way to the elaborate condominium of Major Vostov.

The condo was probably an extravagance, but Major Vostov philosophized that what Dantilev didn't know wouldn't hurt him. It was beautifully furnished with three bedrooms, of which the Major selected the best for himself, a large family room, dining room, and a fully equipped kitchen. Fortunately Lieutenant Shadosevil was an excellent cook and enjoyed preparing meals, surrounded by all the modern conveniences in the kitchen. Food was plentiful and relatively inexpensive, compared to the poor markets in Moscow. They ate well.

Upon arrival at the condo the sharpshooter, a Senior Sergeant, advised the Major he could see no problem in carrying out his proposed assignment. He saw no need to tell of his close call with Cape Security. It was now well into daylight hours and Sergei thought to himself, 'Thank God something is going right on this assignment'. The Major thanked the Sergeant for his report and offered him a drink of vodka. The Sergeant replied that he did not drink anything when he waspreparing to fire a trying shot, even though he saw no need for any concern. He asked for a light breakfast and then retired to his bedroom to contemplate his upcoming effort.

Major Vostov readied his secure phone, with its American made scrambling device, for his daily report to Colonel Dantilev. The Sergeant's announcement of his readiness for the highly risky shot gave him a feeling of satisfaction. The Major decided this was probably as good a time as any to report his plan for use of explosive rifle bullets to destroy the two erected stages. He thought, 'Finally Colonel Dantilev will be pleased at the news of how well things are going'. There appeared very little likelihood of discovery before the American's hopes of superiority would come crashing down. He did not think Colonel Dantilev would disapprove of his plan.

It was May third, with the launch scheduled for T-0 at exactly 6:45 AM, only six weeks away. General Mayfair almost beamed at the appearance of Walt Crawford, slightly disheveled, but obviously ready to tackle the task before him. He was just 6' 2", carrying a hard-muscled, 190 pound frame, dressed in coordinated slacks and shirt, purchased from an expensive New York shop. He carried himself with a confident air, but without arrogance. He did not appear to be 40 years old and was frequently taken to be in his mid-thirties, or younger.

Because of Walt's unique abilities to assimilate highly technical information and to perform well in the most difficult of assignments, he had become a well known trouble shooter for any of the military branches of the United States government.

His current assignment was for him and his Team to support the highly classified launch of the most recent design of destroyer spacecraft. He was to anticipate troubles before they became a deterrent to the launch. General Mayfair believed in Walt's abilities to solve whatever problem was given him. His trust was based on intimate knowledge of Walt's prior assignments. Though nothing had happened to impede the operation to date, he knew that foreign espionage agents had been sniffing around.

The General told Walt of progress made in the operation and its current status. Walt had been briefed on the astonishing design of the deadly spacecraft before leaving Washington. He absorbed the design implications as he had driven from Washington to Cocoa Beach. He still found it difficult to believe the capabilities told him.

He thought to himself, 'Every nation in the world would give their eyeteeth to have this knowledge. With what I know, I had better watch my back while I work this program.'

After having been advised of all that had transpired during the spacecraft preparations for launch, he busied himself with details of the missile itself. At about the time the two missile stages were being enclosed within the launch tower he felt saturated with so much detail he could take no more. He realized that he would soon have to bring his Team on board and it would be necessary that he brief them. Walt thought to himself, 'If I absorb much more my mind will be completelyoverloaded.' It was critical that he have his information correct in order that he could properly brief his Team, it was time to stop. He bid General Mayfair goodnight, checked out of the Operations Center and drove to the motel to get a quick bite to eat, then to his room for a well-earned rest. He tumbled into bed and promptly fell into a deep sleep, leaving his clothing lay where it fell as he disrobed.

After only 5 hours of sleep he awoke feeling much refreshed. He knew that in a few hours time he would feel the effects of not enough rest. He thought to himself, 'I must find time later to get a few more hours of sleep'.

Fortunately his body was able to recuperate and function at his normal intense pace with much less rest than an average person, due to having studied several oriental mind-controlling exercises. He had received training in Yoga, Zen and other introspective mental exercises, allowing him to function at the necessary high level expected of him for extended periods without rest.

Upon awakening he retrieved his clothing from where it had fallen and tidied up the room. He then showered, shaved, dressed in a tailored set of lemon yellow colored coveralls especially treated against static charge, bearing his name and the Team logo Fixit. Yellow was the color that the Team would wear to distinguish them from others.

He placed a call to his friend Jack, to verify the Team would be ready to roll upon notification. He received his expected affirmative answer, and asked Jack to have Nat assemble the Team and stand-by. Walt advised Jack he would call him with destination information and a timetable.

That done, he headed for the motel restaurant. He ordered a large breakfast of orange juice, rye toast, three eggs over easy, a large slice of ham, and hash browns. While waiting for it to be brought to his table, he drank two steaming mugs of black coffee. He rapidly consumed all that was served him, left the restaurant, and headed for his Cobra parked in front of his ground floor room, chosen because of its location adjacent to a breezeway.

He made a detailed examination of the Cobra and finding nothing amiss, started the 427 cubic inch engine and permitted it to warm up briefly. Feeling more like tackling the situation he knew he would have to face, he was almost jubilant as he pulled out onto the highway and headed south towards the Base Operations Center.

He was checked in to the Base Main Gate and drove the short distance to the Operations facility. He stopped in one of the parking spaces reserved for senior personnel. His unique status as a government employee entitled him to the privileges of a full Colonel, his grade being that of GS-15 in Civil Service. He had been given a badge with his photo and special coded numbers imprinted thereon, attesting to his security clearance of "Top Secret", and permitting him access to any activity or function associated with "Absolute", as the program was named. If successful, it would alter political thinking worldwide.

CHAPTER 2

THE GATHERING OF SCIENTISTS, ENGINEERS, budget people and a smattering of highly placed Department of Defense managers was at an impasse. The long polished conference table was littered with documents, coffee cups, reference material, and copious notes. Heated discussions and vociferous arguments had punctuated this assemblage. The meeting had come to a halt, awaiting the decision whether to proceed with the project. The decision was a major milestone and critical if the project was to see fruition.

The three star officer, Air Force Lieutenant General Stanley Canfield and his Army counterpart, Major General Michael Gates, a two star general officer, had just left the meeting for a private discussion, accompanied by a privileged few, who were permitted to go with them into the small, sound-proofed office adjacent to the large conference room.

General Canfield looked at his aide and asked, "Has this room been swept?"

"Yes sir, I verified Security did a check and found the room clean less than ten minutes ago," he replied.

General Canfield turned to General Gates and asked, "Mike, what do you think? Are we going to be able to pull this one off?"

General Gates thoughtfully scratched his chin and answered, "Stan, this is the most difficult and most expensive operation ever undertaken by any government in the world. I hope to Hell we are doing the right thing to proceed with this program. Yes, I see no alternative to acceptance of the program as presently proposed. I believe we would be remiss to not go ahead with it."

"You are right, of course, but we'll have to recognize the impact we are going to make on other programs," General Canfield said. "We are going to be the most hated guys around," he further commented.

Turning to the senior fiscal representative he asked, "Well Sam, where do we stand on the money tree?"

The Colonel from the Budget Office replied, "Sir, as you know, the President has given his 'go ahead' to the Department of Defense to proceed, once the details have been ironed out. The Secretary of Defense has designated you as the Program Manager, so it's your call, if you are satisfied that we can do it."

"God forgive me for what I am about to do," the General said and continued, "Unless I hear anybody say anything to the contrary we are about to embark on a most dangerous effort to saddle our country with, one never undertaken by any nation before."

His audience in the small office was silent, mute testimony to his statement. He led the somber group back in to the conference room, where all those around the table looked at the grim face of the General.

The chatter of conversation ceased as the silent group returned and took their seats. Before he spoke, every man and woman present shrunk within themselves, as they understood the decision about to be announced. The General stood at the head of the long conference table, and for a hushed moment, silence prevailed as he gathered himself for the breathlessly awaited announcement.

He slowly looked around the table, assessing each person's demeanor and the anticipatory face of each, before he spoke, saying, "Each of you has had a special part to play in the unusual program we have jointly conceived. We must jointly bear the responsibility for what we are about to do. Never before has any weapon of war been so able to dictate who can inflict such casualties upon another nation. It is incumbent upon each one of you to protect the information you now have. It is imperative that you maintain the highly classified nature of this project. No slips, people!"

His emotion was evident as he completed his remarks. "We will proceed with development of this destroyer spacecraft. Do your best to make this bird one that is capable of stopping nearly any weapon from being launched against us." His shoulders slumped as he departed.

The murmur of excited conversation resumed following the exit of the general officers and the senior staff. After they had absorbed the fact that they were to go ahead with development, the engineering staff huddled to determine their next step.

That they effectively had an almost unlimited budget was so new, they could hardly contain themselves. The chief engineer cautioned them that it was hardly true. Just because they had the go ahead, did not mean nonessential design components could be added. Once they had settled down from their initial excitement at the prospect of actually launching the spacecraft they had conceived, work commenced in earnest.

The various teams returned to their laboratories and clean rooms to start the assembly of those components which had been built under preliminary authority of the Defense Department, in anticipation of the go ahead. Two versions of the spacecraft would be built, one as a test article of basic weapon components and the other, the flight article, the actual spacecraft to be launched.

At a number of military headquarters a collective sigh of relief was evident when the decision to proceed was received. Additional conferences would be needed, but none as critical as the one just completed.

The Military Chiefs became allied with the Civilian Chiefs of offices of the National Aeronautics and Space Administration, known as NASA.

Each top official had been tasked by the President of the United States, by edict to the Department of Defense and NASA, to do their best to assure that the project known as "Absolute" became a reality.

As was usual, concerned foreign agents were quick to become aware that a highly secret operation had been undertaken by the United States. The very function of secretiveness imparted awareness that something major was being embarked upon. Nothing specific was known, but with the amount of funds authorized by Congress and approved by the White House, it was difficult to keep it secret.

Fortunately, the purpose of that funding could not be uncovered so readily. Only a handful of people were privy to the details. As design and development took place, the secret aspects of the program became more and more difficult to maintain. Gradually slips were made, bits of information were put together, and those so desperate to know were partially fulfilled. The gleaning of these bits produced a picture that was being tediously assembled by KGB agents and several lesser powers.

A program technician breathlessly lay back from his love-making and remarked to his girlfriend, "This is the first time I've a chance to be with you for a week, and it will probably be like this for a while yet. We had better take advantage of what time I have before I have to go back to work on that damn project I'm tied up with. None of us are going to have much free time from here on in."

He immediately regretted his remarks and said to her, "Please keep what I just said to yourself." He had quickly lost his desire to make love to her again.

She was not so careful when at lunch the next day, with her group of other secretaries, she commented, "Boy, will I be glad when Bill gets through working on that damn thing they have, and has a little more time for me."

Her remark was noted by an inquisitive secretary who was being paid for anything she could pass on to her contact. It didn't seem to be unpatriotic to her, and she needed the extra money she received each week. Fifty dollars was a significant boost to her modest income, and as the weeks went by she reported seemingly unimportant comments made by the secretaries at their daily luncheon gathering.

When she became reticent about telling what she had heard, her contact became more aggressive and demanded she get replies to questions he had her pose to Bill's girlfriend and to the other secretaries. As time went on she was becoming more enmeshed in the scheme her contact had set up. She was warned she was being paid to produce, and failure to do so could result in her superior becoming imformed of her transgressions, or something even worse. She feared for the loss of her job and the dire threat given her, so she continued to pass on what she heard.

Her pieces of information, answers to carefully posed questions to the friendly secretaries at lunch, coupled with bits obtained here and there, resulted in a somewhat clearer picture of progress being made on Absolute. Now, not only the KGB was digging for information, but several other nations were becoming equally inquisitive. The United States was becoming an unwilling host to agents from a number of other countries.

As the American program developed, fear became more evident in other nations, in not knowing what was about to be laid upon them. This same fear drove the

KGB to extreme measures to obtain any information they could, from any source available. They were rapidly approaching the point where they would expend whatever effort was deemed necessary. Wet work was coming in vogue. Clandestine projects were the order of the day, for those countries trying to learn the truth of what was about to be forced upon them.

The Washington office of Colonel Mikael Dantilev was not able to keep the bits of data so far collected, to themselves. They too, became the subject of intense foreign scrutiny. Foreign agents also collected bits of information from that office and put it together. None-the-less his office became the Russian focal point to try and identify exactly what was being developed by Absolute. Spy work was becoming very convoluted.

More agents were becoming embroiled in the search for reliable data. This effort was costing a great deal of scarce American dollars to the KGB. Colonel Dantilev felt vindicated as the picture became clearer to him. His superiors were satisfied he was not wasting precious American dollars, but they did insist on being regularly briefed on whatever progress was being made. Their newest concern was trying to keep what they had learned to themselves.

The United States Military Program Office was forced to bring the CIA and the FBI into the picture to a limited degree, to try to counteract foreign incursions. It was a losing battle, too many variant U. S. offices had become involved to maintain the level of secrecy originally contemplated. Too many legitimate people needed to know selected parts of the program to be able to keep up the pretense that a major classified operation was not being implemented.

It was decided to salvage what security could be had under these circumstances, and to go forward with the best level currently obtainable. This, in itself, was actually quite an effective operation.

Very specific knowledge about the program was difficult to obtain, not to mention very costly, for even the smallest morsel of data.

The CIA and the FBI were together able to be an effective deterrent to the casual release of information.

They were able to close several loopholes, causing selected people to be detained pending investigative formalities. Security became even tighter as the launch date came closer. Whispers were silenced when friends seemed to disappear without a trace. Words such as 'Protective Custody' were heard here and there.

General Mayfair was painfully aware that security had become a major problem. He also recognized when seemingly open loopholes appeared to be closing. He felt much more at ease from a security standpoint, as launch preparations were undertaken. As each milestone was achieved he breathed a little easier. He knew that he could not truly rest easy until the spacecraft was finally in orbit and operational.

Walt Crawford had become an integral part of the launch team.

He had attended all pertinent briefings, particularly those having to do with spacecraft testing. He had personal concerns that the type of testing available after the craft was mated to the upper stage of the missile might not be sufficiently adequate to prove it would properly function after it was in orbit. He planned to set members of his Team to the task of verifying that tests were actually accomplishing all that was reported. Their positive answers would be encouraging and could be passed on to General Mayfair.

The design and build phases permitted detailed testing during assembly of the spacecraft components. The solar arrays were able to generate the necessary power requirements, and their durability was remarkable. A design breakthrough was used that appeared to allow unbelievable longevity of the solar cells. The real capability of the craft was in its disrupter device. It involved a means by which a beam of energy could be directed over great distances, and to a remarkable degree, be made to curve around the earth to destroy a pre-selected target. The use of Global Positioning System, or GPS parameters, greatly facilitated achieving pinpoint accuracy.

The generation of the energy beam was unique, involving interaction of accelerated particles within a coalescing device, which in turn, multiplied the encapsulated energy particles on an exponential basis, with a seemingly unlimited level of energy being produced. The resulting beam, from its yoke and focusing magnets, was steerable to a fairly precise degree by miniscule inputs to the magnets. The marrying of microelectronics and unique control capabilities enabled the system to be operated by reasonably intelligent people without having to understand how the system worked. Reasonably well-qualified technicians could operate the system in the field.

What was not completely understood was why power increased as distance to a target increased, up to a certain point, then it seemed to deteriorate. Fortunately that distance appeared to be in excess of 50,000 kilometers. For example, at a range of 8,000 kilometers, an input at the yoke of one kilowatt produced several thousand megawatts of power at the output terminal, which traveled on a beam to its terminus. As the power at the yoke was increased, the corresponding power at the test distance resulted in an exponential increase at its terminal point producing a stupendous explosion. Anything at the terminus would be completely destroyed. Inherent in the spacecraft design was an ability to track a very small moving target, hence the expectation that any detected launch could be quickly tracked and destroyed Current detection systems were already capable of discerning the launch of even very small missiles, and was easily convertible within the destroyer spacecraft. With a reasonable source of input power the options for subsequent output would be staggering. Solar array panels currently existed and now enhanced, permitting their use as a power source in the final design. A real killer spacecraft had been conceived.

The disrupter device was tested in a high flying B-2 Stealth Bomber at 45,000 feet above western Missouri, and was targeted on a small 30 foot long craft, floating in the far-away Pacific Ocean, 300 kilometers south of Hawaii, a distance of 7425 kilometers. When triggered, the beam flashed over the western states, curved out over the ocean and struck the small boat with a devastating blast of energy, destroying it completely. Not a shred of the little vessel was left intact. The ocean around the target boiled in a large cloud of steam, visible to the tracking ship twenty five kilometers away. It was a spectacular explosion, also visible and recorded by the remotely controlled monitor aircraft flying overhead. The destruction was recorded for later analysis. Observers were awe-struck at the complete disappearance of the target. Recording devices were unable to discern the narrow beam as it flashed from the test aircraft out to the hapless target. The time from initial triggering of the disrupter until the beam struck the small boat was measured in fractional seconds. Escape, once targeted, would have been highly improbable.

Reviewing engineers were both elated and flabbergasted at the total success of the test. Upon landing of the high flying B-2, the on-board test engineer was queried as to whether he had increased the planned amount of power to be used. His response was that the procedure was followed exactly, minimal input power had been applied to the accelerator, as called for in the test parameters.

The principle designer exclaimed, "Oh, there is joy in Mudville tonight!" The sentiment was echoed by the military managers as well. At last there would be something to use against those who would use terrorism to gain their ends.

It was difficult for the design people to come down from their high, so much effort, frequent failures, and very long hours had been involved in this project. However, it was realized that much more work lay ahead before this weapon could be placed into an operating spacecraft, and successfully launched into orbit. The elation was put behind them as they went back into their labs to work even more fervently.

———————

All were thankful that adequate funding was actually available to see it through to its operational development and ultimate deployment. Additional testing would be needed to verify solar cell arrays would unfold properly and orient themselves toward the sun, after the spacecraft was in orbit. Would they be able to generate enough power to operate the system, or would they be dependent on long–life batteries as a power source? The B-2 test had used the plentiful power available from within the aircraft. Would ground-based dummy loads be adequate to accept the test discharge necessary before launch? Engineers set themselves to identify what further testing needed to be accomplished

———————

The intricacies of funding were not well-understood by most of the engineering people associated with the program. One category of funds was allocated to design, another to testing, another to support personnel, yet another to purchase of equipment or for the manufacture of components. The categories seem to go on and on. Scientists and engineers were happy to leave funding to the fiscal people and just hope that there would be money available when it was needed.

The highly successful test had been monitored by more than the United States, satellite passes had been altered by at least three nations. A number of agents had been able to discover the date planned for the test and as a result, Japanese, Russian and French satellites had been relocated to a position over the Pacific Ocean, as was a reconnaissance satellite of the United States. It was fortunate that none were in close enough proximity to impact one another. All recorded the destruction of the target. The foreign nations became alarmed at what had been observed.

Each waited breathlessly for an announcement from the Americans. When the announcement came it was terse to an extreme. It stated, "The United States conducted a successful test in the open reaches of the Pacific Ocean south of Hawaii, on Tuesday, 14 May". Nothing was said explaining that it would be nearly a year before Absolute could be called an operational weapon, and many more milestones would need to be first met.

Colonel Dantilev was advised of the test results and disbelieved the report. The monitor data reached his office at the same time it was being reviewed by the head of the KGB. He talked at length with that senior staff, and was charged with responsibility for taking necessary action to obtain pertinent information about the American program. He was to report a plan of action within the week.

CHAPTER 3

THE ELDER CRAWFORDS, WHO UNKNOWINGLY would become the parents of a brilliant young man destined to be important to his country, lived in rural Arkansas. They had a deceptively large home on the outskirts of a small town called Springfield. Jonathon Crawford was a sizeable man, standing at six feet one and weighing two hundred muscular pounds, obviously one not to be indiscriminately trifled with. He was confident and not easily turned from a formed opinion. Occasionally he could be quite brusque with fellow workers, if he felt he had cause. On the other hand he was exceptionally gentle with his children, two boys and three girls. He disciplined with a firm hand, but always fairly and with an explanation for whatever punishment was meted out. He unabashedly showed his affection, not just to his children, but his love for his surprisingly beautiful wife of twenty six years. They made a charming couple, always willing to help with community projects, or to friends in need. He was a successful business man, having made prudent investments and diversification of his assets.

Jonathon met his wife-to-be while in college, both juniors at the University of Maryland, in College Park, a bustling small town of some 20,000. It was a typical college town with many young students, professors and university support personnel. It was an upscale University, earning high regard for those who completed degree programs. The town abounded with apartment complexes, frat and sorority houses, and a large assortment of fun-filled beer parlors and inexpensive places to dine. Many of the students occupied dormitories to save money where they could. All in all it was a delightful background to foster friendships and enjoy campus life. The University itself was a large collection of ivy-covered brick buildings, with wandering walkways, benches, gently rolling grounds, beautiful landscaping and several athletic facilities.

Jonathon met his wife to be at a dance sponsored by her sorority, both attending without dates. He noticed her standing with a group of young women chatting among themselves. She was not a petite girl, beautifully endowed with a figure envied by many. Her hair was a light brown, almost blond, with lovely highlights that glistened in the moving lights of the overhead mirrored ball. She had captivating eyes, as blue as the sky, quickly noticed by even the non-observant. As the girls talked, she gently moved to and fro in rhythm with the sounds of the orchestra. The music had changed from a pounding beat to a slow melody.

On an impulse, Jonathon slowly walked over to the group, causing a lull in the conversations as the girls looked at him, assessing his acceptability. He was Captain of the La Cross team, a standout player well-known to the student body.

He singled out the very attractive girl and, holding out his hand, asked her to dance with him. She promptly accepted and as they swung away in perfect unison, identified herself as Barbara Lundquist and asked his name. He told her his name, Jonathon Crawford.

He immediately became aware of her firm body as he held her. It was obvious from the very beginning that something special happened as soon as they started to dance. Their blue eyes made contact and she unabashedly allowed herself to be held close. He knew that this girl was unique, a feeling came over him that he had never before experienced. They danced together the rest of the evening and talked to one another as if they had known each other for an eternity. As the evening ended he asked if she would accept his fraternity pin, and although they had just met for the first time, she accepted with the firm knowledge that this was the man for her.

They finished college and shortly after graduation they married. He accepted a job offer in Arkansas at the firm headquarters of Delta Electronics, a multifaceted company firmly entrenched in the development of early electronic hardware. Their efforts put them in the forefront of modern microelectronics. The company was well established and produced so many different devices it became necessary to open new plants and divisions to market their products.

Jonathon became an integral part of the firm, planning and integrating many of their advancements and in the process distinguished himself greatly. He was rapidly advanced in positions of corporate responsibility. The firm prospered and was able to become a premier force in the electronics field. Branch offices were established and staffed with people trained in part by Jonathon.

Initially, Barbara worked as a teacher in the local elementary school, where she became a favorite of the youngsters she taught. Together they made their first home a place of comfort and relaxation. In the first five years of their marriage she bore him two sons and three daughters. Together they decided that though they dearly loved the kids, five growing children were enough. He visited a doctor who agreed to perform a vasectomy for Jonathon only after he interviewed Barbara and Jonathon together. Their appetite for sexual pleasures was not diminished afterward, and they continued to enjoy one another as much as ever. He was able to reduce the amount of road trips he made and they improved and enlarged their home. A workshop and garages were added making it finally complete to their ultimate satisfaction.

The eldest son was named Walter, after Jonathon's father, the next son was called William, after her father. Similarly the daughters were named after the grandmothers, the first named Sara, after her mother, the second Bertha a name the child abhorred and which ultimately became Bertie, and lastly came a daughter Jocelyn, so named because Barbara simply thought it was a nice name, and of course Jonathon agreed.

The children excelled in school, all earning high scholastic marks. As might be expected, they all also participated in athletics, showing extraordinary skills and aptitude at whatever they tried. Walter had grown into a robust athlete, earning letters in football, baseball, and was throwing the shot and discus at record distances for a high school senior. Scholastically he showed prowess in mathematics, chemistry and languages. He set high marks for his siblings to surpass. He graduated from high school with honors and was the class Valedictorian. He was a welcome candidate for several good colleges.

He liked the University of Maryland where his father had matriculated, and was interviewed there by the Athletic Director. That astute man could foresee a valuable asset for several sports as well as in academia, and offered Walter a full athletic scholarship, surprisingly to play La Cross first, and baseball second. After consultation with his parents he accepted, and became a standout La Cross player for the University of Maryland. During baseball season he played third base on the varsity team, even though he was but a freshman.

Walt, as he came to be known, completed his Bachelor of Military Science program in less than three years, a program he chose after his freshman year. Military Science was a bit unusual, but appealed to him because of its unique diversity and opportunities available in the Military. Later he pursued an advanced degree in another unusual discipline, Celestial Mechanics, learning a great deal about space programs in the process. His thesis for his advanced degree was unusual for a college student, being on the order of defining new criteria for applying certain hypothetical orbital parameters. His premises were found to be accurate by a well-known space scientist.

He looked forward to a military career after excelling in the ROTC program, earning the gold bars of a Second Lieutenant. Upon completion of his advanced degree, he applied for, and was commissioned a First Lieutenant in the U. S. Army. Shortly thereafter he requested airborne training, and was sent to Fort Benning, Georgia. Because of his athletic skills he was able to withstand the rigors of the demanding physical fitness program associated with becoming qualified as a parachutist. On one of his training jumps he found himself drifting beyond the drop zone and over a farmer's field. When Walt spied the farmer at work below him he shouted loudly, "Watch out, I'm going to hit you"! The farmer looked left and right but saw nothing so he dismissed the shouting. At about two hundred feet Walt again shouted, "Look out below I'm gonna hit you". The farmer looked skyward and fell over backwards as Walt hit the ground right next to him. The parachute billowed out and gently settled over them both. The farmer cried out, "Oh my God I've died and gone to heaven".

Walt was apologetic saying as he lay next to the man, "No sir, I kinda misjudged my landing, I'm sorry if I scared you," and quickly gathered up his 'chute and left the fuming farmer fearing he would be reported. Upon completion of his airborne training he was assigned to the 82nd Airborne Division.

After varying assignments of airborne duties he wrangled acceptance for training as a Pathfinder, a jumper who parachuted into a prospective target for airborne assault. An entirely new set of physical hardships was endured successfully and he discovered the fear present at parachuting from very low altitudes, barely enough height for his 'chute to open, release his static line holding eighty pounds of gear just below his reserve parachute, and get ready for ground impact. After his first Pathfinder jump he wondered why was he equipped with a reserve parachute, there would never be time enough to open it before ground impact. He supposed it must be psychological! He wore his parachute jump emblem proudly.

After being promoted to Captain, he saw the horrors and underside of fighting during his early assignments. His first combat was in the mountainous regions of Afghanistan, where he sustained his first wound, a Taliban sniper rifle shot struck him in the lower right side of his chest. The bullet passed completely through leaving an entry and an exit wound. Though wounded, he killed that sniper and went on, wiping out several more Taliban. He had returned fire in spite of having been hit, and actually captured a group of enemy militants. He was awarded the Bronze Star with "V" device for valor and a Purple Heart for his wound. He next participated first hand in "Desert Storm," the throwing back of Saddam Hussein's forces out of Quwait. He again distinguished himself there, being awarded the Silver Star for courage above and beyond the call of duty, where he faced Hussein's Republican Guard forces before they ultimately collapsed at the onslaught of U.S. troops. He was twice wounded during Desert Storm, resulting in being awarded two more Purple Hearts.

During his tour in Iraq he was promoted to Major and again later to Lieutenant Colonel upon his return to the United States, where he served as an action officer in G-3 Operations, in the Pentagon. Here, his earlier college studies came into play and his broad knowledge of how space was a peculiar entity of its own, became a valuable bit of knowledge. He served with distinction in this assignment and was awarded the Legion of Merit for his outstanding efforts. He now had a considerable array of ribbons on his uniform.

Though in all probability he would have been promoted to full Colonel, had he stayed on active duty beyond his twenty years of service now completed, he felt a need to do something new, and asked to be separated from the military service. A General officer tried to dissuade him from his decision to retire, asking him to remain in the Army, to no avail. After twenty years in the Army he was once again a civilian, albeit a most peculiarly qualified person to be a civilian.

Walt Crawford, a civilian. He hardly knew what he really wanted, it was more like he knew what he didn't want! He visited home with his parents for a few days and realized after all this time he was still single, though he had known a few women intimately here and there, none had found a place in his heart. He was at loose ends, almost at a standstill, not knowing exactly what did he really want.

He talked candidly with his father, seeking an idea, a direction, or was he seeking solace from the agonies of war and the ugliness of maiming and death. Jonathon, his father, served as an excellent sounding board, suggesting Walt might embark on an entirely new walk of life. What qualifications did he bring to the bargaining table? Was he willing to take on a new direction? Walt was aware that he was blessed with the ability to assimilate information and react quickly and produce responsible actions or recommendations. Where was there a market for such abilities? The answer was obvious, Washington, the United States Government!

He knew how he needed to go about selling himself to 'Uncle Sam', but a simple résumé would not suffice. He rummaged around the big house until he located a place to set up. He needed a video cassette recorder, a bare wall to display maps and charts, and lighting to produce a professional quality video tape. He set up a desk in front of a light-colored bare wall, found a swivel chair and minimal typical desk accoutrements. His father owned a fine VCR, and his sister Jocelyn loaned him flood lamps. He was ready to begin preparing a script of sorts. By this time his whole family was involved in helping him in his effort to make a good tape. His script was edited and re-edited by his father, his mother, and his sister. The final product was well-polished and he closeted himself to memorize it.

When he was finally prepared to record his 'résumé', he had a ready, critical audience of his parents and younger sister Jocelyn. He had posted maps on the wall showing the various places in the world he had served, and framed commendations and awards adorned the wall as examples of the multitudinous things he had accomplished during his storied career in the military. His dialog was terse and to the point, no wasted words. He alternately stood, using his pointer to touch the many places on the maps where he had served, and then resumed sitting at the desk. He painted a picture of himself as a quick study, able to assimilate complex projects or ideas, and physically fit enough to handle the most difficult of situations. It was a bold and possibly slightly egotistical narrative, but spoken by a man with great presence and confidence. Upon completion, his family audience broke into spontaneous applause. He thought, 'that would have to be deleted from the sound track.'

Copies were quickly made and he busied himself determining to whom he should send his 'masterpiece.' His first act was to send one copy to his recent superior in the Pentagon, beyond that, he was unsure of to whom else should he send a copy. He had no need to worry, for his past superior, Major General John C. McIntyre, was delighted and immediately had the personnel department make up a contract for Walt's services on a long-term basis. The contract called for him to report for duty as a GS-15, to serve on 'special projects' as assigned by General McIntyre. Over the next two years he was sent to all corners of the world, primarily as a 'trouble shooter,' seeking out problems and offering solutions thereto. He had gathered together a group of highly specialized people with whom to work. With General McIntyre's approval he had formed a small company which he dubbed 'Fixit,' who helped him solve the often difficult problems given him. He was eminently successful and became well known for his prowess in solving several significant dilemmas. His last assignment was in India, where he had successfully helped to negotiate an agreement permitting U.S. aircraft to over-fly previously restricted air spaces controlled by India. He was thinking of where should he go for a well-earned vacation. His planning was short-lived. General McIntyre sent him an electronic message alerting him to a new assignment.

Walt was called to Washington and told his new assignment would be to the program known as 'Absolute,'

Top Secret in nature and critical to the Nation's welfare. He was briefed by the principal scientist and several engineers. He was ordered to report within two days to Major General Billy Mayfair at Patrick Air Force Base, Florida. He immediately went to his apartment and commenced packing for an expected extended absence.

He contacted his close friend, 'Gentleman' Jack Johnson, a valued member of the Team Walt had developed, and briefly explained he would be away for an extended period. He offered the use of his apartment to Jack.

In retrospect he asked Jack to meet him at the apartment if he was interested in a new project. General McIntyre had given him the option of selecting personnel of his own choosing to participate in this highly classified operation. Knowing Walt, Jack accepted with alacrity, and agreed to meet him in an hour's time.

After being told of the operation, Walt asked Jack to remain at the Washington apartment and have Nat, his 'good right hand,' gather the Team together in anticipation of the job ahead. He explained the apartment was available for a brief period while he traveled to Florida to determine just how the project was moving along and where did he and his Team fit in. Before departing, Walt wanted verification that each member of his Team of specialists was available and ready for the important work ahead. He asked Jack to keep trying to reach Nat, his coordinator. Walt had left messages on her voice mail but had yet to hear from her.

The Team was a carefully selected group of people with highly specialized talents. Walt had realized early on that although he considered himself able to handle many tasks alone, there were times when he needed to call upon uniquely qualified people for special aspects of some of his jobs. Over the months he had selected men and women he knew to be reliable and trustworthy to serve with him. Effectively he had organized his group into a small company. When he realized this he decided to name his group 'Fixit.' His contract with the Army was modified to include his Team of professionals. Their salaries were commensurate with those of equal skills in major corporations and each had been cleared for 'Top Secret' access.

He channeled his choices of whom to use on specific tasks through his 'Executive Officer,' Natalie Morse, in turn she contacted each of his selected people and advised them of the times and places they were to be and the general nature of what they were to do. Walt placed a high degree of trust in 'Nat,' as he called her. She was not only a valued Team member whom he utilized to alert and bring other Team players in to a designated location, she also had a photographic memory, able to keep a mental catalog of all Team names and various contact telephone numbers. Aside from that, she was also able to handle a gun and could use in-fighting techniques to an exceptional degree. In one sense she thought she loved Walt, but knew that it was not reciprocated She would not hear of any kind of deprecatory remarks against Walt. He prepared to depart after assurances that Jack would be able to reach Nat and give her Walt's instructions.

Walt used Jack Johnson frequently in various roles. He was a fearless combatant in a barroom brawl, seemingly unfeeling of any personal injury, and quick to assess what was needed in emergency situations. He was Walt's closest friend. It was believed by the others that Jack would lay down his life for Walt without a whimper. He was talented in handling explosives and ordnance devices. As might be expected, Jack was an enormous man, standing at six foot four and weighing close to 230 pounds, all muscle, and only four percent body fat. Though immense, he had a gentle touch with exceedingly sensitive feeling in his fingers. His capacity for holding his liquor was legendary. While he enjoyed having drinks, he would become a virtual teetotaler on the job, never permitting himself excess liquor.

Other members of the Team included Kim Shirakawa, an absolute genius with computers. He was often found talking to his computer as though he expected an answer. He too, was loyal to Walt, without reservation. It was said that Kim could wheedle information out of a dead computer, he lived and breathed to be as one with any type of computing device. He was Walt's expert in the use of 'bugging' devices. Like Natalie, Kim was adept at martial arts.

Another man considered to be essential was Joseph Miselli, an easy going man, capable of surprising skills. He could repair any engine no matter its heritage, and if a vehicle was drivable he could coax real performance from it. On more than one occasion he had made their escape from 'sticky' situations possible. Joe was somewhat deceptive. He was soft spoken, but the old adage about 'speak softly but carry a big stick' fit Joe very well. He was not a person that would be noticed under most situations, and this trait fit very well into the needs of the team. He spoke several languages aside from his heritage-learned Italian, being fluent in Russian, French, German and a smattering of Arabic. He often parodied a stumbling, drunken Italian, speaking imperfect English, "Ima jussa poora Italiano." Walt thought highly of him.

The last regular Team member was a voluptuous woman of indeterminate origin. She claimed her mother was a hooker who consummated a hot affair with an unknown father. She had a rather fetching name, inconsistent with what she would have you believe, Constance, or 'Connie', as she preferred. Though she had a passport like all the others, and except for Walt, only Natalie knew her real last name. None of the other members pressed her and were satisfied to call her Connie. Like the others, she too carried her own weight. She was adept at street fighting and could down an unsuspecting man in seconds. Aside from that, she too, was skilled in the matter of languages, learning in the shadowy hallways of prostitution to speak Russian, French and Czechoslovakian fluently and Spanish reasonably well. She could turn herself into all manner of persons, unrecognizable to even the Team members. Using theatrical makeup she prepared disguises when needed by the team. She too, controlled her emotions where Walt was concerned. Having been rescued from a halfway house, she felt obligated to do whatever was required of her by the Team. Each of them held her too in the highest regard.

These people were all regarded as family by Walt, and who had genuine affection for each other, as well as for Walt There was mutual trust among them, earned in many close working relationships, often in dangerous situations. They instinctively knew to whom to turn for specific help in trying circumstances. Every one of them had complete trust in Walt, and vice versa.

CHAPTER 4

AFTER WALT SIGNED IN TO the Operations Center he reported immediately to General Mayfair and upon seeing his tired countenance asked, "Sir, have you been able to get any rest?"

He replied, "I have a little room here in the Ops Center with a cot where I can catch forty winks now and then. I was able to snooze about three or four hours after you left. Did you get any sleep at the motel?"

"I was able to get several hours, thank you, and got a pretty good breakfast at the motel restaurant before I came back here," he responded.

The General told Walt, "There is coffee at the snack table, get a cup of coffee, then try to get yourself up to date from the data we have on the operations boards. After that we will talk."

Walt moved over to the backlit boards, which displayed all the current information as it occurred. Several uniformed men were at the boards entering data as they received it over their headsets. Cryptic comments were made as data was received, acknowledging receipt of a specific message. Each man had an up-to-the-minute copy of the procedure in progress. The reports came in "page 42, Step 21, or page 43 Step 56 'complete', or 'in progress', or 'started'. In this fashion they were able to quickly verify how the operation was progressing. The procedure was controlled by a senior representative of the responsible company and monitored, step by step, by a field grade officer of the Air force, usually a well qualified major.

Later, control would shift to the Launch Control Center, when the preparations for the actual launch would get under way. In the interim, all the preliminary operations were handled at the Ops Control Center. At the moment, and for some time to come, this would be the place where current activities were tracked and kept in proper sequence.

Walt stood at the displays for several minutes, absorbing what he could see on the boards. He mentally projected what should occur as certain milestones were met. When he felt he understood how things were progressing, and thought he could reasonably accurately project when important milestones would be achieved, he turned from the boards, ambled over to the large coffee urn and drew himself a mug of steaming hot coffee. He carefully sipped from the hot mug as he approached the General and asked if they could now talk.

The General turned toward the back of the Ops Center where there were a number of desks and chairs. Bookcases lined the walls with telephones and computers on every desk. The computer screens were bright with colored displays and graphs. The bookcases were filled with thick binders and technical books. Some of the phones were extensions of the headsets in use by the uniformed men at the displays. Open reference books and binders littered the desks and note pads lay covered with hastily scribbled information. Most of the desks were occupied by Air Force officers and shirt-sleeved civilians. One desk had been set aside by itself in an alcove for the General, it too, had computer displays.

Hanging from the walls at strategic locations, were large screen color television sets, which could display whichever camera was selected. There were two television sets which responded to a special camera controller on the General's desk, allowing him to select a camera to show any of the Operations Center displays, or critical locations of the launch complex, including the launch vehicle enclosed in the mobile tower, as well as pictures of whatever was desired. It could also display the various consoles in the Firing Room, formally called the 'Launch Control Center,' during launch countdown.

The remote cameras could be zoomed in to close range when needed, allowing viewing of critical operations, or even the individual meters, gauges, and specific indicator lights on the control consoles. The two TV screens were adjusted so they could be readily monitored from the General's desk. The open doors of the mobile structure were displayed on one on his monitors, while the other showed a status board from the far end of the Operations Center.

The General and Walt turned to meander back to his desk and then sat facing one-another, both were solemn faced, with obvious concern for the momentous task facing them. The General explained his current plan for the operation, and brought Walt up to date on his thinking. It was imperative that Walt and his Team be 'on the same page' with the General.

After a few minutes of discussion General Mayfair asked, "Walt, is your Team ready to support this operation?"

"I have asked them to assemble and wait for my instructions on what is to come next. We are ready for whatever happens, I hope!" he answered, and added, "As soon as you give me the word I will get them on the road and on their way here."

"This effort will last for several weeks at least. Maybe longer, if things go wrong. Will you be able to have all five of your Team here to participate?" He eyed Walt quizzically.

Walt replied, "If I can have access to a secure phone I can get them started immediately. After my Washington briefing I instructed my people to get our hardware and equipment together and be ready to move on my call. Will you want them on base or should they get quarters in the local area?"

"I'm sorry Walt, but there are no quarters left on base. We have all kinds of people involved in this, and most of them are using the base facilities, so I guess you had better make arrangements for quarters nearby. That Astronaut Motel ought to have something."

"That is where I am, I already told them I might need more rooms," he replied. He used the phone on the General's desk and activated the scrambler before he called his own phone number in Washington.

When Nat answered he asked, "Scrambler on?" and when she confirmed it was, he said, "We are on to support the operation. Go ahead and move the Team to the Astronaut Motel here in Cocoa Beach. They will be expecting you and have rooms ready for the Team, Thanks for getting things lined up and seeing to assembling of the Team and all the preps. I will be looking forward to having everybody here in a couple of days. Is everybody on board with no hang-ups?"

"Ready to roll," was her quick rejoinder, "See you in a couple of days."

It was a strange assortment of vehicles that headed out of Washington and started south on I-95. It consisted primarily of five Sport Utility Vehicles for the passengers and their gear, each towing a highly specialized trailer loaded with the unique equipment deemed necessary for the mission and an alarm system activated by the driver when stopped. It was midday when they departed, picking up speed as soon as they were on the Interstate.

Walt turned to the General and said, "We're all set. They will be here in two days time and stay at the Astronaut Motel. All I need to do is to call the motel and confirm." He made the quick call and told the clerk to set up the requested five rooms, preferably all next to each other and close to his room, as prearranged. Fortunately there were vacancies adjacent to his room, one with an adjoining door to Walt's room. He knew that Nat would occupy it.

The General sat back in his comfortable executive chair and looked piercingly at Walt. He brought him up to date on all the activities so far accomplished. Walt was intimately familiar with the spacecraft to be launched, probably even more than General Mayfair. However he had not been privy to the results of the airborne test of the system carried out over the Pacific Ocean. Upon hearing how the target had been totally destroyed, a smile broke out on his face. He did not interfere with the General's train of thought and listened with rapt attention as the General continued with his explanation of how much progress had been made. After some thirty minutes of uninterrupted talk, the General sat forward and said to Walt, "That about brings you up to snuff on where we are right now."

Walt was totally fascinated with the dialog and smiled in response to General Mayfair's unabashed grin. "How about them apples," he proudly spoke to Walt.

"I can hardly believe we have come such a long way," Walt replied and then continued, "I can see we need to be very alert to cut short any attempt to sabotage this launch. Has there been anything happen so far?"

"We know there are several foreign agencies trying to find out what they can," the General said, "But we have been able to keep a pretty tight lid on information. Our people have been indoctrinated so often they are sick of hearing about it. I'm assuming your people will be subjected to the usual security briefing."

"Yes sir, they know they must go through the orientation and indoctrination," he replied, and then continued, "With your OK I'm going to head out to the launch complex and refresh my mind as to the overall layout." "Go ahead, but have Ops let them know you are coming." was his response.

Walt strode over to where the Major in charge sat and asked, "Stoney, any problem with me being at the pad now? I'd like to go out and get the lay of the land again."

Major Stonewall Jackson, being well acquainted with Walt, said, "Sure, Walt, just be sure you have your badge with you. You can't even get in the Cape Main Gate without it, much less on the complex."

Badge in hand, Walt left the Ops Center and remembered his car would have to be tagged to get him on the Cape and the parking area near the complex gate. The Base Security Office was manned twenty four hours a day so he had no trouble getting the proper sticker for his car. Once he had the decal he headed north on Highway A1A, through Cocoa Beach and the city of Cape Canaveral and the several miles around Port Canaveral and east to the main gate of Cape Canaveral Air Force Station, an Air Force operated test facility. After being checked in to the Cape he continued north past Navy facilities, the main industrial area housing Range Operations and other complexes, finally arriving at the complex where 'his' bird was being erected, he was already feeling proprietary towards this launch vehicle, as it was being prepared for launch.

He entered the Complex Operations Building and introduced himself to the Lieutenant Colonel in charge. He approached and said, "Sir, I am Walt Crawford, on special duty with General Mayfair. I hope I'll be working closely with your organization for this launch."

Lieutenant Colonel Jason Comisky stood and shook hands said, "The General has explained in detail about you and your Team. Frankly, I'm glad to have you with us. Please call me J.C., and that doesn't mean Jesus Christ, although I get a fair amount of razzing about it."

He turned and introduced Major Bill Holloway, as the one who really carries most of the load in getting the 'bird' up and in place in the mobile launch tower.

Walt replied in kind saying, "I'm Walt to everybody, and we will try to stay out of your way as much as possible. I am the only one of my Team here now, but as soon as the rest arrive you can meet them. Can I make a tour of the complex and structure without getting in anybody's way?"

Major Holloway, though obviously tired said, "Sure, I'll run you around to whatever you want to see," and added, "J.C., as soon as I get through I'm going to go get some rest before things start up again tomorrow."

He then turned to Walt and said, "Come on, I have a jeep right outside and we can get started."

Walt advised him, "I am reasonably familiar with the place, but it has been quite a few months since I was here last."

The tour encompassed the high pressure gas facility, each of the four propellant 'farms,' the Change House, where protective garments are donned, the lower reaches of the flame bucket, the launch pedestal, the umbilical tower, and finally, the tower itself where they used the elevator to carry them to the upper reaches, which would later enclose the spacecraft, and finally climbing down the twenty five levels via the different stairways. He was able to see the first and second stages of the partially erected vehicle close at hand.

Walt expressed his genuine appreciation for the detailed tour and as they drove back to the complex gate, asked if Bill would like to join him in a nightcap before heading to his quarters. Bill accepted and they signed out of the complex and climbed into Walt's Cobra.

He said, "I hope the open breezes are all right with you, it is a nuisance to put the top up."

Bill expressed his pleasure at being able to ride in the Cobra and did not mind the open air at all. Walt was able to hit the throttle on some of the open highway en-route back to Cocoa Beach, much to Bill's delight. They stopped in a late night bar and leisurely consumed two drinks each, while they casually probed each others personality.

They mutually decided it was time to call it a day. Walt drove Bill to the Base dropping him at his Bachelor Officers Quarters and bidding one another good night. Each decided the other was a well qualified individual and had good feelings, in terms of becoming a real friend. As he drove towards his motel he thought, with people like J.C. and Bill, the road ahead appeared much less bumpy.

CHAPTER 5

NAT WAS THE MOST EXPERIENCED member of the Team in determining the make-up of needed equipment and materiel for their assignments. In this case she called upon each member and explained what she knew of the forthcoming task. They then sat down and determined which of their large inventory of highly specialized items of equipment each thought would be needed. After each Team member had prepared their individual lists, they cross-checked with every other Team member to verify the absence of duplication. They then had a round table discussion to insure all aspects were addressed insofar as they knew the project to be. Nat and Jack were the most well-informed, Jack having been briefed by Walt before his departure, and they made the final determination of what was to be taken.

Based on a number of prior missions together, they felt they could make a fairly accurate estimate of their needs. They also knew that the best of plans laid with incomplete prior planning information might necessitate a later re-evaluation and possibly a return to their secure logistics warehouse to augment their original package. If this came to pass it meant one of the Team would need make a mad dash back to Washington, with one of the SUV's and a trailer. It was always an argument to decide who should make the trip. Invariably Walt had to decide who should go.

He would quietly and dispassionately discuss the issue with each of them and after a logical examination of the situation, actually induced them to make the decision themselves. As always, they felt sheepish over their petty arguments. The person who could best handle the revised requirements always stepped forward to make the trip if it was required.

Aside from this minor event, each of them had the highest regard for the skills and abilities of each other. They knew that when the chips were down, any one of them would do anything for the other. The men knew that in a difficult situation, the women were as reliable as the men. The women were equally confident of their skills and would have no fear in counting on their male counterparts for support when needed. Together they were a remarkable group of people, a cohesive unit that could function under the most difficult of circumstances. Each placed complete trust in Walt Crawford, and espoused a common, unshakable belief in him. Walt reciprocated that trust and belief.

En route, the Team took only brief rest stops to stretch their legs and to eat. While driving they were in communication with each other via short wave radio. They were careful to stay relatively close together, maintaining adequate stopping distances between vehicles based on their speed. In actuality they pushed the speed limits only slightly. They could not afford to be delayed because of a ticket through careless driving. They changed lead vehicles periodically so that they had a fresh pair of eyes keeping a careful watch for speed traps. Each SUV was outfitted with the latest in driving comforts, including modern radar detectors with laser, Ka and X-band devices, they also had a display system in each SUV showing accurate GPS maps and their routing. Each had a winch at the front bumper, a heavy duty trailer hitch at the rear and four-wheel drive, as well as high intensity driving lights and yellow fog lamps. Each was equipped with a heavy-duty rear bumper and a sophisticated alarm system. They were indeed a pleasure to operate.

They made one stop for an overnight rest and proceeded onward at an early hour.

More than once other motorists and truckers took a second look at the unusual convoy of fast-moving vehicles. Others tended to avoid them, and leave plenty of road clearance around them. When they stopped at one roadside truck stop and pulled their SUV's in a single file in close proximity to each other, a big cross-country rig stopped unnecessarily close to them.

Jack approached the driver and said, "Say fella, don't you think you are a little close here? How about moving away just a little?"

The driver ignored him, and climbed down from his cab and started toward the restaurant. Whereupon Jack started to climb up to the rig's cab. The driver turned back and said, "Mah man, get yo ass offa mah truck!"

Jack stepped down and turned to the driver and replied, "I'm not your man and if you don't move this rig I'll do it for you." He menacingly clenched his very large fists and took a step toward the driver.

The driver suddenly realized just how big Jack really was, and that his rude remark had offended him. He decided prudence was the better part of valor and obligingly climbed back into his cab and rolled his 'semi' to the complete opposite side of the parking lot.

They took turns staying with their vehicles at each stop, calling it 'guard dog' duty, and brought a sandwich and drink out of the restaurant after the others had eaten, for the 'guard dog'. The unfriendly trucker incident had occurred at a stop near the intersection of I-26 and I-95, just west of Savannah, Georgia. They had no further problems the rest of the way.

Their next landmark was the intersection leading to Florida's State Road 520, going east to Cocoa Beach. After turning on to SR 520 they realized they were almost there. In less than an hour's time they pulled in to the parking lot of the Astronaut Motel. Their total travel time had been less than the two days estimated. They had called Walt via cell phone to alert him as to their arrival time. He was there to greet them with open arms, having been concerned for their safe arrival. Though they had been 'on the road' for about forty hours, they were keyed up at arriving without real incident.

Before their day was done they needed to park their trailers and unload their sensitive equipment in a secure location. Walt escorted them to the Base and got them checked in through Security. A Military Policeman took them in tow and led the way to the secure storage facilities. After placing the trailers inside special garages and unloading equipment from the SUV's, they were thankful to return to the motel, where they entered the restaurant and sank into comfortable seats. Walt ordered a round of drinks for everybody and when they had had a chance to eat a leisurely meal he suggested they get a good night's sleep and be prepared for a lengthy briefing in the morning.

After seeing that they were all comfortably settled in their individual rooms he retired to his room. Instead of going to bed he sat at his table and laid out a pattern of necessary briefings they would be required to attend. He knew that aside from a common detailed briefing for the entire Team, it would be necessary to set up specialized sessions for the particular qualifications of the individual members. Once he had a plan for the next day's activities he turned on his TV to get the latest news There not being anything of interest after listening for thirty minutes, he too went to bed.

The next morning they gathered at the restaurant again just before seven AM. They occupied a large table for six and joined in animated conversations over breakfast. All were in good spirits and ready to hear Walt's detailed briefing. He pointed out it would have to wait until they could assemble at the Base Ops Center. They finished their breakfast, mounted their SUV's and Walt led them to the Base. Before they could enter it was necessary for each to be photographed, fingerprinted, and have a verification made of their existing background check. The Base Security Personnel handled this in an expeditious manner and soon they all had shiny new photo badges and appropriate decals for their vehicles.

It was almost ten AM before they were assembled in the Operations Center awaiting introduction to Major General Mayfair. While senior rank was not new to them, they nonetheless fidgeted in anticipation of meeting General Mayfair. Walt had advised them that the General was a good man to work for and not to be overly concerned. They assembled in the impressive Ops Center, near the General's desk and waited while he completed a telephone call. He turned to them and smiled pleasantly. He was in shirt sleeves, and except for the visible stars on his jacket on the back of his chair, and the two small stars on each side of his collar, there was no outward indication of his rank.

Walt introduced each of his group, explaining their individual function and specialty. "This is Jack Johnson, Jack is qualified in just about every aspect of explosives and ordnance devices, and he has been known to open many supposedly secure safes. Natalie Morse is my executive officer. She can memorize things you wouldn't believe, she pretty much speaks for me in my absence. Here is Kim Shirakawa, he knows electronics and computers inside and out. Next to him is Joe Miselli, he is a mechanical genius, can make any engine purr like a kitten, and finally this is Connie," he deliberately omitted her last name.

Each of them shook hands with the General, Connie being last, held his hand slightly longer, looked demurely at the General and said, "Charmed, I'm sure!"

He almost laughed out loud, and said, "Me too," though he could not help but notice her beauty. He then spoke seriously and added, "I am delighted to have all of you with us on this mission. I feel you will be an asset to us in several ways. After you have been briefed, Walt can fill you in on just where we are now and how we will function."

The General had his Operations Chief present a formal classified briefing and when he was through he reminded them, "What I have just detailed for you is classified 'Top Secret.' I know all of you have the appropriate security clearance, but I want to say anyway, what you have just heard is classified for good reason, please be careful what you say, where ever you are."

Well over an hour had passed and Walt was anxious to complete the Team's orientation. He asked the General if they could be excused in order to go out to the launch complex for the rest of their briefing. The General peremptorily waved them away, his mind already shifted to other concerns, as he went back to his phone.

The team trooped out to the parking lot and all but Nat piled into one SUV. She joined Walt in his Cobra at his request and they headed out on to the highway, turning north toward the Cape. Walt carefully observed the posted speed limits as they drove away from the Base and through Cocoa Beach, Cape Canaveral and the port area. He was in radio communication with the other vehicle and assured them they would have an opportunity to see the complete area at a more leisurely pace in short order. The route was indeed a fascinating place with a multifaceted ambience, very much worthwhile visiting at another time.

En route Walt used the time to discuss some of the details of the mission with Nat. He asked her to repeat what he told her to the rest of the team. He explained at length about the design of the spacecraft and the enormous capabilities with which it was endowed. She listened with rapt attention when he described the results of the test done out in the Pacific Ocean. She only offered a brief question here and there during his recitation. He talked steadily during most of the drive to the Cape, stopping only when they were halted at the Main Gate for a check of their badges and vehicle decals. It was a forty five minute drive to the Launch Complex from the Base Ops Center, and as they came to the complex gate he remarked, "I'll have to finish a little later on."

The rest of the team quickly unloaded from the SUV, joining Walt and Nat as they walked toward the Complex Control building. Inside they were introduced to Major Bill Holloway and Lieutenant Colonel Jason Comiskey, who having been told of the exploits of Walt and his group, were pleased to welcome them to the Complex.

Major Holloway made a quick check of their badges and said, "If you are ready for a tour of the complex, let's get going. It's going to take about an hour to give you a good understanding of what we have here."

They immediately stood and started out after the disappearing Bill. They each obtained their hard hats from the SUV and joined Bill. Since their SUV was not equipped with a spark arresting muffler, a small truck was used and with Major Holloway at the wheel as they drove through the Complex gate and started their indoctrination.

After a little more than an hour had passed they returned from their tour, greatly impressed with what they had seen. All were excited by the sheer massiveness of the missile, even though the spacecraft itself had not yet been brought to the site.

They appreciatively thanked Major Holloway, who responded by saying. "Please call me Bill, we are generally informal around here."

The Team members immediately gave him their individual first names with a chorused reply, not readily understandable. Nat then repeated their names and a brief commentary about each. It was obvious that a real rapport had been established. Team questions posed were intelligent and pointed, indicating a good knowledge and understanding of the program.

Nat thanked Major Holloway on behalf of the Team and expressed genuine appreciation for the tour. She said to him, "Bill, I know I speak for Walt and all our Team when I say how much we have learned from you, and we hope we are able to provide something in return."

He retorted, "From what I'm told, you folks will be involved up to your ears before you know it!" He was aware that the Team would interface with, and be exposed to known foreign espionage efforts.

Nat looked at him quizzically, but said nothing in response. She thought to herself 'Walt has not told us everything we might expect.' She knew that Walt would tell them everything they would need to know when the time was right. Walt was waiting for them to complete their orientation and tour of the launch facilities to insure they could comprehend the enormous scope of the task ahead.

After handshakes all around they loaded up into their SUV for the trip back to the motel, to join up with Walt who had already departed.

CHAPTER 6

WALT WAS WAITING FOR THEM at the motel. As soon as their SUV pulled in to the parking lot, Nat herded them to Walt's room where they sprawled out comfortably. He motioned for them to not speak. He then asked Kim to get his detection equipment and perform a check of his room to determine if any 'bugs' had been installed during their absence.

Kim retreated to his room to pick up the portable unit he kept in his personal belongings. He quickly calibrated the unit and did a sweep of Walt's entire room and bath. He then stepped outside to see if he could detect any devices affixed to the walls. Since Walt had a room at the end where only a passageway abutted, it was an easy task to verify no obvious tampering had been done. Nat's room was next to Walt's so Kim asked Nat to let him run a perfunctory check in her room.

All this took but a few minutes before Kim said. "No bugs, unless it is something pretty sophisticated."

Walt said, "You all have gotten a very broad brush briefing on the program and you should have a good understanding of what they are trying to do. In a nutshell you can see that this very special spacecraft is to be launched from the Cape in the not too distant future. Our job is to help assure we have no foreign interference. Of course, there are the normal protective measures already in place by NASA, the Air Force, the CIA and FBI, and many other agencies as well. But, there are known foreign agents already here, looking for any information that can be had. You all know how these things can get out of hand. We are to independently try and forestall any threats we can find."

Nat interjected, "They don't want much, do they?"

Whereupon Walt responded, "As a matter of fact they want a helluva lot, we may be all over the country chasing down who knows what. You might as well know now, that somebody may try to stop this launch by whatever means possible, including killing if needed."

The Team immediately became subdued, realizing they were once more being called upon to perhaps risk their lives to defend their country's assets. There was nodding of heads and collective murmurs of assent.

Nat stood and spoke, "I think I can speak for all of us Walt, we pretty much knew we were getting into something especially sensitive. You know you can count on each of us to do our best."

"As always," echoed Jack.

Walt looked at each one of them individually, receiving an affirmative nod of the head. He then said, "I figured you were all kind of 'gung ho' to get in on this fantastic program. Here's what I would like each of you to take on."

"Nat, you and Kim can head out to Whitman Air Force Base in Missouri, where they have the test set-up they removed from the B-2. I have already made contact with their Operations Officer, a Lieutenant Colonel Charles Donohue, and they will be expecting you in a couple of days. Get a look at what they have done with the test set-up, size, number of components, any other pertinent technical data and especially the security situation. See if the test set-up is the same as what will go in the spacecraft, and whatever else you can collect.

Give yourselves one week and then return here. I don't need to tell you how sensitive this is, so be sure you carefully protect all info you collect. OK?" He added, "Stick around til I finish lining up every one else, that way you all will know what the others are doing."

Nat and Kim looked at one another and each nodded their understanding.

"Jack, will you get with Bill Holloway and arrange a tour around the perimeter of the exterior Cape fence. Also see if you can get the Security guys to show you how they operate so we won't cause any interference or set off their alarms. The Cape is a big place and it abuts the NASA launch area, so you may need to coordinate with them also. Bill Holloway is knowledgeable in this area, so he can help you considerably. When you feel you have the complete picture you can bring me up to speed, OK?'

"Gotcha, boss", Jack responded.

Walt turned to Joe Miselli and said, "Joe, we are going to need some vehicles that are equipped with spark arrestors, probably one or two jeeps will be enough, unless our SUV's can be properly set up, but that's probably a long shot. No vehicles are permitted on the Complex unless they have the proper safety equipment."

Joe thought for a moment and replied, "I've already gotten friendly with the Base motor pool guys. They hate to let us civilians use their equipment. I know the NCO that runs the motor pool. Maybe I can use my charm on him."

Walt said, "I am sure I can get an OK from General Mayfair for you to contact the motor pool people, if you need me to."

To which Joe asserted, "Let me give it a shot first."

Turning, Walt faced Connie and said, "If you try make out with General Mayfair, I'll be in real trouble, but what I'd like you to do is be my interface with the General, at least at first, until I can tell where I'll be or what I'll be doing. After that you will be the Team contact. Have you got our portable scramblers in the equipment trailer?'

She said, a trifle brusquely, "We have everything we'll need, including our scramblers."

Walt replied, "Bear with me Connie, I'm really up to my ears with so much information that I lost my mind."

She was immediately contrite, and said, "Sorry boss, I've got it all covered."

They departed to their rooms for necessary packing and later reassembled to have a quick review of each team members' actions and to estimate time schedules. Connie recorded everything on her laptop computer, and verified each of them could remotely interface with her computer.

Within an hour they started out on their assigned tasks, taking with them a schedule for check-in times, and a mental picture of what each of the other team members had been told to accomplish.

Nat and Kim, being the only team members expecting to travel, drove to the secure trailer storage area to select the equipment they thought essential for their trip. They had access to each of the team trailers, permitting them to select what they needed from the entire team inventory. Within an hour they were under way, using a single SUV and towing one of the trailers. They headed north on A1A to SR520 and then west to I-95, once on I-95 they drove north at the maximum speed limit, 70 miles per hour. They drove around Jacksonville on the by-pass until its intersection with I-10, where they turned west. They took turns driving, keeping up the rapid pace, stopping briefly to have snacks and coffee. After passing Tallahassee they decided they should soon stop for the night.

They passed Pensacola before they finally stopped at a roadside motel and asked for a single room with two beds. The innkeeper smiled knowingly and gave them a room where their vehicle was well illuminated and immediately outside their room. Satisfied that their parked vehicle was relatively safe, they entered the small restaurant and ordered a substantial meal. After consuming one cocktail each the meal was placed in front of them. They quickly devoured the food, not having had a real meal since breakfast, and returned to their room.

Nat started removing her clothes until she had nothing on but her panties and bra, though she was exceedingly attractive as she stood there, Kim appeared to take no notice. She announced she was going to shower and 'hit the sack'. Kim went outside and verified their SUV and trailer were OK and set the alarm system. Upon re-entering the room he sat down in a comfortable chair, and turned on the TV to catch the latest news.

Nat finished her shower and returned to the room and asked Kim,. "Anything new on the 'boob tube'?"

Kim shook his head negatively and said, "OK if I shower now?"

She had already slipped into her pajamas in the bathroom and had dropped into the other chair before she replied, "Sure, I picked up after myself, so it's ready for you."

Kim went in the bathroom and could be heard singing softly as he showered. He too put his pajamas on before returning to the room. They chatted briefly before he got into one of the beds and promptly fell asleep. She watched the news for a few minutes before she too bedded down for the night.

Immediately after listening to each team member review their assignment Joe went out to his SUV and headed for the motor pool on the base. He was confident of his task, having already met the senior NCO assigned to the Base Motor Pool. He parked his vehicle just outside the gate to the motor pool and sauntered inside, asking a passing harried mechanic in greasy coveralls, "Hey, Sarge, where can I find old 'Redneck Billy' about now?"

The sergeant replied, "He's over in the main building", pointing at a nearby large corrugated building.

Joe mumbled a thank you, ignored by the sergeant, and walked to the main building. Once inside became impressed with the modern lifts and test equipment plainly visible. It was obviously an up-to-date facility, capable of performing extensive mechanical repairs to all, or any of the vehicles in the base inventory. He spied the windowed office in one corner of the structure, and correctly assumed it would be where he would find Senior Master Sergeant Billy 'Redneck' Romanelli. Joe sauntered over to the open doorway and asked "Is there an old son-of-a-bitch here named 'Redneck'?"

Romanelli, hearing the loud remark turned and said, "Damned if I don't get the worst kind of visitors in here!" The two met and embraced with considerable enthusiasm, each smacking the other on the back with resounding thumps.

"If I know you like I think I know you, you came here wanting something," the immaculately clad Romanelli spoke, in a false menacing tone. Then in a sincere clasp of Joe's hands in his own strong grasp, said, "You know I will do whatever I can. We have been told to 'cooperate' with you guys, by the 'front office' no less."

Joe said, "I wasn't sure it was you when I heard who was running the motor pool, but I'm sure glad it is you. We may need to equip our SUV's with required safety stuff that will allow us to drive on a launch complex."

"That might be a substantial job," Romanelli replied. "It means spark suppression on your ignition systems and a special muffler, at the very least. You would be better off using approved government vehicles. And they are in damned short supply."

They walked outside and he said to Joe, "Let me take a look at one of your SUV's and I'll know better which way to go."

Joe drove his SUV inside the motor pool shop and positioned it over a hydraulic lift, whereupon it was lifted high in the air and the safety lock engaged. Romanelli started looking the undercarriage over from front to back without a word being uttered. He then lowered the vehicle, opened the hood and all the doors, as well as the tail gate. He quickly examined it and said, 'OK, your electrical systems meet our requirements, who ever selected these units was really on the ball, all the electrical systems are code 5. All you need is a special muffler. Who ever bought this baby knew what he was doing." He called out, "John, go get one of those spark arresting mufflers and hang it on this truck."

Joe was impressed and said so, "Billy, you really do know how to get things done, but I've got four more of these SUV's, just like this one. Can you take care of them too?"

"No problem, bring them on, they told me about your trucks, all five of them are special cases, according to my Motor Officer," was the quick rejoinder.

While they talked, the special muffler was quickly added to the tailpipe of Joe's SUV.

Jack had called Major Holloway and arranged to meet him at the Complex gate. Jack explained what he had been tasked to do and asked if Bill could help him. Major Holloway told Jack he was not all that familiar with the Cape fencing and called Security Headquarters to seek help. One of the Security Sergeants was about to go off duty and offered to be an escort. Major Holloway and Jack drove to the Headquarters to pick up the

Security Sergeant. He was waiting at the Ops Desk and introduced himself as Sergeant Jim Hutchinson. As soon as introductions had been made all around, Jim, as he asked them to call him, pointed out that the Cape was a pretty large place.

He showed them to a wall-mounted map of the Cape, whose size came as a surprise to Jack. They then sat down and examined the overall picture and decided it would not be appropriate to tour around the entire Cape. Jim pointed out it would take the better part of a full day to do that. Instead, they determined that since access was generally difficult without proper identification, they need only examine that part of the Cape in relative proximity to the launch complex.

The logical demarcation was the road leading to Kennedy Space Center, KSC. There was a large expanse of water also limiting entry to the area of their concern. Jim pointed out that the water portions were regularly patrolled by the security forces of both KSC and the Cape. At the north was another line of demarcation delineating KSC versus Cape property. It had guard posts manned by both KSC Security and Cape Security.

Jack toured some almost inaccessible ground and drove along a roadway adjacent to part of the fencing enclosing the Cape. He noted that one or two places afforded an excellent view of the complex, though it was a several hundred meters away.

They did not notice the tracks left by Senior Sergeant Karamoski's departing vehicle only days before.

Kim awoke first at the break of dawn. Nat became aware of Kim moving around but judiciously allowed Kim to dress and then yawned and spoke to him., saying, "Hope you slept well. Are you going to check the SUV?"

Kim replied, "Yes, I'm going to take a quick look and will be right back."

Intuitively Nat knew that Kim would take enough time to allow her to dress. She then said, "As soon as you get back I'll be ready and we can go to breakfast."

Kim first looked out the window and noted nothing seemed out of order. He opened the door and stepped outside to make a visual check of their SUV and trailer, shutting off the alarm system. A quick examination showed nothing amiss and Kim stood for a moment breathing the fresh air before returning to the room. Nat was dressed in the Team coveralls and looked quite fetching.

Together they walked to the motel restaurant for breakfast. He too, wore the yellow Team coveralls with the small "FIXIT" logo on the left breast in bright red. They made a striking duo.

Following a good breakfast they climbed into their SUV and headed West on I-10 again. They continued westward passing Mobile, Alabama through Biloxi and Gulfport, Mississippi, until intersecting with Interstate-12 which took them to Hammond, Louisiana, there they turned North on Interstate-55. They knew that I-55 would take them to Memphis, Tennessee, where it would cross the Mississippi River into Arkansas. Just before coming to a small city outskirts they broke again for another meal. The rest stop offered prepackaged sandwiches in reasonable varieties and bottled drinks, upon which they stocked up. They added ice and put their purchases in the chest cooler.

Continuing beyond Memphis, I-55 stretched northward before them in a graceful rise and fall of the highway. They decided to press on and try to get nearer to St. Louis, Missouri. The Interstate was smooth going and they made excellent time, being careful to avoid exceeding the speed limit, fearful of being delayed unnecessarily. At Cape Girardeau they decided they could put up for the night and get an early start in the morning. The next morning they were under way at dawn, skirting around St. Louis, they headed West on I-70 to the turn off to Fulton and on to Jefferson City, their destination.

They immediately drove to Whitman AF Base to find the B-2 Base Operations officer, Lieutenant Colonel Donohue. They were required to check in at Base Security where they were expected. A quick call brought a young lieutenant to escort them to Base Operations. They were impressed by the numbers of large aircraft lined up on the tarmac, including several B-2 Stealth Bombers.

Inside the Ops area they were introduced to Lieutenant Colonel "Chuck" Donohue, who made them feel welcome. He said, "The test equipment has already been removed from the aircraft, but it is located in one of the labs where you can still see it."

"Will security be a problem?" asked Nat, concerned that they would not be able to assess the security controls, as Walt had requested.

"No, your clearances came through yesterday," he replied. Then continuing he told them the test set up was soon to be dismantled and later shipped to NASA, Huntsville, as back-up hardware. "That means you only have the rest of today and part of tomorrow to do your thing," he said in a reluctant tone.

"However, the science and engineering people are still here and can answer just about any question," he explained. "Good thing you got here when you did or you might not have been able to see anything," he added.

"Scotty, take them over to Hanger J, everything is still laid out on benches so the science guys could examine every thing, I saw the video of the test, it was spectacular," he exclaimed. "After you are through with what you want to see, I will set up a viewing of the tape for you both. We have a small viewing theater there in Hanger J."

Scotty shook hands with first Nat then Kim and asked, "Are those coveralls ordnance approved?"

They both responded at once, "Yes they are, the tag is in the collar."

He laughed and said, "I thought they would be, I don't need to see the label."

As they exited the hanger Scotty told them, "Your vehicle is safe where it is, just lock it up and no one will bother it."

Kim replied, "I lock it and set the alarm every time we leave it, company ground rule."

They climbed into a jeep and Scotty drove away at a rapid pace, seemingly with no regard for safe limits. They pulled up to a barbed wire topped fence around an innocuous appearing building with armed guards posted at each corner of the fenced area, each one carrying a lethal looking weapon at the ready. They climbed out of the jeep and were halted at the entrance gate where a pair of alert guards eyed them suspiciously. Scotty explained that this was Hanger J, a facility for accommodating Top

Secret projects, and that they would be subjected to a search of their person.

They emptied their pockets of everything and placed it in a small plastic box which was marked with their names and placed on a rack for later retrieval. They were then very professionally and thoroughly patted down without regard for the fact that Nat was female. It was obvious that these guards were only concerned with doing their job. Their badges were exchanged for a special iridescent badge and a tape with their name printed thereon stuck on their garment. They were finally permitted to enter.

As they entered the building they were once more stopped and required to sign in. The log contained spaces for their name, company, security clearance, badge number, and authorizing escort. They opened the inner door to a sterile facility, though not classified as a "clean room". The room was brilliantly lit with several men in lab coats working around a long bench. The device spread out along the length of the bench, were a series of small compact frames holding what appeared to be miniature electronic components, all tied together by bundles of wires and metal-clad stainless steel hoses. The wires terminated in coupling joints, some appearing to be 'jury rigged' contraptions.

Since this was test equipment, clean standards were not required. The equipment appearing to be 'jury rigged' hardly looked like something from a highly specialized weapon.

Kim looked at it aghast, this was the weapon to end all weapons? The construction offended his sense of well-soldered joints and mother boards, where finished products were neat and tidy, no loose wires. How could something like this work as described, the weapon to end all weapons?

Nat, on the other hand, was impressed by what she saw. She was anxious to talk to the design people. She had no preconceived notion about how the weapon should look. She looked at Kim, startled by his expression, and said, "What's the matter Kim, you look like something is wrong." Kim did not reply.

Together they approached the bench, while Scotty talked animatedly with a tired appearing older man dressed in a lab coat. In a moment Scotty brought the man to where Nat and Kim were staring at the device.

Scotty said, "Nat, Kim, I would like you to meet Doctor John Bowman, the principal scientist associated with the program, Doctor please meet Natalie Morse and Kim Shirakawa. They are members of Walt Crawford's Team of specialists." Scotty seemed to be on his best behavior.

Doctor Bowman said, "I'm delighted to meet you, I've heard many tales about some of your exploits. I met Walt in Washington, and I must say, he is a most impressive individual. I understand you and Walt will be involved with helping to keep us out of trouble from some of the bad guys."

Nat replied, "We hope we will be able to contribute in some measure."

Kim said, "I thought I knew electronics, but I must confess I have never seen anything like this. Is this the actual unit that performed the test in the Pacific?"

"Yes, this is it, but we had it assembled a lot differently," he replied. He then started to walk them through how the system operated, soon realizing these two were not off the street nincompoops. He was like an animated boy explaining how it worked, though in some regard they simply did not understand everything he said Surprisingly, they did comprehend most of what he told them.

After thirty minutes he stopped and asked if he was boring them. They replied in unison, "No way, not at all."

He said, "Of course you understand this test device is not at all how the flight version will be configured." The doctor went on, "Oh sure, I keep forgetting you know how things like this are a poor example of what the real article will look like."

Kim mumbled something sounding like an assent, but like Nat, he had no idea what the final craft would look like. Kim did remember to ask, "Doctor, have you given any thought as to how the power output of the real spacecraft can be accommodated in a dummy load?"

Doctor Bowman looked at Kim with new respect and replied, "We have some special 'horns' that will match up to the output device. We think they will accommodate the power, but only minimal input will be allowable. We are confident that if it works at minimum, it will accept the entire power curve. If we were to use a higher input it would probably destroy the entire area, spacecraft, launch vehicle, and the Launch Complex."

Kim looked at Nat and shrugged as if to say, 'How are we going handle that?' Instead he asked, "Doctor Bowman, how long before this will be in flight configuration?"

"The spacecraft frame has already been built, based on what the actual flight hardware needs. It is at Huntsville now. It won't exactly be little, but we know precisely how much weight and room is needed. It is well within the nose cone dimensional limits, and lift capability of the launch vehicle. Some assembly has been started and now we can go ahead with the rest. It will be assembled at the Huntsville facility in the large clean room," he sounded very confident. "We even have a shipping container that will fit in the C-5A for air transport to the Cape when we are ready."

Nat and Kim both came to the same conclusion at the same time. They were appreciative of the opportunity to see the test article, but they had expected to see something that approximated the launch configuration. In retrospect, they realized that this test device only served to validate that the design would operate. They discussed what the flight unit would be like and asked Doctor Bowman if he could show them anything concrete about what the ultimate flight article would be like.

Doctor Bowman replied, "We'll ship the test unit to Huntsville now as back-up hardware and later on to KSC, but come on over to my lab and I'll show you the drawings for the actual spacecraft."

They accompanied him through the exit procedures, recovering their personal belongings and followed his car out of the classified area to a large office structure. Parking their SUV in an available space they followed him to an elevator, where they were once again halted and subjected to much the same security measures as for the spacecraft building. Once in his laboratory, they could see by the various test equipment and visible apparatus that they were in a very special place. A number of experiments were in progress under the watchful eyes of serious-faced scientists and engineers. They moved to an office at one side of the lab and were ushered inside and seated on stools before a large drafting board. Already spread out were drawings of the spacecraft, but covered with opaque sheets of plastic.

The doctor lifted the plastic and before them was a series of technical schematics, as well as several actual pictures of the craft in all its glory, flying high in space. These were artists renderings of what the flight craft would look like. He set the pictures aside with a dismissive motion, saying, "Here are some of the integrated drawings of the actual flight configuration."

Neither Nat nor Kim could comprehend the voluminous amount of detail the drawings depicted. They asked to see a drawing of the external appearance and how it would be mounted on top on the missile third stage. He showed them to another drafting table, where an engineer politely laid out that drawing for their viewing. The drawing was unimpressive, until Doctor Bowman went through a detailed description of the various components and their inter-relationships. Though his description was very lucid, they realized they did not need such a detailed explanation. They thanked Doctor Bowman and the people to whom they had been introduced, and explained that further discussion was not necessary.

Nat and Kim retreated to their SUV and prepared to depart, first calling to Connie on their portable scrambling system, explaining they had completed their mission, and would return to Cocoa Beach with details for Walt and the rest of the Team. Connie dutifully recorded the call on her computer for relay to Walt.

They checked out of the base main gate and started their return trip. Kim ruefully said, "We sure didn't need to bring the equipment trailer, or anything else, for that matter. It was really interesting but, too technical at this stage. Shipping that test unit to Huntsville is going to give them a complete set of spares, I guess."

Nat nodded her assent, and said to Kim, "Why don't you try to get forty winks while I take the first shift driving back." Kim obligingly reclined his seat back and dozed off as Nat pushed the speed limits, mentally trying to put what they had seen in some sort of order. She thought of how they should present all the information given them to Walt and the rest of the Team. They took turns driving, with occasional stops for a brief rest and to eat. Neither wanted to stop until they had covered nearly a thousand miles. They finally stopped at a roadside motel for a brief rest and started out again with but a few hours of rest They arrived back in Cocoa Beach, tired but pleased they had made the trip without incident.

Walt said, "Kim, I know you are tired after your run, but will you make a sweep of the room before we all talk again."

Kim immediately got his equipment and made the required checks. He reported, "All clear, Walt."

The rest of the Team came in to Walt's room, which had been furnished with several more easy chairs, and settled down to hear the reports from each of the other Team members.

Walt said. "We are all anxious to hear from your trip Nat, so how about you and Kim telling us what you found at Whitman."

Nat looked at Kim, who nodded at her to start. She began, "It's a helluva lot further there than we thought, but we had no trouble en route or getting in to the Base. They were expecting us and were very hospitable. Security is very tight, but our clearances were in good order, so we had no problem in that regard. We met Doctor Bowman, who was very nice to us. He took us in to the classified areas and showed us the actual beast they fired from the B-2 It had already been broken down and we saw the disassembled hardware spread out on work benches. Not especially impressive, but it is the one that was actually used to destroy that little boat."

She closed by adding, "Doctor Bowman showed us the video of the actual test, that little boat was totally destroyed, the ocean even boiled."

Kim picked up with the narrative and said. "The doctor did tell us that the flight hardware will be assembled in Huntsville labs. He took us into another secure lab and showed us the drawings of the flight configuration, both pictorials and actual detail drawings. He assured us all was well and the actual spacecraft design will fit within the nosecone. Oh yeah, he was not concerned about the weight, said it was well within the capabilities of the missile."

Connie verbalized a thought, "Now would be a lousy time to find out it was too heavy, they should have figured that out a long time ago."

General discussion ensued and each of the Team members gave an account of what they had learned. Walt terminated the session, but reminding them of the hour and that the days ahead would be demanding. He bade each of them goodnight and after they had left for their own rooms he remained at his makeshift desk and contemplated what lay ahead.

CHAPTER 7

AGENT BORIS MOSHILEV, OF THE disbanded KGB notoriety, recorded the departure of Nat and Kim on his Palm Corder, as they left Whitman AFB in Missouri, entering the time, hour and date of their leaving. As he sat outside the main gate he could see their faces through his binoculars, noting their look of bemusement. He was anxious to know if he would be able to hear any discussion between Nat and Kim. He hoped his planted device would pick up their voices as they drove away toward St. Louis. He started his vehicle and pulled out onto the roadway, keeping about one half mile behind them, being cautious to not be seen. He hoped Kim would not run a sweep of their SUV to detect the miniature device he had affixed to the top rear of its roof. It blended in with the roof rack on the SUV and was indiscernible to the casual eye.

Kim had not made a sweep to check for 'bugs'.

Boris and his companion, a muscular woman with not unattractive features, were in a non-descript Chevy pickup with a camper on the bed. The sliding rear window of the pick-up was open to the camper interior permitting the two to converse. Inside the camper they had set up the most modern equipment available to them from a large sporting goods store and an internet supplier of surveillance equipment. She monitored their listening equipment as they drove along the highway. It was inconceivable to them that such equipment was available to purchase without government approval.

She could hear the discussion between Nat and Kim about not having needed to bring the equipment trailer with them and thought, 'What have they seen, did they not observe the test set-up?' Suddenly she became alert as she heard the brief comment between them about the need for moving the test article to Huntsville as a back-up unit very soon.

Boris continued to follow about a half mile behind being careful to not attract attention. Natasha passed what she had heard to him as he drove on. She adjusted the receiver volume to allow Boris to hear any further conversation between Nat and Kim.

The brief comment between Nat and Kim about the movement of the 'test article' was the highlight of all they heard during the rest of their trip.

The woman was deceiving, in that she held advanced degrees from Moscow University in electronic engineering and psychology, a strange combination. Boris had specifically asked for Natasha, knowing she was fluent in English, and capable of mimicking the voices of females to a level so nearly perfect, that even persons familiar with someone were easily deceived, particularly if it was a telephone call.

Boris also noted Natasha had a healthy sexual appetite and he was not loath to avail himself of her female 'charms.'

It was a matter of convenience for both of them, inasmuch as they traveled as man and wife, and no eyebrows were raised as they checked in to the same motel as had Nat and Kim..

Boris and Natasha had breakfast at a table near Nat and Kim, but picked up nothing of note as they listened to their conversation. Neither Nat nor Kim noticed the pair or the old pick-up parked at the motel. Within minutes after Nat and Kim's departure, Boris and Natasha were on the road not far behind, following them all the way to Cocoa Beach.

They registered at the Astronaut Motel, explaining to the clerk, they would be a few days while they saw the sights associated with the famous launch site of missiles. They appeared to be just another couple vacationing in the area.

Colonel Dantilev congratulated Agent Moshilev on his report advising of the transfer of the spacecraft test equipment from Whitman AFB to the NASA test facility at Huntsville, Alabama.

A bold plan was set in motion by the Colonel, which would shock the United States beyond belief. The convoy of vehicles transporting the test spacecraft to Huntsville would be hijacked. Accompanying personnel and guards would all be killed in order that there be no one left to identify the transgressors. A small group of trusted people were brought together to work out details. There was little time for planning, but there was an adequate supply of 'wet work' personnel, some mercenaries, and some from within KGB resources.

The move date of the test spacecraft had been identified as ten days away, leaving little time to test the viability of their plan. The route was one used on other occasions for movement between Whitman and Huntsville. It was not a road frequented by individual travelers, much preferring the high speed Interstate highways.

Discipline was essential to the concept of the planned hijack. Fortunately discipline was not a real concern for the Russian, those who did not conform could be easily dealt with, harshly, if not worse.

Dantilev himself conducted the briefing of the hijack group, insuring strict response to orders. He sought assurance that his group could react to unknown, un-preplanned situations. He availed himself of one of his own staff, Captain Sgedy Skelsin, a veteran of clandestine operations, to head the group. Skelsin would not hesitate to shoot his own men if they questioned his orders. The plan was simple, a group in front of the convoy and another group behind it. A simulated breakdown of a truck to block the highway, preferably just beyond a curve of the road, would cause the convoy to halt, if only briefly. This should be all the opportunity the hijack group would need to stage their attack, it would have to be swift and sure. Kill everybody in view of the hijack, no one to report what had happened. Colonel Dantilev reminded them their substantial pay would be dependent upon their success.

The move was planned by Air Force Military Police to take place at night and did not utilize major highways. This followed the practice of avoiding routes well traveled, since the Military Convoy would have several vehicles.

One large tractor-trailer carried the actual equipment and was preceded by a small truck leading and another following, each with an armed guard plus the driver, a total of three vehicles and six men including the drivers and the young officer in charge, riding in the cab of the primary tractor-trailer.

The ambush occurred just past midnight, after the convoy had rounded a curve, when the hijackers had one fast-moving pickup overtake the convoy, then slowed down pretending to have motor trouble, while a second pickup approached from the rear. Each pickup was manned by heavily armed men carrying machine guns and rocket propelled grenades. The lead pickup rounded a curve and slowed to a halt on the roadway, effectively blocking passage. The driver dismounted and approached the convoy lead vehicle asking for help, when the Air Force driver opened his door, the pickup driver shot him at point blank range. This was the signal for the others to open fire, killing everyone almost immediately. The convoy guards did get one spray of bullets off, killing one of the pickup drivers. It was all over in less than two minutes.

The assassins dragged the dead bodies from the convoy trucks, climbed in and started the tractor-trailer rolling down the roadway, followed by their pick-up trucks and the Air Force vehicles. The deserted highway was the scene of carnage seldom seen before. Seven bodies lay in the ditch along the side of the road. The one mercenary killed carried no identification linking him to the perpetrators. He would not join in the revelry voiced by the successful hijackers later that day!

An abandoned farm with a large barn was utilized to conceal the Air Force trucks. The spacecraft components and equipment was transferred to a single large closed-bed truck, with misleading advertisements painted on its sides, attesting to a moving company as the owner. The Air Force trucks were left in the barn, to be discovered days later when investigators tried to determine how this had happened. The slaughter of six unsuspecting Airmen would be difficult if not impossible to keep from the press, and the seventh man, the mercenary's body, yielded no clues to help in determining what had happened.

The Military Police unit at Whitman AFB waited for the call that all was well from the convoy, due every fifteen minutes. When no call came, the NCO in charge of monitoring the convoy's progress called the Base Ops Officer to report loss of communication from the convoy. Emergency procedures were immediately implemented when the loss of communications was reported. Efforts to contact the convoy were without response.

An Air Force Security Team was dispatched via helicopter to the last reported position of the convoy. Although the helicopter was a fast moving Huey 'chopper,' time was irretrievably lost while the helicopter was en route. Some fifty five minutes later the emergency team reported their arrival and passed on the report of the gunned-down bodies of their fellow Airmen and the one body of the hijackers.

The Whitman Air Force Base Criminal Investigation Detachment immediately sent their team of investigative specialists to the hijack site by fast-moving cars. With the cooperation of state Highway Patrols they sped to the scene in record time.

––––––––––

Doctor Bowman was aroused and informed of the hijacking incident, to his bewilderment. How could such a thing happen? He was astonished that his 'child,' his dream had been stolen away. He tried to rationalize that without knowing a great deal about the experiment, having the test hardware was not tantamount to making the test unit operate. He realized that any competent scientist could understand the system, given enough time to study the hardware and given time would understand how to make it work.

He recalled the visit of the Team members from Walt's group, and their assigned function to guard against loss of the spacecraft. He called Lieutenant Colonel Donohue, the program Ops Officer, and said, "Chuck, the worst has happened......".

Before he could go further Lieutenant Colonel Donohue interrupted him saying, "I know, the report just got to me here at home." He then continued saying, "We will need to get in touch with Walt Crawford right away."

Doctor Bowman said, "If you don't mind, would you do the calling, I am rather distraught at the moment."

The stern-voiced officer replied, "Of course, I understand, I think I have all the available information. I will contact him right away." He then turned to his wife, still in bed but now wide awake and said, "Sorry honey, I have to go to the office and work a little problem."

He dressed quickly, using the phone to order a driver to pick him up at his quarters in five minutes. The car was there with the door open, as he exited his home. He nodded his appreciation to the driver and asked to be taken to the Base Operations Center. It seemed everyone on the base knew about the hijacking, even at the lateness of the hour, although the convoy departure was supposedly classified.

He entered his office where the lights were already in full illumination and his senior NCO was standing at the ready. He told the noncom to get Walt Crawford on the line as quickly as possible. M/Sgt Delahanty had already gotten the number and was ready to punch it in at a moment's notice, at a nod from the officer he depressed the buttons and passed the handset to Lieutenant Colonel Donohue saying, "Ringing, sir."

Walt was aroused by the phone ringing, and realizing the lateness of the hour, was immediately alert and responsive. He answered, "Crawford here, how can I help you?"

Lieutenant Colonel Donohue answered, "Walt, this Chuck Donohue, please call me on a scrambled line ASAP, you have my number".

Without further word Walt hung up, contacted Kim and said, "Emergency Kim, come on over here right now and set me up via scrambler to Colonel Donohue at Whitman."

Kim grabbed his ready bag and went directly to Walt's room, he entered without knocking since the door was unlocked. He quickly made a sweep of the room interior and then went outside to make a quick sweep of the exterior. He reentered and activated the scrambler system and looked inquiringly at Walt for the number to call. Walt read off the correct number for the Whitman Operations Office, which Kim promptly entered and asked, "Speaker phone?'

Walt nodded and the connection was quickly made. "Donohue here," was the first words on the speaker.

Walt immediately replied, "This is Walt Crawford, I have part of my Team here listening to you on a scrambled speaker phone. We are secure, you can speak freely."

Donohue gave a complete rundown on the events so far reported, and after a few minutes of narrative he asked are you recording this?" Walt answered in the affirmative and he continued with all the details so far known.

Walt asked for the location and was given precise map coordinates, Donohue then added, it is about halfway between Florence, and Athens, in Alabama on US 72, just East of Rogersville. Nat had entered the room and gestured to Walt questioningly, should I get the rest of the Team in here? Walt nodded affirmatively and she went back to her room to arouse the rest of the group.
The Team quickly assembled in Walt's room in various stages of dress, all wide awake, aware that a major event had occurred.

Walt summarized what had occurred and then asked Kim to play back the recording of Donohue's call. They listened with rapt attention to the detailed recounting of the hijacking, the killings, and the lack of evidence as to where was the test unit.

After the recording had been played through twice, Walt said, "We will want to check out that area and video tape the scene, or at least what ever is left by the time we get there. Maybe Chuck's troops videotaped it before everything was moved. Nat, Kim, you saw the test unit, how much space is needed to haul it around?"

"Depends on how big a truck they used, one truck would make it. I am sure it would fit into one vehicle in spite of they way they had it spread out," Kim said.

Nat added, "From what Donohue said, it was one good-sized truck, I assume he meant a semi-tractor trailer type".

Walt noted, "Chuck did say they used one semi-tractor trailer rig. So you are right on."

"I'll contact Chuck again and see if they videotaped the scene," he added then went on, "In the meantime, Nat, you and Jack head up to the scene and look around, talk to whoever is available. I'll want Kim here, since he is aware of what the test unit looks like. Connie, you will have to continue to track everybody and coordinate their reports. Each one of you must maintain contact with Connie, I don't want to lose track of anybody, keep her notified of where you are and what you are doing. Connie, I'll depend on you to keep me updated as much as possible. Joe, you'll have to pick up on the Cape security that Jack was following, he did pass on what he had discovered so far, didn't he?"

Joe said he and Jack and all the others had discussed each others activities and he could pick up what he needed from Bill Holloway.

Walt said, "Kim will you take care of getting all this info in to safekeeping? I must get out to update General Mayfair."

The Team desire to see some action appeared to be well satisfied. Walt cautioned them, "Be safe, and Connie will let each of you know when we can get together to update everybody, I hope we'll reassemble here in two or three days."

"Connie, check on that Whitman video taping and let Nat and Jack know if you can give them anything else," were his parting words. With that he hastened out to report to General Mayfair.

CHAPTER 8

JACK DROVE THEIR SUV AT a pace just above the speed limits, keeping a careful check on the speed detection equipment in the vehicle. As he approached any slight rise in the highway he slowed until he had crested the slope, avoiding being caught by a radar beyond visibility of their on-board detectors. Florida being relatively flat, he had little concern for these slight grades, and their detectors were very reliable. Nat relaxed as much as possible, knowing that she would be driving later on. From experience they knew to spell one another, covering considerable distances in the shortest possible time. Their route had been laid out on the GPS dash-mounted display system.

Connie had thoughtfully gotten the motel kitchen to fix sandwiches while they absorbed the news. The pair passed Jacksonville before daylight and were well on the way to just East of Rogersville, their destination. After only one stop to top off their fuel they arrived in good time and found the Air Force Investigative Team still on site. The highway had been blocked by the Alabama Highway

Patrol, both East and West of the grisly scene. Lieutenant Colonel Donohue had advised the investigators to expect them and to provide full cooperation. Jack was almost deferential as he introduced himself and Natalie to the lead investigator, a Captain Phillip Johansen.

Jack said, "I am Jack Johnson and this is Natalie Morse, I hope we don't present a problem to you, but we are here to help in any way we can, we are working for Major General Mayfair down at the Cape."

The Captain replied, "Not a problem, I've been told you were coming and to be completely cooperative." He continued, "May I see your identification please?"

Jack and Nat promptly complied, showing their special identification cards as well as the Cape badges recently issued them. They both had donned their yellow coveralls with the company logo "Fixit" on the breast and were quite conspicuous in the early morning sunlight.

Captain Johansen commented, "You'll be hard to miss wearing those bright yellow jump suits, but don't worry I'll see that you get access to whatever we have."

Nat immediately asked, "Any chance there is a videotape of the scene?"

The Captain looked at her with new respect and said, "That is the first thing the Security Team did when they arrived on location. We have about an hour or more of tape already in the can. We have a player over there in one of the vehicles where you can view what we have. We videotape as we go along, and you'll get a copy of everything."

She responded, "That is the first thing we'd like to see, and when will it be possible to get copies of what you have. Also, be assured you will get a copy of everything we videotape, that is, if you have no objections to us taping the scene."

"Good deal," he responded. "Come on over to the van and you can get started."

"Our Graves Registration folks have already picked up the bodies, but the tapes will show you each one and where they were dumped," Johansen commented, he then continued, "They will refrigerate the bodies until disposition of the remains is determined. The next of kin have to be notified, but I don't know how that will be handled."

Nat asked, "OK if I start taping the area so our guys will understand what this place looks like from our viewpoint?"

The Captain replied, "Suggest you might want to look at our tapes first, then you will have a better idea of the overall scene."

"You are right of course, can we get started pretty quick?" she asked.

"Come on," he said and turned toward a step van of considerable size, he rapped on the rear door and waited for word to enter. The door opened and a bespectacled Air Force Sergeant invited them in. Introductions were made all around and Captain Johansen explained these visitors are the specialists sent by higher headquarters.

The Sergeant said, "My name is Alvin, and no cracks, please. I'll set up our tape viewer and you can review the tape, then I can make a copy of whatever you want."

Nat smiled warmly at the Sergeant and said, "Thank you so much, it will be a great help to us."

Alvin almost fell over himself as he looked at Nat, admittedly she was an extremely attractive package, as she shook his hand. Her yellow coveralls were tailored to show her trim figure and her zipper was conveniently low to give a splendid view of her cleavage. She belatedly pulled the zipper up a couple of inches with her left hand, while demurely looking at Alvin. He reluctantly released her other hand and showed her where to sit, almost forgetting Jack's presence. Then he also showed Jack to a seat near the viewing machine.

Alvin started the tape through the machine with a smile at Nat and said, "I'll stop the tape whenever you want and you can ask questions of Captain Johansen. I can make copies of what ever you would like, just tell me where to stop, and start, and I can make it as we go along, that way you can take it with you when we're through."

The video scene shown was horrific, in that the dead bodies lay where they had been literally thrown by the hijackers. The body of their own man was treated with no better regard than were the bodies of the Air Force men. Some men lay half on the body of another Airman and half in the ditch, with several inches of mud-colored water. Bloody streaks discolored the water here and there. The uniforms of the Airmen were riddled with bloody bullet holes, some of the faces were unrecognizable having been literally destroyed by impact of multiple bullets. Hundreds of empty casings from the fired ammunition lay every where. Each piece of 'brass' was identified as to type and precise location, then logged by number on a special record sheet.

———————

Before departing, Sgedy had made sure that all were dead by sending bursts of machine gun fire through each body, including his own man, after they had been thrown into the ditch. His eyes reflected a perverse pleasure as he completed that final act. The empty casings from his gun would reveal the kind of weapon he used. The few .30 caliber casings were from the weapons carried by the Air Force guards, mute testimony to the surprise of the attack.

The recording was shown in its entirety, then replayed at a slower rate, allowing Nat and Jack to select pertinent views for transcribing to a separate tape. The versatility of the machine was amazing, they would have one tape with the views they had selected and another copy of everything the Air Force and CID cameramen had taken. Alvin was so taken with Nat that he would have given her the entire machine, had she asked for it.

A burly civilian wearing what appeared to be hunting gear entered the van unbidden, to the chagrin of Alvin, who stated , "I told you to knock before coming in here, you never know what I might have in progress."

He responded by saying, "I could hear all of you talking, besides they told me outside it was OK," he continued, "Captain I got some news for you," indicating they should step outside.

"It's OK, George," said Captain Johansen, gesturing toward Nat and Jack, he continued, "They are in the know on this, they are part of that special team from Washington, you can speak freely, but let me introduce them first. This Ms. Natalie Morse and this is Mr. Jack Johnson," Captain Johansen spoke in a forceful tone, as if to say 'mind your manners,' he continued, "This is George

Gregory, of the Whitman AF Base CID, that's Criminal Investigation Detachment, what have you got, George?"

"We have discovered where they left the Air Force vehicle. The truck is in a vacant barn just down the road from here," he stated, and continued, "We have isolated everything so we can get track imprints and anything else they may have forgotten."

Jack asked, "OK if we come along?"

Johansen said, "Any reason why not, George?" who jerked his head, indicating they could come along.

Nat and the Air Force cameraman both picked up their gear and headed for their vehicles. Jack got in their SUV as Nat climbed in the passenger seat, and they proceeded down the road behind the CID jeep. Less than two miles later they turned in on an unmarked dirt road leading to the abandoned farm Shortly, the CID jeep halted and they could see the large barn just ahead.

Yellow tape marked the boundaries of the scene and they see could plaster casts being made of tracks exiting the barn.

Jack asked, "How do they know which tracks to make casts of?"

Gregory responded by saying, "We know the military vehicle had military tires, which are unique, the other tracks had to be from the hijacker's trucks, they are probably standard tires available everywhere, so I'm not sure how much good they will be. But we want to be sure, just the same. They will be through in a few minutes and then we can go in and look around." Nat had videotaped their brief journey to the barn and continued taping the entire area while they waited. She and Jack noted that the CID personnel were efficient in doing their task, and Jack asked Captain Johansen if the CID people would make a report, and would it be available to them. Gregory heard him and replied affirmatively in his taciturn manner.

It was hours later when it appeared investigative actions were drawing to a close. Nat and Jack tried to not show their weariness as Nat followed the CID Team and Jack stuck behind Captain Johansen. The barn interior had revealed no additional clues.

Surprisingly it was Gregory who said to Nat, "You folks must have had a helluva day driving all the way from Florida to here, then traipsing around this damned mess. We are about through here, but it will be days before the analysis is completed. If you can give me an internet address I'll send you the report when we have the prelim done. It will be several weeks before a final report can be finished."

Nat looked at him gratefully, and replied, "You are very kind to have let us dog you around here, we are truly appreciative. Please send anything you can to General Mayfair and it will get to us."

Gregory responded, "Will do. I know how it is to try to pick up on a thing like this, you'll get everything in a day or two."

She was completely baffled by his sudden acceptance of their presence and said, "I take it you've been through this before a few times."

Though he did not say it, he was impressed by the no nonsense attitude of this pair of 'outsiders,' and particularly by the knowledge implicit in their few questions. He recognized the questions posed were appropriately inquiring. He said to her, "Yeah, and I'll bet you two have seen your share!"

Nat and Jack thanked Captain Johansen and Gregory for their cooperation and told him they would send copies of whatever was produced by the 'Fixit' Team to Whitman.

They parted on mutually respectful terms and slogged their way back to the SUV. With Jack behind the wheel they turned East toward Athens and in a few minutes of rapid driving they were at the outskirts of town. Jack turned in at the first decent appearing motel where they registered, asking for adjoining rooms.

She opened the door on her side and asked if Jack would care to join her for a cocktail at the restaurant. He laughingly accepted and they walked to the restaurant while still in their 'slightly soiled' garments. They caused a slight stir among the other diners as they entered, but taking no notice they followed the host to a pleasant appearing table, laid out with a white tablecloth, sparkling glasses and gleaming flatware.

Jack played the gentleman, and pulled out her chair for her, saw her seated, he then whipped out her napkin and lay it in her lap with a flourish He then seated himself and asked, "What is your pleasure, madame?".

She smiled coyly and said, "Jack, I'm too pooped to pop, order what you will and do the same for me, I'll be grateful."

He replied, "I suppose I should get a report off to Walt right away, but I don't think he'll mind a few minutes delay while we get a drink and something to eat." He looked at Nat and added, "Do I look as tired as you?"

She nodded and said, "I agree, let's get something before we die of hunger." A waiter had appeared and took their order for drinks and dinner, and quickly returned with their cocktails. After a surprisingly few minutes he reappeared with the steak dinners they had ordered. They sipped their drinks as they ate their steaks with relish, enjoying the fine meal.

Following dinner they walked back to Jack's room to make their call to Walt. He answered on the first ring, obviously anxious to know what had happened. Jack had routed the phone through the portable scrambler device and confirmed Walt was on a scrambler. Jack spoke for several long minutes, interrupted occasionally by Nat to interject a comment or observation. He offered as closing remarks that they had received outstanding cooperation at the scene and had videotapes of just about all there was to be had. As he finished he added he and Nat needed to get a little rest and then would be on the way back in the morning.

Had the circumstances been different they might have indulged in sexual foreplay, but neither felt the inclination to initiate anything. Both were too tired to do anything except to get some sleep. When they awoke in the bright morning sunlight all thoughts of indulgence had left them. Though they had indulged on previous occasions, it was only in a casual sense, neither did more then satisfy a mild sexual craving.

The next morning they left early and found themselves in Cocoa Beach after seven hours of fast driving, albeit not within posted speed limits.

CHAPTER 9

WALT WANTED NAT AND JACK to get some rest before they briefed the rest of the Team about the hijacking on the road between Whitman and Huntsville. But, true to form, Nat and Jack were ready to give their briefing immediately upon their return. Walt insisted they take enough time to clean up before they begin. He asked if someone could order some coffee and a snack for them before they started. In anticipation Connie had already ordered a pot of coffee and sandwiches for delivery to Walt's room as soon as Nat and Jack had arrived back at the motel. Connie had an unerring feeling for what was needed at the right time and place.

They both accepted the proffered moment to wash up and get the dirt removed from their trip. It was less than ten minutes later when all were gathered in Walt's room to hear the results of their trip. Jack was still toweling his face and neck when he joined Nat already in Walt's room, and declared himself ready to talk. As usual, Walt had asked Kim to run a bug check before they started.

After Kim had done his check he said to Walt, "We have visitors, Walt," and then said, "Look at what I found in the truss area over this room." He held up a small electronic device no bigger than a pack of cigarettes. Kim placed the device in a metal box and then said, "No more conversation until I run a detail check of this room and at least Nat's room next door." Walt nodded his assent and Kim promptly completed the check with no more devices being found.

Walt belatedly motioned for silence and indicated Kim should follow him outside the room. Once outside Walt said, "Kim, can you replace that device like it was before you removed it?

Kim replied, "If they are not too sharp, I can put it back where it was, but if they were listening or running a recorder, they will know I took it away."

Unbeknown to Boris and Natasha they too had company anticipating their arrival. A covert French agent had been tasked to plant as many listening devices as possible while all the Fixit Team members were away from the motel, as well as in any other areas offering potential information.

Kim and Walt were experienced in coping with such happenings and found no such devices. Unknown to Boris, a bug had been planted on the wall of the room next to theirs. Room 111 was occupied by two men from the French espionage service, the Sureté.

As luck would have it, the French covert agent was interested in the attractive young bikini-clad females enjoying the motel pool and missed the return of Nat and Jack as well as the bug installation. He had delayed trying to plant one on the Fixit Team accommodations, but he did leave the recorder running on the Boris 'bug.'

Kim quickly reinstalled the foreign listening device planted by Boris. He had no way of knowing if the device was connected to a recorder, so he wrote out a quick message explaining what he had found, and not to discuss anything of a sensitive nature. He passed it around to each team member.

In order to not alert the listeners to their discovery the team continued to indulge in idle chatter that would reveal nothing.

Walt said, "I think I'm going to head out to the Ops Center, I'll see you all later," at the same time silently indicating they should also go the Ops Center.

After checking in and assembling in General Mayfair's office area, he briefed the General on what had happened. General Mayfair was extremely upset at the development and voiced his concerns. Walt responded by saying, "Sir, it was only a matter of time before we had to expect something like this. You will need to alert your in-house security so they are aware we have foreign agents in the area."

The General spoke to Major Jackson, "Stoney, get our security people and the complex folks up to speed on this latest intervention and be sure our security level is now at increased awareness."

Major Jackson responded, "Right away, sir." He called the senior NCO to his desk and alerted him with an admonition, "Get on it right now!"

The NCO went around the Ops Center, alerting those present of the current situation. He then changed the settings on the Alert Status Lamps from a master control panel, changing all area Alert Lamps to the new settings. The settings ranged from green, All Clear; to flashing red for Imminent Danger; with stages in between of yellow, Alert; flashing yellow, Increased Alert; and red, Danger; and finally the Imminent Danger, flashing red. An audible tone sounded each time he switched from one status to the next. He set the lights to flashing yellow, jumping from green, All Clear, past the intermediate condition of Alert, directly to flashing yellow, Increased Alert, in accordance with the General's orders. The audible tone, a raucous sound throughout all the affected areas, was intended as an attention getter, insuring that everyone knew the alert status had changed.

The Ops Center was immediately deluged with calls seeking confirmation that the status change was correct Word was spread rapidly so that every guard and all responsible personnel had been notified within the course of a few minutes time. Guard post personnel not previously armed were suddenly equipped with weapons, .9mm pistols, sub-machine guns, and M-16 rifles, all with live ammunition, were in evidence.

The General requested his staff assemble to be updated to this new threat. The military response was swift and sure. Officers were noted wearing web belts with holstered pistols on their hips. Building entrances were staffed with uniformed Airmen carrying loaded sub-machine guns or M-16 rifles. Suddenly those who had forgotten their ID or badges were denied access. Security became tight!

The new security measures pleased Walt tremendously. He was given a desk in the Ops Center near General Mayfair and a TV installed on the desk giving him access to the many cameras around the various areas. It came with a list of camera locations and instructions on channel selections. He was informed a telephone would be installed within 24 hours.

The Fixit Team had a new focal point for coordination. Walt asked Kim to set up one of the Team scramblers for use when the phone was installed. Nat appropriated two extra chairs and placed them at the desk, and set up one of their desktop computers, as well as a portable laptop for backup. The Team worked swiftly with practiced precision.

General Mayfair made mention of the speed and efficiency with which Walt's Team had established themselves in the Ops Center, to which Walt responded apologetically that he was remiss in not telling the General it was how they always tried to fit in.

The General laughingly responded, "I just hope you don't take over my whole Ops Center."

"Sir, it's not too much different than the last time I worked for you, I think. We just have it down pat now."

"I am glad to see you appear ready to actually support us," General Mayfair responded.

Walt explained that their desk would be manned continuously, if at all possible, but there might be times when it would be difficult to do so. In such cases they would do their best to keep the General informed of their actions. He added that most of the time he hoped Nat or Connie would be there, especially during any critical operations.

Walt explained that he hoped they would soon learn more about their new unknown visitors. "As soon as I have a handle on who these people are, I will pass it on to you. That way your people will know beforehand what to expect if they try to breach your Air Force security."

Walt started detailing instructions to his Team, with an immediate goal of determining the scope and size of the incursion, and whether there was more than one agency at work. He assigned Nat to be the initial team interface at the Ops Center, and took Connie aside to brief her on her newest role.

He told Connie, "Put on your Russian ears, I want you to see if you can determine just what we are working against. See if anyone suspicious has checked in to our motel. I smell the fine hand of our old friend Colonel Mikael Dantilev in this mess.

"I'll bet he had something to do with that hijacking. It is just the kind of bold stroke he is capable of setting in motion." Walt continued, "Somehow he must have found the details for shipping the test satellite from Whitman to Huntsville."

After chasing a multitude of thoughts around in his mind, Walt said, "Connie, have Kim go over their SUV with a fine tooth comb to see if he can find any kind of planted bug from their trip. Maybe he can find something." He then continued, "If we have a visitor at the motel, just maybe you can smoke him out."

Connie prepared to stretch out on a chaise lounge at poolside. She delighted in showing off her magnificent body for any and all to gaze upon. She had on a wide-brimmed hat and wore reflective sunglasses, permitting her to look around without seeming to do so. She slid her thigh-length cover-up off her shoulders in slow motion, revealing a very scant, luminescent yellow bikini. The top barely contained her well-proportioned breasts and the bottom was just enough to hide her well-rounded behind, and a miniscule "V" in front suggested, rather than hid, her private parts. The brilliant color combined with her voluptuous tanned body instantly became the focal point of every pair of male eyes around the pool.

She stood hesitantly next to her chaise, turning slowly on her spike-heeled shoes, seemingly seeking someone to apply the sun tan lotion in her hand, to her long shapely legs. She was tanned to an even golden brown over the visible portion of her body. She shrugged and placed the lotion on the pool deck and stretched out on the chaise.

Almost immediately three young men approached her chaise, one boldly saying, "Would you like me to rub some lotion on your back?"

She replied, "You look like you want to do more than just put lotion on my back". She then looked at the youngest of them and asked, "Would you do it for me?"

The other two reluctantly turned away as the young man awkwardly applied the lotion to her back. She spoke gently to him saying, "They look like dogs in heat," and then continued, "Are you from around here or just visiting?"

He mumbled a reply that he lived in Cocoa Beach and worked at the motel cleaning the pool and doing odd jobs for the summer. He silently finished applying the lotion, being careful to not let his hands stray.

Connie realized this boy might be useful in getting information. He would not arouse suspicions as an employee of the motel. She coyly started to cultivate his acquaintance. She asked him if he could get her a cold drink, or was the bar open yet at this hour, 3:00 PM she noted.

He quickly relied, "My name is Bobby, and yes, I can get you whatever you want from the bar, but you have to charge it to your room." The words came tumbling out in a rush, and he repeated much more slowly, "Sure, I can get you whatever you'd like."

"Please get me a Tom Collins, charge it to my room, and add a couple of dollars for a tip," she said as she took off her glasses and looked him straight in the eyes. Her stare was disconcerting and he blushed as he rose to go for her drink.

He quickly turned back and asked, "What is your room number Miss....?"

She laughingly responded, "I'm Connie and I am in room 103."

He quickly went to the bar and opening the door he strutted in saying, "You guys don't know how to do it," the message aimed at the two young men who Connie had brushed off.

The bartender knowing the boy, accepted the order for Connie and made a tab for her room. Bobby returned to Connie with her Collins in a frosted glass, carrying it on a tray with cocktail napkins and a coaster upon which he carefully placed her drink saying, "Here's your Collins Miss Connie, I didn't put any tip on the charge, it's my pleasure to serve you."

Connie with her unnerving stare said, "How sweet, I thank you very much." She then engaged him in idle conversation, eliciting all kinds of information. He explained he had lived in Cocoa Beach all his life, but that he had traveled extensively with his parents. He had just recently graduated from high school and had been accepted by Florida State University in Tallassee. She gently steered his conversation to the people registered in the motel, finding that he was an astute observer of people. Without prompting he described the two people that had arrived recently, explaining that they seemed to have plenty of money, but drove an old Chevy pickup. He noted a peculiarity in that the pickup seemed to run like a clock, even though it looked like a dog.

Connie's interest immediately picked up and she asked Bobby to show her these people. He stated that they were in room 110, across the breezeway from Walt's room, and pointed them out sitting under an umbrella at the other end of the pool. It was apparent that the man had already noticed Connie and was still eyeing her speculatively. The woman was not totally unattractive, but with seemingly plain features. Connie thought, she could use a good makeup artist.

The woman was dressed in slacks and a snug fitting T-shirt, revealing a nice figure, muscular, though not entirely unattractive. The man was well-dressed in slacks and colorful sport shirt, he also appeared fit. Though he wore sun glasses, Connie could feel his eyes appraising her, and speculated whether he was involved in some clandestine operation.

Connie wondered aloud within Bobby's hearing, "I wonder what that couple is really like", and then again for Bobby's benefit, "I'll bet they have something in their room."

Conspiratorially Bobby said, "I've got a master key to every room, sometimes I have to move stuff in and out, I could check them out, they look shifty to me."

"You wouldn't." Connie said teasingly, "Or would you?"

That was all that was needed to get young Bobby involved. He wanted to have Connie think he was special. He said, "They are both just sitting there, they would never know I was in their room. I'll be right back."

With that he stood and went to the far end of the pool into the bar and out the opposite end. He was not noticed as he casually walked to their room just out of sight of their view. He entered and gasped as he saw the electronic equipment open on the table. He quickly decided he had best get out pronto, and left the room more quickly than he had entered. He rapidly walked around the building housing the bar, and strolled back to Connie, handing her a towel, as if that had been the reason for his disappearance.

He sat down on the next chaise and blurted, "There's something going on all right, you should see the electronic stuff they got in there."

Connie's mind kicked into high gear and she stood up and excused herself to Bobby, explaining, "I've had enough sun and I think you should forget what you say you saw in that room," inferring maybe he had had too much sun.

Once back in her room Connie Immediately called the Ops Center to report what she had uncovered. She activated the scrambler once she was connected to Nat

117

and said, "Nat, Walt was right on when he figured we might have somebody on to us. The people in 110, just across the breezeway from Walt's room, are loaded with electronic gear. They are probably the ones responsible for the bug over his room. I haven't been able to pinpoint anyone else yet, but I wouldn't be surprised if we have others."

Nat was quick to record Connie's report and said, "I'll let Walt know right away, and then let General Mayfair in on it". She continued, "I'll see if Walt wants to have Kim return the favor and plant something to hear what they have in mind."

Boris and Natasha had just returned to their room and Boris said in Russian, "The recorder is not running, I thought you were turning it on" He looked at her reproachfully.

"Why me? You are the one deciding who does what." was her rejoinder. "You always tell me if you want me to do something."

Disgruntled, he replied, "We are supposed to be an experienced team, Natasha, we must always be sure nothing is overlooked. You know how we work, back me up, always, OK"? She nodded her understanding aware that they may have missed something for which she could have been blamed.

The misunderstanding behind them, they mutually came together and embraced. The hot rays of the sun worked its sensuous warmth and the understanding embrace became more intimate, rapidly degenerating into pure lust, one for the other. They quickly removed their clothing, each expertly fondling theotherineager anticipation. They were unmindful of their failure to turn on the air conditioning, as perspiration glistened on their naked bodies, stumbling, as they tumbled onto the bed. He nibbled on the nipples of her breasts arousing her to a new level. He finally entered her with a violence that caused her to gasp with pleasure. They repeatedly climaxed in a crescendo of passion, finally laying spent on the twisted sheets.

The French Sureté espionage agent was not so derelict as to fail to activate his recording device. He was chagrined to hear the Russian had not recorded the device he knew they had planted over Room 101, he thought to himself, those two are not what I had expected. He continued to listen with amusement to the recorded sounds of their passion, thinking that he would like to have had the young woman in the yellow bikini at the poolside.

Such pleasantry would have to wait for a bit, but might be had, judging from some of the scantily-clad women lounging around the motel pool. More than one of them appeared to be willing and quite well-suited for an amorous encounter.

Being by himself, awaiting arrival of a second Sureté agent was wasted time. Without help he would have difficulty installing another listening device to hear anything from Room 110, occupied by the big American obviously in charge of the group he had been told to monitor. He had seized the opportunity to surreptitiously see the motel register, and according to it, the man's name was Walter Crawford. The Frenchman knew that he had heard that name before, but for the moment he could not recall where.

———————

Kim thought that if he could create some kind of attention-getting event perhaps he could slip into Room 101 and check it out. When he discussed the situation with Connie she suggested that maybe she could get Bobby to pull a fire alarm or something. Kim seized upon the idea as viable, but concerned whether they should implicate young Bobby. Connie pointed out that he was already implicated when he entered Room 101 at her suggestion.

Kim bowed to her irrefutable logic, and they called the desk asking if Bobby could bring some towels to Walt's room. In a few minutes Bobby knocked on the door and gushed to Connie, when she opened the door, "Here's the towels you wanted."

Connie drew him inside asking if he would please come in. Belatedly, she introduced Kim, saying, "Bobby, I'd like you to meet someone very special. This is Kim Shirakawa. He and I are special agents of the U. S. Government. Since you entered that room I have inadvertently involved you in something I should not have done. But I did. Now I have to ask you if you would like to join us and work for our Team?" What she did not tell him, was that if he declined he would be put in protective custody for an indefinite period and she would be at fault. Connie knew that she had blundered and she would have to explain it to Walt, accepting that she had erred.

Bobby was overjoyed at the prospect of such an opportunity. Both Kim and Connie explained he would have to obtain his parents permission to participate, when he interrupted saying, "Do you mean they have sign an OK or something?"

Connie said, "Before we go any further would you mind waiting outside for a minute, I have to call someone." She looked sheepishly at Kim and added, "I have really screwed up on this one." Kim silently nodded his agreement.

She immediately called the Ops Center asking if Walt was available. Nat sensed something amiss from the tone of Connie's voice and quickly asked if this should be on scrambler.

Connie replied in a low voice a single word, "Yes."

Walt came on the line and said, "What's the problem, Connie?"

Connie quickly explained what she had done, adding that Bobby seemed like a promising youngster. She described all she had learned about the boy and took full responsibility for her misdeed.

Typically, Walt accepted that a wrongdoing had occurred and concerned himself as to how best to compensate for the mistake. He did not chastise Connie, rather he accepted that the exigencies of the situation needed to be dealt with.

He turned and had Nat ask the General how quickly could he get a temporary clearance for a person. Walt continued the discussion with Connie until Nat returned from speaking with General Mayfair The answer was that he, the General, could grant an interim clearance for limited access. Walt then asked Connie to give Nat the requisite information on Bobby for submission to the

General, he turned the phone over to Nat to complete the necessary action.

Walt excused himself telling Nat, "I am going to the motel to see what we have first hand," and departed the Ops Center.

He thought to himself that perhaps we all need a refresher on handling security as he sped north towards the motel. He continued to wear mufti, foregoing the brilliant yellow jumpsuits worn by the Team, rationalizing no need to over-advertise their presence. He decided to have all Team members to don civilian attire, except when directly supporting operations on military locations.

He parked his Cobra in the parking slot near his room, walking through the breezeway to his room's entry facing the pool. Inside he found a moodily silent Connie sitting upright in a chair, now wearing her cover-up, and Kim in animated discussion with the dark haired young man.

Walt smiled as he strode forward into the room with his hand outstretched in greeting to Bobby, saying, "I am Walt Crawford, I am responsible for the Team you have just been told about. With your permission I will ask for a security clearance for you from the General we all work for."

Walt was pleased to note the firm grip Bobby had as they shook hands. Bobby was slightly taken aback at the straightforward attitude shown by Walt, but quickly replied to Walt, "My name is Bobby, uh, Robert Camden, and yeah I know what a security clearance is because my father's company does a lot of business with Uncle Sam, uh, the government. I don't know why I need a security clearance, but I guess it's O.K." Then asked, "Is it something to do with that check I made on Room 101?"

Walt replied, "You catch on quick, yes, it is because you did that at our request."

"No sir," was the quick rejoinder, "I did that on my own, not because Connie asked me to." He had sensed Connie was in disfavor and did not want her to be chastised.

The phone rang and Kim answered, "Kim here," and after a moment, "Good, I'll tell him," and hung up. He turned to Walt and said, "Nat says the General has granted an interim access for Bobby, and he will issue the necessary paperwork right away."

Bobby's eyes opened wide, recognizing that something unusual had just transpired. He thought to himself, 'Boy, am I tied in with real hotshots! With a second thought occurring on top of the first, I had better be on my toes for these guys.' He was sufficiently discerning to know that Walt seemed to be very special to Connie and Kim.

Walt asked Bobby, "I assume you prefer to be addressed as Bobby, is that correct?" After the young man's affirmative nod, Walt went on, "I also understand you are eighteen, is that also correct?" Again, an affirmative nod, and Walt asked, "How do we contact your parents?"

Bobby replied, "I really don't know, they are on safari in Africa right now, kinda of dream vacation they have been planning for a long time." He went on, "They have literature about the Safari Company at the house, I think. If you want I can go home and look for it."

Walt rationalized in his mind, he is eighteen, somewhat a legal age, and his parents did leave him home. I wonder if he has a responsible adult somewhere. He voiced the question to Bobby, "Do you have someone looking after you?"

"Not really," he replied, "I'm supposed to go to John Godfrey, the motel owner here, he is an old friend of the family, if I have a problem. Mr. and Mrs. Godfrey are my Godparents. I have a room here and I eat in the restaurant."

Walt perked up thinking he could query them, when Bobby dashed his hopes by saying, "They aren't here either, they are in England for another week."

"Well, Bobby, I guess you will have to be responsible to me. Do you think you would have any trouble with that?" asked Walt.

"No sir, none at all," was his response.

Walt proceeded to give Bobby a basic outline of his Fixit Team and their function here in Cocoa Beach, without telling him about the spacecraft aspects of their operation. He explained that the General was granting an interim security clearance based on what Bobby had told them. He emphasized that if the background check now in process revealed he had lied about anything, the repercussions would be severe. The check in progress was intended to permit Walt and his Team to accept Bobby into their confidence. He cautioned Bobby that there was a significant degree of hazard associated with becoming a member of the Team. Walt concluded his briefing by asking Bobby to carefully consider his response before accepting any role with the Team.

Bobby unhesitatingly responded, "I understand what you have explained to me and I am honored to be allowed to become a part of your Team." It was a far more mature a response then any of those present had expected, and drew a smile of satisfaction from each of them.

Walt said. "Welcome aboard Robert Camden, you are now a member of Fixit. We will outfit you with our Colors and acquaint you with our operating procedures. You will be introduced to the rest of our Team later today. While I don't expect you to give up your life for the Team, we do count upon one another in some pretty extreme situations. I trust you do understand that?"

Bobby's response was a bold, "Yes sir, I do."

CHAPTER 10

WALT APPROACHED GENERAL MAYFAIR IN the Ops Center and said, "Sir, I must report an incident caused by my Team, and for which I must accept full responsibility."

The General looked up in surprise and said, "I suppose it has something to do with that request for an interim clearance I gave you earlier?"

"Yes sir, it does," was his reply. He went on, "We inadvertently involved that young man in an effort to discover who had planted the bug over my room, back at the motel. Actually thanks to him we discovered the culprit. It is a pair of known Russians agents posing as tourists."

"I guess I don't see your problem," commented General Mayfair, "If he identified who they were, what's the problem?"

"He is a very bright young man, only eighteen, but has a solid head on his shoulders," Walt started to explain. "And he did give us a real opportunity by what he did. However, his parents are not available to give their O.K.

126

to employ him and his local guardian is in England. I like him and I believe he can be of use to us, but I can't do this without you knowing he is not one of my regular, fulltime employees."

The General smiled and replied, "You do have a dilemma, but I have complete faith that you will find the right thing to do." He continued, "Unless the quick background check now underway reveals something untoward, you may do as you think best."

"Very well sir, I will limit his actions for the time being, but at least tentatively, I might as well bring him on board as a member of my Team," Walt responded with evident relief.

With the exception of Nat, who was at the Ops Center, on the Fixit desk, all the rest of the Team had assembled in Walt's room. All were conscious of the bug over their heads, and tried to carry on normal conversations without revealing awareness of the listening device Connie noticeably abstained from talking.

Walt returned from the Ops Center, entered his room and greeted everyone jovially, much to Connie's consternation. He commented that he had a very pleasant talk with General Mayfair in the last hour and that the General was pleased with his report about visiting Whitman Air Force Base. The Team looked at each other in bewilderment, why was Walt telling them this knowing the bug was still over their heads.

He finally said, "Give me a minute to wash up and we can all go to dinner together." He pointedly looked at Connie to be sure she understood she was expected to accompany them regardless of her personal feelings.

Once seated in the motel restaurant he looked directly at Connie and said to her, "Connie, we all err at one time or another, I want you to put this behind you and realize you are a part of this Team for good reason. You do understand that?"

In a rare show of emotion, tears glistened in her eyes as she nodded, unable yet to speak. A waiter took their orders for drinks and quickly returned with them. The other members each raised their cocktail glasses to Connie in an unspoken acceptance of her contriteness. Young Bobby did not understand what had gone wrong but he was sufficiently astute to recognize she was not being punished for whatever it was that she supposedly had done. He was unaware of the part he had played in this internal drama.

In an afterthought Walt said to Bobby, "Bobby you have been accepted as a member of the Fixit Team, however in deference to your age you are not to drink any alcoholic beverages until you turn twenty one. Do you think you can accept that?"

Bobby blushed and replied, "Yes sir, I'm not into drinking or drugs.".

"Good." said Walt. He then added, "I guess we had better get you some of our standard gear and clothes and let you know just how much you will be paid. What sizes do you wear?"

Bobby grinned and said, "You don't even have to pay me, I'll work for nothing as long as I can be part of you guys. I'm five foot ten and I weigh about one sixty I think, but I'm not too sure about what sizes I wear."

Walt smiled in response and said, "Everybody gets paid on the Team, and Connie, can you figure out sizes and order things for him? Let's head back to my room and we'll go on from there."

Connie looked pleased at being given something to do even if it was a bit mundane. After they had returned to Walt's room she looked at Bobby appraisingly and said, "I can guess pretty close, but let me look at what he you're wearing and maybe they will have the sizes in them." Then to Bobby, "Give me your shirt and pants and we'll see what they show," then realizing the boy was about to disrobe, added, "I'll check your collar and then you go in the bathroom and check your slacks."

He blushed as he realized he was among adults, and he was expected to act like one. He walked over to Connie and knelt down so she could see inside his collar, and was pleased when she found he wore a size 15 collar and 32 sleeve length. He went into the bathroom and quickly returned saying, "They are 33 X 30, if that makes sense to you."

The Team laughed at his naiveté.

Connie smilingly said. "That's close enough, I'll call our supplier and he can express them here." Then to Walt, "What equipment, does he get any weapons?"

"No ammo for his pistol yet, he'll have to get some weapons instruction first, but you can set him up for a hard hat and our standard stuff," Walt replied.

"I've done a lot of hunting with my Dad and I have fired everything from a 30.06 Springfield rifle to a Winchester Model 12 shotgun and a Colt Hi-Standard pistol," Bobby proudly proclaimed.

Once again the Team smiled knowingly as Walt explained, "That's nice, but not exactly what I'm talking about." He went on, "We deal with mostly military weapons, foreign guns and some very sophisticated ordnance. That will take time, but we will qualify you in the personal armament we use a little later on. In the meantime, you look to be about the same size as Kim, perhaps he can loan you a set of coveralls."

Kim quickly reacted and said, "Sure thing, I can spare a couple of our jumpsuits temporarily. Come with me Bobby and we'll see if mine will fit you." He led the way and took Bobby to his room. With typical Team understanding he knew Walt wanted to say something not intended for the youngster's ears.

As soon as they had departed Walt explained that the Team would have to keep track of Bobby since he had been inadvertently embroiled in a Team action, and the best way to do that was to accept him as a limited member. He cautioned them, "Be careful in involving Bobby in anything hazardous. We must be sure he doesn't get hurt."

Walt told Connie, "Would you take over from Nat at the Ops Center please, I would like to get her here and bring her up to date on this Bobby situation. She can brief him on paperwork and arrange for his pay."

Connie, delighted to be occupied with the assignment to the Ops Center, obligingly jumped up and said, "I'll get out there right away and let her know about what I did with Bobby and all."

Walt's quick rejoinder was, "No, I will tell her what I want her to hear in my own manner."

Everyone was still cautious in what they were saying because of Walt's concerns. They left his room, leaving only Connie still present. She stepped forward and hugged him holding him for a moment. He hugged her in return, unconsciously reacting to her closeness. She reached up and pulled his head down to her and kissed him passionately. He responded by sliding his hands downward to her well formed buttocks, cupping them and squeezing them.

She moaned saying, "Walt make love to me," and started to unbutton his shirt, he did the same to her blouse, slipping it off her shoulders as she unfastened her bra. His shirt was off and she pressed her voluptuous breasts against his chest, he felt there was no turning back at this point. It had been months since he had been with a woman and here was the most desirous female he had seen urging him on.

He spoke saying, "I know I will regret this in the morning, but what the hell I can't stop now."

They moved to the bed, falling upon it in their haste to have one another. They enjoyed one another's sensuality and satisfied their need then were suddenly aware that they had let lust overwhelm them.

As the love making waned he realized he had violated his own rules, sex with one of his Team was unthinkable, yet he had done it without thinking. He looked at Connie and said to her, "Connie I don't know if I brought this on or was I just weak, regardless, you know as well as I do, that it was wrong. Now, what to do about it?"

"Oh Walt, I am so sorry, it was me, I just lost control and deliberately tried to have you make love to me, please forgive me, I promise I will never let it interfere with the Team."

He replied, "Maybe you can, but can I. Get dressed," he brusquely ordered, "I'll have to think about this, I certainly don't want to lose you as one of my Team people."

Once again, Connie realized that Walt was a unique person, knowing that she had made a mistake, but accepted the fact that the mistake was not revocable, and his course of action would be to minimize the effect. She was grateful that he did not berate her, knowing that she would not forgive herself. He had selected her to be on his Team, because she was a very real asset, not a liability as an outsider might have thought. She knew this man was a rare breed, and she knew she would do anything he asked of her.

When Nat had returned to the motel and entered Walt's room, Kim and the others joined in at Walt's room where he turned on a high pitched audio device not audible to their ears, causing all conversation to be a 'white out' to the listening device planted over their heads. Walt briefly recounted the entire bug incident to Nat, neither embellishing nor leaving anything out. Nat recognized the seriousness of the situation and accepted the course of action Walt had chosen without comment, nor would she recriminate against Connie, recognizing that any one of them could have erred under the same circumstances. The information obtained through Bobby's misadventure was obviously invaluable.

Kim returned to Walt's room with the boy in tow carrying the yellow jump suits from Kim's wardrobe. Kim had Bobby try on a set of the brilliant yellow coveralls with the "Fixit" logo on the chest, and discovered it was nearly a perfect fit. The amount of time Bobby had been kept occupied by Kim was deliberately stretched to several minutes, instinctively knowing Walt wanted a few minutes without Bobby being present. Walt thanked Kim and sent the boy off to his own room with instructions to report to back at eight A.M. the next morning.

Walt then instructed Kim to remove the overhead listening device using much show and noise. He wanted to be sure the Russians were aware of the fact that it had been found and removed. In truth the Russians fully expected that it would be only a matter of time before its discovery.

Boris turned his recorder off with the comment, "I knew they were aware of our little 'ear' as soon as they started that damned 'whiteout' gadget. I would like to know why they recruited that young boy. He must know something."

Having been disappointed before, Boris was not one to be particularly upset. Things like this were to be expected, seldom do things go precisely as desired.

He spoke to Natasha saying, "I am going to bathe and then we can go to the restaurant for dinner."

She nodded her agreement and hurried to get in the bathroom before he started to undress. When she returned, he gazed at her naked body and rapidly removed the rest of his clothes. She was as eager as he, but this time he was unhurried and gave her great satisfaction. Boris was an accomplished lover and seemed to know when savagery was appropriate and when to be slow and purposeful. Two hours later, sated, they dressed and strolled unhurriedly to the restaurant.

Kim went to the motel office and asked to see the manager. The clerk on duty said, "I'll get her for you, just a minute, please, is there any thing I can do for you," she queried, aware of the angry appearance of Kim. She called out, "Marie, come in here, please, a man wants to talk to you."

When she arrived Kim said to Marie, "Did you know that one of your motel guests was up in the roof area and stuck a listening gadget over Mr. Crawford's room?" He was loud and demanding and looked very unhappy. "I am going up there and remove it and I need a ladder to get up there."

Marie became quite flustered and told the clerk, "Get Bobby to get him the ladder and help him to do what he wants."

Having accomplished his purpose to make a show of anger, Kim walked back to the breezeway under the trap door accessing the truss area and waited, knowing that Bobby was in Walt's room. He made a great racket in moving a table under the opening and climbed up in the roof trusses. In a moment he reappeared with the electronic device in hand and told Marie, who was standing nearby, "I'm just going to keep this to show to Mr. Crawford."

She was so upset she hardly knew what to do or say, as she acquiesced. Kim entered Walt's room and closed the door. Several people had gathered outside wondering what was happening. As quickly as they had gathered, they dispersed, still knowing no more than they had before, and Marie retreated to the motel office without elaborating.

Kim, however, realized he too had not done as Walt had asked him much earlier. He immediately went to his own room to pick up his detection equipment and went out to his SUV to verify the absence of 'bugs'. As he ran the wand over the upper rear roof line of the vehicle the detector emitted a chirping sound. Stepping up on the rear bumper of the SUV he immediately found the small, unobtrusive device attached behind the cross rail of the cargo roof rack. He removed it with great chagrin, realizing he had not checked to find anything since he and Nat had left Whitman Air Force Base.

He tried to remember, had he and Nat discussed anything of a sensitive nature en route back to Cocoa Beach. He vowed to himself not to be caught lacking again, dreading that he must now inform Walt of the second failure of a Team member. The thought never crossed his mind to not report what he had discovered. He realized that Walt had earlier asked him to verify the absence of a bug on his SUV and he was further remiss in not having done so sooner.

As he reentered Walt's room he found Nat already present and being brought up to date. He shamefully faced Walt and said, "Connie has company, I have screwed up too."

Walt looked at him sharply, it was not in character for Kim to have mentioned Connie's failure, Kim was truly 'hang dog' appearing. He said, "O.K. Kim let's have it, what now?"

Kim mutely held the bug up for Walt and all the Team members to see, "I failed to run a check on our SUV when we left Whitman," he said.

Walt was taken aback by this revelation, it did not seem possible for two highly regarded members to have slipped up on such a routine matter. He wondered, 'Had he somehow failed also?' To his credit, he did not lose his temper, though he gritted his teeth momentarily. He said, "Call Connie, tell her to join me and all of you," and as an afterthought, "Include Bobby, he might as well hear this too, and I want to get everybody in one SUV, and we are going somewhere quiet to have a little chat."

When all had assembled he said, "Get in Kim's SUV and follow me, we will drive someplace where we can have a little private discussion."

Walt climbed into his Cobra and led the SUV out of the motel parking lot onto A1A and turned northward. He drove through the town of Cape Canaveral, around the port area and on the long approach road to the Cape Main Gate. When he was about halfway to the Cape Main Gate he pulled over on to the shoulder of the isolated road, climbed out and sat on the hood of his Cobra.

He waited until they had gathered around him and said, "I didn't think I would need to say this but it appears to be necessary. Never before have I had to ask you to be more alert, but never before have we had problems indicating carelessness." He hung his head and asked, "Have I failed any of you in some way?" He raised his head and looked at each of them in turn, including the new recruit, Bobby. They shook their heads negatively as he gazed at each of them, Bobby took his cue from the others, and shook his head also without speaking.

"I did not think I had placed any of you under any particular strain, at least not yet," he then continued, "Bobby, this doesn't really apply to you, but you might as well understand how we operate." He went on, "I am concerned that we are not sufficiently alert or that maybe I let you think this is unimportant, if so, let me dispel that right now. We are involved in the most important mission ever given us. If anybody would like to be relieved now is the time to speak up."

Heads came up with a shocked expression, only once before had Walt ever talked like this, and that when they first came together as a Team. They spoke as one, "No," and Nat spoke for them all as she said, "Walt, you can count on us, every one, no more mistakes, right?" She looked at each one and received a confirming chorus of "Yes!"

Walt openly breathed a sigh of relief and said, "You all know what is expected of us, let's do it!" Walt smiled in appreciation and added, "Thank you, I'm sure now that I can count on each one of you, I know you are the best!"

There were no recriminations toward Connie or Kim, they realized their error could just as well have been by any member of the Team.

CHAPTER 11

THEY RETURNED TO THE MOTEL with a renewed sense of purpose, realizing that as a Team they had let Walt down, each vowing to himself, 'No more mistakes, if I can help it.'

Walt decided that he would not pursue any further discussions about Team fallibilities for the time being, his comments given to them as a group had served its purpose. The Team seemed to be satisfactorily invigorated again and further recriminations would serve no useful purpose. He was concerned about the incursions already made by foreign agencies. The loss of the test spacecraft to the hi-jacking was something he should have anticipated. He should have had contingency planning in place as a possible occurrence and plans to preclude such an event. He would gather the Team together and 'brainstorm' the situation, maybe he could forestall any future adverse actions. His Team had done so in the past with a high degree of success, one of the reasons he and his Team were in demand.

Walt had spent the past several hours mulling over potential options available to him, he concluded his best choice would be to call the Team together and review the current situation. Perhaps they could come up with a means to recover the lost test spacecraft. He hoped he was not expecting miracles.

The Team members were in their own rooms, each with thoughts of how to regain lost integrity. Nat was the first to be called by Walt. He explained that he wanted the entire Team to gather to assess their current situation and to determine a new course of action. He avoided any mention of the lost spacecraft. He asked her to assemble the entire Team, necessitating an explanation to General Mayfair as to why no Team member would be in the Ops Center for a short time.

After talking to Nat, Walt called General Mayfair and when the General answered his call personally, Walt asked, "Do you spend all your time at the Ops Center, sir?"

General Mayfair replied, "Just about all of it, I'm even sleeping here now. You didn't call to pass the time of day, Walt, is there something happening?"

"I would like to have all my people here with me for a few hours if you think it would be OK to not have someone there for a bit," Walt explained; he went on, "I would like to have a 'brainstorming' session."

General Mayfair, sensing that Walt must have something afoot, immediately said, "Of course, I'll tell Connie to report to you right away. Please keep me informed if you come up with anything."

"Yes sir, you'll be the first to know."

Night was falling as the Team gathered in Walt's room. All were present, even young Bobby, as Walt stood and looked around at each of them, they knew he had something special to discuss when all were brought together at once. He opened his remarks by saying, "You know I would not ask all of you to gather at once without good reason, tonight we must come up with some kind of a plan to recover the spacecraft that was hi-jacked. Think for a couple of minutes before we start documenting anything."

"Kim, are we clean here, no more bugs?" Walt asked.

"I took the liberty of running a check before we started," Kim responded, "No bugs, we're clean", he added.

"Good, I'm glad you're ahead of me," Walt said. "All right let's get started," he continued, "Let's review what we know and then we can run the videotapes from the scene. We have several to look at, those that Nat and Jack shot, as well as the ones from the investigators at the scene."

A brief discussion ensued, primarily reviewing Nat and Jack's trip and their reports upon returning. Kim set up the video player and connected it to the TV as the discussion went on. A review of the videotapes recalled the horror of the massacre that had taken place on that isolated bit of highway in Alabama. It was a grim reminder of the callous nature of the killers who had stolen the test spacecraft.

Nat was the first to speak and commented that she would contact her acquaintances in the services intelligence community to see if any leads were forthcoming.

Her comments were followed by Jack, who recalled that the Whitman AF Base investigators had said they would inform the Team of any leads they developed. Nat volunteered to call Dr, Bowman, at Whitman, to see if he had learned anything and immediately recalled that Lieutenant Colonel Donohue, the Whitman Ops Officer, might also be a good contact.

Ideas were put forth and rejected as thoughts flowed to and fro. Connie, quiet and unspoken, but obviously resourceful, had immediately started recording the conversations on Kim's audio recorder and began listing potential actions on her note pad that might be taken. Not much escaped Walt's attention as he observed Connie initiating the recording and notes. He was pleased he had not had to ask someone to do so.

Almost two hours had passed before they realized that anything had been accomplished. Walt rapped for attention as the last of the videotapes were viewed. They came back to reality with a start, not realizing that much of anything had been accomplished. He asked Connie to review what she had been able to record. The others were moderately surprised that any consensus had been reached and that anyone had recorded their comments, much less that a possible course of action could be laid out.

Connie read from her notes, "First item; Nat is to contact intelligence services to determine if they have any information; second item; Jack is to check the Whitman AF Base investigators to determine if they have any leads, third item; Nat is to contact Dr. Bowman to follow up with him, and then to contact Lieutenant Colonel Donohue for any leads. I personally think it might be prudent to more carefully review the videotapes step by step, to insure nothing else is missed, and also, wasn't there a lieutenant from Whitman at the scene that worked with Nat and Jack?"

Jack responded, "It was a Captain, and yeah, he would be a good person to talk with, I will get back with him, his name was Phil Johansen, as I recall."

Walt took charge and commented, "All right people, we have a plan of sorts to start with, let's get going on these initial steps and then we'll meet again to see where do we go from there. It's late now, and we will be unable to talk to anybody at this hour, so let's start first thing in the morning. Remember to use scramblers where you can, if you use the phone system. We can also work better from the Ops Center, so we'll head out there after an early breakfast tomorrow. We'll meet at the restaurant at 0700, get some rest now, because you may not get much in the next few days."

With that the Team said their 'goodnights' and departed to their own rooms. As was the case with most of the others, Walt had difficulty sleeping, turning over in his mind the actions laid out. He wondered, 'Had they missed anything important that might yield a clue to the spacecraft's location?' He drifted off to a restless sleep and awakened at 6 o'clock in the morning.

Walt showered and shaved and donned the Team brilliant yellow jumpsuit as he prepared to meet the day's challenges. The Team members were of a common mind as they too, dressed in the Team colors. It was an unspoken allegiance, each having similar concerns that severe opposition lay ahead of them.

None were surprised at the unspoken feeling that all shared and displayed their emotion in wearing the Team colors. They made an unusual appearance to the other early morning diners in their eye catching flamboyant coveralls when they gathered for breakfast at the restaurant. Kim had suggested to Bobby that he too, should wear the yellow jumpsuit he had given him. Bobby had taped over Kim's name and printed his own on the tape.

Each was somewhat subdued in that they had not been able to come up with any additional ideas to further the investigation. Because others were present in the restaurant they kept their voices somewhat muted. After all seven Team members had placed their breakfast orders they looked to Walt to initiate the conversation. He glanced at each of them in turn, thinking 'How fortunate I am to have this dedicated group of people to work with.'

He forestalled any discussion of their problem by saying, "I sure hope all of you got a good night's rest," and then added, "Enjoy your breakfast, then we'll head out to the Ops Center."

He ordered a hearty meal and asked for a pot of coffee to be left on the table. Following his lead each member chose a breakfast of their own liking, and managed to relax slightly. After an unhurried meal they drove to the Base and entered the Ops Center, where they gathered around the Team station and noted there were several messages waiting for them. Nat assumed the chair at their desk after looking at Walt and receiving an unspoken word to do so.

She opened the messages quickly, scanned them, and passed them to Walt, who in turn scanned their content and passed them on to the Team. Two were from Whitman AF Base, both addressed to Nat; one was from the CID Investigator, George Gregory, the other from

Captain Johansen, Base Operations, his, referring to Gregory's message advising that Gregory had uncovered some information. Gregory's message asked for Nat or Jack to call him 'at the earliest'.

Nat activated the scrambler and called Gregory's number. He answered after the first ring with an abrupt, "CID, Gregory." Nat identified herself and asked if a scrambler was necessary, Gregory immediately changed his gruff demeanor and told her to hold while he activated his device.

After only a brief moment Gregory came on the line with a courteous, "Good morning Nat, it is nice to hear from you."

Nat replied, "Thank you George, it was nice of you to contact us. I hope you have something useful for us. We have been reviewing tapes and notes without much coming of it. Don't keep me in suspense, what have you got?"

He replied, "Some of our people up the line picked up a possible I. D. on the truck they used. We think it was a rental out of Washington. We picked it up from the rental place and have it in isolation up there pending a look see by us." He then went on. "I think you folks would like to take a look at it. One of our guys found a high quality aircraft type bolt on the floor of this truck and immediately tied it to our request for help to find a vehicle that had been used to transport a spacecraft. We had suggested a rental truck might have been used."

As soon as Nat had repeated the message to Walt, he stepped over to General Mayfair and informed him of what had been said.

General Mayfair said, "I suppose you'd like to get up to Washington in a hurry, right? I can get a courier jet to haul you up there, if that is what you'd like."

Walt replied, "You are reading my mind sir, this may be the break we are looking for. Can I send one of my people instead of myself?"

"Of course, I'll alert them to expect your man at the airfield in an hour, is that about right?' responded General Mayfair.

"Sir, if I can, I would like to send Nat, she is qualified as a jet pilot, also she has seen the test spacecraft, and as you know she is a fine investigator."

"No problem, she can make it to Washington in a couple of hours," he replied, "Have her at the hanger and check in with the scheduler there."

Walt asked Nat, "Do you need anything to take with you?"

"Not much, just a laptop," she replied, then to George Gregory, who was still on the line, "I'll be on my way to Washington inside of an hour, can you set me up with a contact there?"

"I'll have a guy to meet you when you arrive, at the Air Force Hanger at Dulles, how's that?" he asked.

"You're a sweetheart," she quickly responded.

Walt said to Jack, "Jack, will you take her over to the air field where the courier jet is standing by, take my Cobra if you would like, and tossed him the keys"

Jack and Nat immediately departed.

As they arrived at the passenger area an Air Force Sergeant was waiting for them and asked, "Are you the passenger we're supposed to get to Washington pronto?"

Nat stepped forward and said, "That's me, what plane are we using, looking toward a large cargo aircraft."

The Sergeant laughingly said, "There's your ride warming up on the runway," pointing to a jet fighter aircraft gently hissing as its engine began its 'run-up' in power, "I have your gear and helmet here, please sign this manifest and you can get going," he continued. Obviously the General had told him Nat was a qualified jet pilot.

Nat quickly donned the flight suit over her coveralls and tugged the helmet over her curly hair. She looked pleased at the prospect of riding in the fighter and promptly affixed her name to the sheet. She thanked Jack and told him she would call back as soon as she learned anything. She walked over to the boarding ladder and climbed up to the top step and shouted her name to the pilot who grinned appreciatively and waved her in to the back seat. As soon as she had settled in the cockpit confines she immediately made her intercom connection and reintroduced herself to the pilot. The ladder was taken away as he lowered the canopy and latched it.

Almost before she knew it the plane was taxiing to the end of the runway, where it halted momentarily as the pilot set his brakes and started advancing the throttle. Within seconds they were rolling down the runway and upon reaching rotation speed, they were suddenly airborne.

The intercom crackled and the pilot said, "I didn't believe it when they told me I had a passenger to take to Washington, much less that it would be a girl. Anyway I'm Mike Cassidy and I am delighted to have you."

Nat keyed her intercom and responded. "Thanks, but it has been a long time since I was a 'girl'. I really appreciate the ride, it has been a long time since I was last in a fighter."

Nat gave him a brief summary of the Team responsibilities and that her own experiences as a pilot were a couple of years back. They climbed up to 30,000 feet and Mike suggested she should don her oxygen mask. She had already done so as she observed the altimeter climbing rapidly. She listened quietly as Mike made his calls to ground controllers, relishing the trip. She was surprised at how quickly they approached Washington, it seemed they had hardly reached cruising altitude before he was calling Washington ground control requesting landing instructions. Upon landing he rolled left and right through several taxiways before finally coming to a halt before the Air Force hanger.

Nat checked her watch, it had taken only and hour and fifteen minutes for the flight and more than five minutes taxiing to the hanger after landing. She had forgotten how fast the plane was traveling as they touched down.

A jeep rolled up to the plane with a boarding ladder and within minutes she was removing the flight suit and helmet. As she handed the equipment to the Air Force NCO with the jeep, she got her first look at Mike, her pilot. She thought, 'My God, he doesn't look any older than Bobby.' He carried his briefcase and helmet to the jeep and told the NCO Nat was expecting to be met by a CID man.

The Sergeant said, "He just arrived, we didn't know who he was supposed to meet," and looking at Nat, added under his breath, "I wouldn't mind helping her myself."

Nat said to Mike, "I appreciate you flying me up here, it really is important to our investigation, thank you so much."

He replied, "It was a pleasure, if you have any time while you are here I would like very much to have you join me for dinner, or drinks or whatever. You can contact me through the flight office right here at the hanger." He jotted the number on a slip and handed it to her. She tucked the slip in her pocket, thanked him again and turned to the CID man and introduced herself.

CHAPTER 12

NAT LOOKED AT THE MAN before her and thought, 'He certainly doesn't look very friendly.'

The agent stepped forward and said, "My name is John Bossidy, George Gregory said I was to pick you up here and take you over to the warehouse to see the truck we picked up." He added as an afterthought, "Would you like to get a cup of coffee or something? How long have you been in the air? Maybe you need a break or something!"

"No thank you, I'm fine, I would like to see the truck to determine if we can get any idea of where the thing it was carrying went, as soon as possible would be nice."

John said, "I have been briefed on the hi-jacking and we are all trying to figure that out. Our experts are still checking the truck for any other clues."

They were talking as they approached his vehicle, a non-descript appearing, dark blue, four door sedan. He opened the passenger door for her to be seated then went around to the driver's door and climbed in. While the exterior was casual in appearance, the interior was totally different. Inside it was immaculate, with dark tinted windows obscuring vision from the exterior. It was equipped with a flashing blue light with a magnetic base, allowing it to be placed on the roof. The dash had been modified to accommodate a complex radio transceiver. John turned the radio on and spoke briefly, saying he had picked up the "passenger" and was en route to the warehouse. A curt "Roger" came over the speaker.

He drove with an expert ease, in moderate traffic, skillfully handling the powerful car. Although Nat was generally familiar with Washington, she had no idea where they were, or where they were going. After numerous turns they entered an industrial area with rows of large warehouses. As they approached a barbed-wire topped fenced, John pressed a button on a ceiling-mounted console garage door opener. A large gate rolled back permitting their entry and he closed it behind them. He parked the car near a small personnel door to the warehouse and got out of the vehicle, went around and opened the door for her to climb out.

He spoke to Nat saying, "Here we are, come on and I'll take you to George."

They entered the building and again she was surprised to note the cleanliness and careful order inside. The floor was fenced off into fenced cubicles, in one was the suspect truck. As they entered the cubicle, George Gregory emerged from the truck, and jumping down said, "I'm glad you made it so quickly, I've got a couple of things to show you." He shook her hand warmly and he commented to John, "This is the lady I was telling you about, be good to her and she might help us."

It was obvious that Gregory held Nat in considerably high regard. John was mildly surprised at the effusion Gregory exhibited to Nat. He thought, 'This gal must really be something to see old George loosen up like that.'

Inside the enclosure, Gregory led Nat past the truck, to a work station against the warehouse outer wall. High intensity lamps shone down over the work bench. Laid out in trays were several items. In one was a quarter inch diameter bolt about two inches long. It glittered under the lights inside the tray as it lay on a green, lint free cloth. A large magnifying glass lay on the bench near the tray.

Gregory explained to Nat, "This bolt is high tensile strength stainless steel, it has a number on the head signifying it is suitable for aircraft quality requirements. I have checked with Dr. Bowman and he said it is the same kind as used on your missing spacecraft, but he has no idea from which part of the spacecraft it might have come, we found it in the bed of the truck, kind of stuck in a corner," Gregory went on, "I gave the cab of the truck a careful examination and found a number of cigarette butts on the floor. I also examined each of the butts and discovered they are not of any standard brand used by us Americans. They appear to be a type used in Europe, Galoises', they are in that tray," he said pointing to the tray," and went on, "A French brand available everywhere in Europe," he went on, "We checked for prints without much luck, they were pretty much smudged."

"The best news of all is we have found where this truck was leased. They didn't even try to hide their identity when they leased it. We have interviewed the woman who did the paperwork and even have the name on the credit card they used and a description of the guy. The card is one of several held by the Russian Embassy right here in Washington. The rental agency was pretty alert on this rental, the guy wasn't sure how long they would need the truck, so they paid for a month in advance. The address they used is the Embassy itself, which jibed with the credit card address."

Gregory continued with his dialog, "We have been checking to see if they have rented any property which might be suitable for assembling the spacecraft. Dr. Bowman told us it was not assembled as a single unit, so we know they would need a place to put it back together. So far, no luck, but we'll keep at it."

Nat, excited that so much had been learned, asked for a phone so she could inform Walt of the progress made. Gregory led her out of the fenced cubicle to an office area within the warehouse

He said to her, "This phone has a scrambler on it so you can call back to Cocoa Beach, or Patrick, or where ever you people are set up."

She looked at him gratefully and proceeded to dial the Patrick Ops Center. and when Connie answered, Nat said, "Scrambler, Connie."

Connie immediately replied, "It's on, but let me get Walt on the line."

When he picked up Connie said, "OK Nat, he's listening."

Nat reported all she had been given and added, "Walt, I assume you want me to work with these CID men to see what else can be developed here in D.C., right?"

Walt concurred and added, "I am going to get part of the Team up there with you, ask Mr. Gregory if that sets

OK with him." Nat turned to George Gregory and asked if the Team could come up and work with the CID.

He immediately replied, "If you mean Jack, or anybody like you and him, the answer is yes, we would look forward to working with you again."

Walt could hear the response and said, "Jack, and a couple others, will be on their way later today. I'll keep you posted as soon as we can sort out the details. Please tell Connie where they should check in."

Nat asked George to advise Connie where the upcoming Team members should report, after arriving in Washington. George gave Connie the necessary instructions and hung up.

Gregory turned to Nat and said, "Come with me and I'll show you the truck cab and then we can look in the back if you would like to, although there really isn't much to see. We have gone over the bed with a 'fine tooth comb', and found nothing but that bolt."

Together they left the work bench area and turned to the truck. She climbed up into the cab on the passenger side while Gregory mounted in the driver's side. Once seated he said, "I suspect they must have waited for the spacecraft convoy somewhere near the highway. They probably smoked a few cigarettes, that's how come we found the butts here on floor of the cab. We tried lifting 'prints off the steering wheel and around the vehicle, but without much luck, like I said, they were all too smudged."

Nat sat back and tried to visualize what had happened that fateful day, the horror of the scene came to mind as she mentally revolted at the recollection. She saw again the video tapes of the blood-covered bodies as they lay in the ditch. She could hear the chatter of the machine guns as they fired at point blank range, and the surprised faces of the young men as they were gunned down. She shuddered at the mental picture and was jolted back to reality with a visible start.

Gregory looked at her and was struck at the tears welling up in Nat's eyes. He reached over and gently touched her on the arm and said, "Hang in there, we will do our damnedest to catch these murderous bastards."

She wiped the tears from her cheeks with the back of her hand and replied. "Right now that is our number one priority. Jack and a couple more of our Team will be here to work with you folks," she went on, "Forgive my display of tears, but I just couldn't help but think of the families of those young men so brutally shot. Some of them were just kids."

Gregory said, "Don't forget, we find the perpetrators and we find the ones who took the spacecraft."

Nat was back to herself and observed, "We ought be to checking out some of those Russian Embassy people. I would think some of them would surely want to see the spacecraft, and that might lead us to its location. Can you provide 'tails' to check them out"?

Gregory replied, "We are not supposed to be in the spy business, our charter is criminal investigation, but we belong to the Air Force and we sure as Hell aren't going to let our guys slaughter go unresolved. I'm sure we can bend the rules a little bit and put some of those Russkies under surveillance. Let me get back to my boss and see what we can do."

A few minutes later Gregory approached Nat and said, "Our front office would like to help, but say what you are asking for is really CIA or FBI functions and without their OK we cannot do what you ask."

Nat sighed and said, "I understand, let me call Walt again and see if he can turn things on."

They returned to the office area of the warehouse and Nat asked for the use of a phone with a scrambler. Gregory, annoyed by his superior's action, showed Nat to a properly equipped instrument.

She called the Ops Center desk and asked for Walt. When he answered she explained the jurisdictional 'turf' problem. Walt responded by saying, "I'm surprised their boss didn't tell then to turn the evidence over also. I'll contact the right people in the FBI and see if they can't get on it immediately. I'll call you back in few minutes, give me the number there."

She complied and Walt hung up. She turned to George Gregory and said, "Walt is going to try and get the Fibbies on it."

Gregory immediately asked his Washington counterpart if the local CID had a good working relationship with the FBI. The man, dressed impeccably in a business suit which belied his affable manner said, "I know just the guy to call, give me a few minutes to explain the situation and we'll see what he can do."

The Washington CID agent, A.B. Johnson, dialed a local number and asked to speak to Glen. He spent several minutes trying to tell Glen the details on the 'clear' line. It was impossible so he said something and hung up, and immediately used a secure phone to recall Glen. He succinctly explained the situation, listened for a brief period, thanked his contact, and hung up. Doing a smart about face, he said, "It's in the bag, Glen knew about the hi-jacking, and told me they are already trying to chase down leads themselves. You see, we told them about the clues we uncovered here, and now I hear they are one step ahead of us, they have the Russian Embassy under surveillance full time and have a suspicious location to investigate."

Gregory exasperatedly asked Johnson, "Why in Hell didn't you let me in on it, you act like a son-of-a-bitch, you hear!"

He smiled and replied, "I have a boss too, you know. He wasn't too happy that you people from Whitman Air Force Base were doing an investigation in our back yard. Sorry George, we will work with you from here on in. He then said, "How about filling me in on the role of Miss Nat, what's her function. I don't know her, an introduction might be nice." He stuck out his hand and said, "My name is Agent A. B. Johnson, I'm the senior CID agent here in D. C., I am delighted to make your acquaintance. Believe it or not, I have heard of some of the exploits of your Team, Fixit is the name, as I recall."

Nat replied, "You've got it right, my name is Natalie Morse, and I am one of the more senior members of Fixit. I usually go by 'Nat'. Thank you for getting that information for us, it is very helpful." She spoke in a slightly cool manner aware of Johnson's arrogance, but impressed by his quick understanding of what had happened.

He immediately picked up on her manner and was quick to adjust his attitude. He leaned toward Gregory and said, "Why don't you and Nat here, come with me and I can get you in touch with our Fibbie friends." He led them outside the warehouse to a late model sedan and opened the front passenger door for Nat and closed it behind her as she seated herself. Gregory opened the rear door and seated himself. Johnson had hardly closed his driver's side door before he had the car in motion. Nat immediately reached beside her and fastened her seat belt as did Gregory in the rear seat, the Washington agent ignored the warning chime for his unfastened seat belt and it ultimately stopped, He muttered under his breath, "Pain in the ass, damn ding, ding, ding!"

Nat expected to see a formal Washington granite edifice for the FBI office, but was surprised to see a typical brownstone, one of an entire block, only differing in their dull colors. Their 'chauffeur' entered the driveway along side the building and parked in the rear along side several other cars. They all left the car and climbed a short flight of stairs, where the door was opened from within. The shirt-sleeved man inside greeted them in a friendly manner and shook hands with each of them.

He greeted Johnson warmly, saying, "I knew it was only a matter of time before somebody else showed up on this case." He continued, "I had a call telling me about Miss Morse," and to Nat, "Glad to have you with us, I have heard many good things about you folks."

She smiled and responded, "Thank you, please call me Nat, but I didn't catch your name."

Johnson spoke up and introduced him to her and Gregory, "Please meet Agent Glen Starbuck, one of the best men they have in the FBI."

"I'm just Glen to everybody, glad to know you. I feel I know Nat from reading some of our files, you know, electronic data base tells all, and Gregory your reputation precedes you. I am pleased to meet you. I'm sure we can help in this matter. In fact, we have already identified one of the key people involved with the hi-jack. His name is Captain Sgedy Skelsin, a long-time officer in the supposedly defunct KGB, we think he was the leader of the group that did the hi-jacking. He has been known to be called in for special operations, we have seen him here in Washington and in and out of the Russian Embassy. We know he has worked for a Russian attaché, named Colonel Mikael Dantilev in the past in Europe. He is a known assassin, capable of murdering his own mother, plus sightings in other places make him a likely suspect here."

Nat exclaimed, "It sounds as though the FBI is way ahead of us, I am so glad to hear all the facts you have just given us, it does confirm my boss' suspicions about the Russians. I thank you for the briefing, but I understand the location of the spacecraft is also known or at least suspected."

Glen grinned and said, "I figured that would be your first question. We do think we have the location, we have it under surveillance. Actually we were able to use the info provided by the Washington CID to figure out what happened. We have a good working relationship with them, Art, A.B. Johnson that is, kept us up to snuff as things were developed by you CID men."

George Gregory glared at Johnson for not telling him that he was passing on data to the FBI. Johnson saw the glare and shrugged, as if to say 'sorry.'

Nat intervened by telling Glen that other Fixit Team people were en route, and that they would need a briefing if it could be accommodated. In the interim she asked if she could be shown the suspected location.

Gregory attached himself to the immediate proximity of Nat, recognizing her subtlety was assuming leadership of the entire group. Glen too, recognized her gentle assumption and accepted it as a matter of course.

She asked Glen if the info he had just briefed was available for transmission back to the Patrick Ops Center and if so could it be done in the near future. She also offered to provide Glen with the various videos and recordings that Fixit had generated, a fair exchange she suggested. She then asked if space could be made available to Fixit, perhaps in the FBI building where encoded messaging and electronic devices were commonplace.

In short order a desk was arranged next to Glen's and access to their telecommunications afforded. Before she could ask, Glen offered himself as her driver and escort while in Washington. Nat beamed, things were going nicely.

George Gregory doggedly remained close to Nat, which actually pleased her. She felt protected in his presence. In truth, Glen was also pleased to have him with them. Should things suddenly turn ugly, George Gregory would be an invaluable asset. It was apparent that George was a skilled investigator and was known to be handy in a fight or with a gun.

Nat, George and Glen left the FBI building in Glen's car and drove to the area thought to house the missing spacecraft. Glen was in communication with his surveillance team and carefully avoided compromising that location. They entered a back alley and stopped behind a run down building in a string of tightly bunched buildings of similar ancestry, old and in a poor state of repair. They quietly exited their car, being careful to avoid slamming the doors. Glen opened a door to the building and gestured for them to follow him. He carefully climbed the rickety staircase, keeping his footsteps close to the wall. Nat and George emulated his care as they ascended the stairs. Two men sat in folding chairs in the front of the building, one closely observing the building across the street through an aperture in the forward wall. Glen asked the man observing to let Nat take a quick look. Little was said as the FBI man got up and surrendered his peephole to Nat.

The building across the way was not as run down as the one being used for surveillance by the FBI. She noted the fairly neat appearance and the large garage-like doorway opening in to the front of the building, there was also a smaller door to the right side of the front, apparently used for people to enter and leave the building. As she observed she thought, 'That large door would surely be big enough for a truck to go in or out. I'll bet they took the spacecraft inside and then returned the truck'. She turned to Glen and whispered, "How on earth did you ever find this place?"

He replied in a low voice, "When they returned the truck, the rental people called and we asked them to stall them as long as they could. We were fortunate in that we got their response to an alert we had just sent out to truck rental agencies around 'D.C'. Only because of the quick response did we get this chance.

We almost missed them, they had already left the rental place but we had a description of the car they left in and frankly lucked out in seeing them as they went around the corner. That car led us here."

Nat relinquished the peephole to the FBI observer and whispered back to Glen, "You must live right!"

Gregory was allowed a look through the peephole and then Glen suggested they should leave in order to not compromise their location. He led the way back to the car and after they had departed the area a discussion ensued. Nat asked if any additional items had been brought in to the building, such as electronic test gear, or significant amounts of documentation, which would indicate an attempt to do something with the spacecraft. She had confirmed in her mind that the spacecraft was indeed in that location.

Glen responded by saying, "It sounds like you are sure the spacecraft is in that building. I can tell you that several people have gone in and out carrying large briefcases. But so far, no major electronic equipment that we can detect."

"With your concurrence I would like to defer any overt action to enter the place until the rest of my Team gets here," Nat stated almost as an order.

"I agree," said Glen, and added, "We will continue to monitor the building to assure nothing leaves there."

The group returned to the FBI building where Nat immediately called Walt. She reported all that had transpired and it appeared foregone that the spacecraft had been found. Walt was electrified and quickly advised Nat to await his and the rest of the Team's arrival. He told her, "Change of plans, I will assemble the bulk of the Team and we will depart within the hour, I will bring Joe and Jack with me, Connie will have to man the Ops Center desk on her own.

We will bring two SUV's and one trailer to carry our gear. Ask Mr. Starbuck to advise of where can we billet our people. See if you can get a radio to operate on our frequency and that way you can contact us en route. Any questions?"

She replied, "Negative boss, can do."

Glen had heard all of her side of the call and most of what Walt had said. He commented, "Now there's a guy who seems to get things done in a hurry. Let him know we can accommodate him in our own building, we have a dormitory room we use for just such occasions. I am sure we can provide you with a radio if you know the frequency you need. Just let me know their arrival time, driving, it will take them a while."

In an hour's time Nat's desk was completely set up with recorder, radio, secure phone system and her laptop computer. She was astonished at the speed with which things got done.

CHAPTER 13

"LOOKS LIKE WE HAVE A break in the case. If you can handle this Ops Center desk by yourself for a few days, I will take the rest of the Team to Washington to see if we can recover the spacecraft. I think Bobby should stay here, he can act as a runner for you. He will need to be badged, so you will have to arrange it, I think the General will OK it, please follow up." Walt said to Connie.

Her immediate reply was, "Sure, no problem, can I have a cot here by the desk? That's all I'll need, I can 'cat nap' right here if I need to and Bobby will be handy to have if I need anything, he can spell me now and then."

Walt strode over to General Mayfair's desk and said, "Sir, I think we have a break in the case. I'd like to head to Washington to work the problem. If you approve, Connie can remain here on our desk, if we can give her cot to catch a few winks now and then. I'll be taking the rest of my people with me except Bobby, Connie will see you about getting him a badge."

General Mayfair said, "Consider it done, the Sergeant can get a cot like mine. Are you able to bring me up to speed on what is happening?"

Walt gave the General a complete rundown on the information so far available, but cautioned, "Sir, none of what I've just told you has been confirmed. As soon as I can validate it, I will get back to you."

The General expressed his appreciation and told Walt to do whatever was necessary, whereupon Walt advised Connie to keep the radio on for updates. He questioned Connie, "Can you raise Jack, Joe and Kim for me, get them here as soon as you can, alert them we'll be traveling. Load standard equipment and ordnance."

"Joe is over at the motor pool and I will call Jack and Kim on their cells, shouldn't take more than a few minutes, Walt," she responded She keyed a special set of numbers on her system to ring each of them simultaneously. As each answered she had them stand-by until the others were on the line at the same time. When she had them all she spoke into her mike, "Jack, Kim, Joe we need you here at the Ops desk soonest, Walt will brief you, but Kim pick up an SUV and Joe, you too, but hook a trailer to your SUV, be sure they are gassed and ready for a trip. Walt says to load standard equipment and ordnance."

All three responded, almost in unison. "Roger, wilco, be there in about twenty minutes or so."

As soon as they had presented themselves at the Ops desk, Walt briefed them on the latest developments. Being long-standing members of Fixit they were able to be ready to roll from the motel in less than an hour. Kim drove one SUV with Walt as a passenger, Joe drove the second SUV with its trailer and Jack as a passenger. In the course of the briefing Walt had asked Joe to equip the trailer with an assortment of weapons, grenades, sniper gear, and various electronic equipment. He also included a standard load of protective equipment and routine supplies they had developed from past operations. Walt carried a laptop computer.

Joe acknowledged he had loaded the trailer accordingly and all three rushed to the motel to pick up the balance of needed items.

They departed the motel after including necessary personal clothing and gear each member had assembled from their own experiences and was kept in a special duffel bag, Nat's was included. Considering the speed with which it was all accomplished, the varied and combative capabilities included was amazing. They had included detection devices, sound pick-ups, high-frequency radio transmitters with throat microphones, highly specialized optics, including sniper scopes on special sniper rifles, and a wide variety of weapons and ordnance, booby traps, and an assortment of explosives of several kinds. Explosives come in many forms, some of which are innocuous in appearance and often used in devious fashion.

Both SUV's had multiple antennas to permit broad radio frequencies to be used. Long range communication was available, as well as short wave functions. They were able to reach the Washington radio of Nat with ease. Walt notified Nat they were under way and would keep her apprised of their location from time to time. Joe had seen to the servicing of the SUV's, and with their long-range tanks they were able to travel continuously as long as the driver was able to operate. They drove for four hours and changed drivers, with Walt and Jack relieving Kim and

Joe respectively. At the end of eight hours they stopped for a quick meal and coffee. Aside from periodic stops to accommodate nature's call, a quick meal and gas, they kept a steady pace just above the speed limit, figuring their warning radar detectors would keep them out of trouble. They were able to maintain an average speed of about sixty miles per hour, and in a little under fifteen hours they were approaching Washington, D.C.

As they neared Washington Nat advised them that Glen would send an escort to meet them at the I-95 intersection with the city bypass. The FBI car was readily identifiable to Walt by its unique appearance, a white station wagon with several colored pendants flying from its roof. It too, had tuned its radio to the Fixit frequency and as soon as Walt spied the wagon he called on the radio, "Fixit to FBI, I've got you in sight, do you read me?"

The FBI escort responded, "Roger, fall in behind me and I'll take you the rest of the way. They followed closely behind and spent another half hour in traffic before arriving at the FBI building. It was a reunion of sorts for the Team people before Nat made introductions to the FBI people.

Glen announced, "Nat has told me what you have in that trailer, perhaps you had best lock it up in our garage."

Joe and an FBI man went out to take care of it. Glen showed Walt the dormitory and Jack and Kim brought all the personal belongings in and left them in the dorm. The time had worked out conveniently, they left Cocoa Beach at five in the afternoon and drove through the night, arriving at the FBI office by ten the next morning.

Gen observed, "You sure didn't waste any time getting here, but surely you want a little rest before we do anything."

To which Walt replied, "We took turns driving allowing us to rest a bit, so it wasn't too bad, it would be nice if we could get a little breakfast, or something, then I wouldn't mind taking a look see at what you have."

Glen responded, "We have a kitchen here in the building and can take care of the four of you with no problem, so long as you aren't too particular. Our cook is here and does a decent job with simple meals. How about some bacon, eggs and we have some ham, there's toast too and coffee."

Walt spoke for his Team and said, "I think that would be very nice. Perhaps we could talk at the same time."

"Sure," replied Glen, "I'll have some of my guys join us so we won't have to repeat anything."

In the next few minutes breakfast was served and the dishes cleared by the cook. All of the Fixit crew except Connie and Bobby was present, along with Glen and two of his agents. Glen and Nat briefed the rest of them to insure everyone was working from the 'same page'. Walt expressed his surprise that so much had been developed in the brief period since the hi-jacking.

"It appears we need to verify that the spacecraft is in fact where we think it is, before we go much further," Walt added.

He looked to Glen for his assent. Glen said, "You are right of course. It appears we are on the right track though. We have verified the Russian agent, Captain Sgedy Skelsin, has been in and out of the building we have under surveillance. He is a known murderer and our CIA friends verified he legally entered the country a few weeks ago. At least two others who have entered are known to be of the scientific persuasion, though we are not yet sure of their names. In addition there are four others who appear to be 'hired hands', in the building, we think these men are carrying weapons. They probably have a significant arsenal in there. We have not seen them carry any large boxes in, but they may have had all kinds of equipment in the truck when it first arrived."

He took a deep breath and asked, "Any questions so far?"

Walt said yes, I have a few, "Do you know what kind of a schedule they are following? Are they a single shift type operation? Do we know how many people are there at any given time? Do we know which personnel are inside at any given time? Have you had an opportunity to examine the building for access points? Do they have vehicles at the ready? If so, where are they? How do people arrive and depart?" and then, "I'm sorry, I guess that is too many questions at once, I'll try to go more slowly."

"Not necessary," said Glen. "Your questions have been recorded and we can play them back to be answered one by one, that is, if we can answer all of them. Bill, run them back, then do them one at a time and let's see what we come up with. OK Walt?"

"Let's do that, can we record any discussion and some answers?" Waltreplied, looking at Glen, who nodded.

The questions posed by Walt were played back one by one by Bill.

The speaker came on with the first question, 'Do you know what kind of schedule they are following?'

A discussion ensued with the conclusion that the hijackers were on a nominal daylight schedule, but with no fixed hours noted. Walt observed, "That means we will have to be flexible in whatever plan we make."

The second question come on, 'Are they a single shift operation?' Again a discussion ensued, since the FBI personnel were the only ones involved in surveillance to date, they had whatever information was available.

Glen responded by saying, "My people have noted they seem to have no particular schedule. However, it does appear that they must have established a guard system. The same people have been noted entering at the end of the day are leaving the following morning. Of course we have had them under surveillance for only a couple of days, hardly enough to say that is their schedule. If we watch them for a while longer it might well tell us they have developed a routine."

Walt interjected, "I don't think we should wait any longer than we need before we prepare a plan of action. We cannot wait until they have had time enough to figure out how the spacecraft systems work, and we don't know how long that might be."

"You don't want to go in there like gang busters, do you, I think that would be counterproductive," one of Glen's agents commented, looking at Glen for confirmation.

Before Glen could respond Walt spoke up saying, "Absolutely, that's what we are trying to do here, develop a workable plan that will recover the spacecraft without personnel injury or loss of life. We know they think nothing of killing any one who gets in the way. I appreciate all you folks have done, but the recovery of that craft is our responsibility. I cannot risk loss of life by any other agency. We failed to protect it and now it is up to us to get it back. I would like to think of you and maybe the CIA would help us, in a support role."

Walt's words were chosen with care, he knew that both the FBI and CIA had been told Fixit was chartered to handle any 'dirty work' incidental to attacks on this spacecraft. Logic being that Fixit could be available to plan necessary safeguards during the entire duration of the program. Otherwise it would have meant a severe drain on other agency manpower. Similarly it meant Fixit would shoulder the blame if something went wrong, though in the case at hand, Fixit had not yet been charged with responsibility at the time of the hi-jacking. Regardless, Walt accepted that his people were responsible for recovery of the craft.

Glen looked at Walt appraisingly, aware that Walt knew that responsibility had indeed been defined, also mentally breathing a sigh of relief that the FBI was not to be blamed for the loss. In actuality, the Air Force had been specifically given most of the blame for not providing adequate protection. Air Force had belatedly recognized that there was a test article equally sensitive as was the flight article, and thus had called in Fixit. The transfer of the test spacecraft from Whitman Air Force Base to Huntsville was reasonably protected by routine standards, but failed to consider the lengths a foreign government would go to in order to know what the United States had.

The hi-jacking was not thought to be possible, because it would cause an international furor. The damage was done, and a formal charge that Russia was the culprit, was not diplomatically practical without positive, irrefutable proof they were guilty. In all probability a formal charge would never be leveled at any nation. The real unforgivable crime was the slaughter of the men transferring the spacecraft, it would go down in the annals of history as a dastardly crime.

After the brief discussion, Walt asked, "Can we go on?"

The FBI agent started the recorder at the third question, 'Are they a single shift operation?'

Walt said, "That goes 'hand in glove' with the preceding question. If we can determine that they are on a single shift, we can determine the best time to intercede, or should I say 'bust the door down' and kill 'em?" He went on, "Glen do you and your folks agree it looks like this is going to be a night operation?"

Glen replied, looking at his two agents for confirmation, "I think that is one point we can all agree on right now, yes I think it should be at night. But, we must recognize the additional problems that type operation creates."

"Agreed, no choice but to do it at night," Walt replied after seeing his Team members also nod in agreement.

The machine started again at question number four, 'Have you had an opportunity to examine the building for access points?'

Glen responded to this by saying. "We have not had an opportunity to do much more than establish the surveillance post across from them. And that has only been in operation for two days. We are now trying to run a scan on any phone lines they have, which is in work at this time. But as far as seeing whether we can get in the adjoining buildings, nothing has been done yet. That probably ought to be an early item. Bill, any results from the phone company yet?"

Bill replied, "They said they would let us know today."

"I would like Joe to take a look at their building," Walt stated, then turning to Joe he said, "Joe how about you try your little Italian masquerade who had too much to drink. Think you might stagger past and see what you can see?"

Joe replied, "Why not, I haven't done it in a while but I have all the stuff in my gear. How soon?"

"Go now, as soon as you can get ready. Nat, you take him there, you know where it is," Walt said and added, "I don't have to say be careful."

Nat and Joe left the meeting and went to the dorm where their belongings had been deposited. Nat got out a theatrical make up kit while Joe changed into a disreputable set of clothes. He had a bottle of cheap wine from which he took a gulp. It wouldn't wash to be stopped as a drunk and not smell the part. He stuck the bottle in the outside pocket of his jacket. By the time Nat had finished with the makeup he looked very authentic, she added eye drops to cause his eyes to appear bloodshot as well as sunken, he looked like a drunken bum.

He mumbled in a slurred tone, "Whatta' ya say babe, wanna get it on?"

She laughingly said, "I wouldn't go near you in your condition. Let's go back to the meeting and see if there is anything new before we leave."

Joe shuffled his way back to the meeting area and as he entered he muttered, "Any a youse guys wanna have little sip wit me, fore I gotta go?"

The three FBI men couldn't believe what they saw, Joe was simply not recognizable as the muscular Fixit agent of a few minutes ago.

Glen exclaimed, "If I didn't know you, I would never have believed it. No wonder you people have the reputation you have."

Nat entered behind him and said, "Come on, you dirty old man, before I make you walk all the way," and led the way to their SUV.

As they boarded the vehicle she said, "I suppose you have your radio and throat mike on?"

He pulled the bandana around his neck downward showing the strap of the microphone and said, "Yeah, give me a radio check," as he seated the tiny receiver in his ear. They completed the check without problem, the high quality equipment was in perfect working order. Nat drove him to within three blocks of the surveillance site, and after checking to assure no one was observing them, dropped Joe with the admonition, "Be careful, these guys play for keeps."

There was a coffee shop at a nearby corner and Nat took up position there, using a newspaper to make it appear she was waiting for someone. Joe kept up a low mumble as he shuffled along, actually keeping Nat informed of his exact location. He had a miniature listening device which he hoped he could plant near a window or door of the place. There were few pedestrians in this area so Joe was quite obvious as he meandered along.

He stopped and urinated against a building as a car drove by, it's occupants staring at him in a disgust. As he staggered along the sidewalk he bumped against several buildings along his path, once doffing his hat and apologizing to the building. He started to sing softly to himself as he slowly proceeded along the street, he was using Italian interspersed with English.

He slowed noticeably as he came abreast of the building and actually lurched against the large garage door and caught himself with a muttered curse. Someone inside lifted the blind on the window of the small personnel door. They watched him slowly making his way past the building. When he had moved past the two buildings next to theirs, the watchdog agent observing shrugged, and dropped the blind back in place.

Joe spoke clearly in a very soft voice and told Nat, "I thought sure they were going to come out and see what I was doing, I damned near peed in my pants. I did get a good look at the buildings on either side of them, maybe some possibilities there." He was quiet for a few moments as he gathered himself and then said, "I don't think I should chance another trip past right now, maybe in an hour or so I can make my way back, might have to be a little more 'crocked' though, if I expect to be convincing."

Nat said, "Don't chance anything again for a good while, I'll drive on past and pick you up now. I'm sure Walt and the others would like to hear what you have to say from your little walk."

She spied him two blocks away from the building and after ascertaining no prying eyes could see them, she stopped and he climbed into the back seat of the SUV. Nat suggested they should take trip around the block to see if there were any vantage points to be noted. After completing this circuit discovered an alley behind the row of buildings, however she considered it was not the place to go right then. She returned to the FBI building, where she parked in the rear and they both climbed the stairs to the rear door, which opened as they reached the top.

Bill ushered them back to the meeting room where they all gathered. Nat had radioed in to announce she and Joe were returning. Anxious faces awaited them. Glen insisted they be given a minute 'catch their breath' before giving a report.

While they were gone the rest of Walt's questions had been addressed. The recorder played question number five, 'Do they have vehicles at the ready?' "Meaning can they depart in a hurry if they were alerted," explained Walt.

"They don't have any vehicles in the immediate vicinity," commented Glen, "They would have to get them from some where nearby. Maybe we should try to find where they stage from."

"Excellent idea, let's start on that as soon as we reasonably can," added Walt.

"I think we can handle that one for you," said Glen, adding, "Let's finish up with the questions first."

The recorder started again with question number six, 'If so, where are they?'

"This one refers to number five," explained Glen, "And we have already addressed it."

The recorder started once again with question number seven, 'How do people arrive and depart?'

"By automobile," blurted Bill, explaining. "We have seen them coming and going from our surveillance point."

"Looks like we have a good start," said Walt.

He turned to Joe and asked, "Did you see anything interesting, Joe?"

"I thought you all would never ask. Not only did I find my excursion very interesting, I was able to leave them a little souvenir. When I banged up against that big door I was able to stick one of our miniature listening devices on it." He added, "I'll go out to my trailer and set up the receiver, if one of you gentlemen will unlock the garage door."

The FBI men were flabbergasted, Glen asked , "You mean you planted a bug' on the door, won't they see it, or will it fall off if they open the door?"

Walt smilingly answered his questions, "To answer the last one first, no it is not likely it will fall off, they stick so well they have to be pried off, as to whether they might see it, maybe, but they would have to be looking for it, and yes, he planted a 'bug'! The ones we use are miniaturized and have an ultra high frequency to avoid detection. Unfortunately the battery is only good for a limited amount of time, but it will last plenty long enough for what we must do."

Bill jumped to his feet and said, "Come on Joe, I'll get the garage door for you." and led the way to the garage, where he used a set of keys to unlock the special security system on the door.

Joe unlocked and entered the trailer without inviting Bill to join him. He gathered up the necessary equipment, exited, reset the alarm system and relocked the trailer. He allowed Bill to carry the cabling and speaker, while he carried the receiver back to the meeting area. Once inside they quickly connected the cabling and power and Joe turned the unit on.

At first there was only static until Joe referred to a note and set the receiver to the correct frequency. Joe said, "This is a transceiver but we can use it to see what we can hear."

Sounds could be heard and then voices, but they were not in English. The FBI men looked crestfallen, but Walt merely looked at Nat and asked, "Russian isn't it?"

She nodded and started to translate but stopped before she uttered a word.

She said, "They are using some pretty bad language, it seems whomever is in charge thinks the hi-jackers should have thought to bring along the pertinent documentation. She translated, 'How can we assemble the damn thing if we do not know which part goes where.' and 'We are lucky to have been able to put these first two pieces together.' 'Sgedy, are you sure there was no papers or documentation in their vehicle?' 'To you I am Captain Skelsin, I told you there was no time to search the truck.' 'Did you not search the accompanying men, surely some body must have a manual?' "I had to dispose of the guards, they had nothing, I tell you.' 'I go to the Embassy now, good bye.' Nat translated, "Or as they say in Russian 'Das va danya!.' It sounds like they are getting ready to quit for the day."

A phone shrilled in another room, dragging everyone's attention back to the present. Bill signaled for the other agent to answer it. He called out, "Bill or Glen it's the phone company."

Glen said. "I'll take it in here, Charley." and turned to a wall-mounted phone and speaker system, He pushed the flashing button and spoke, "Starbuck here."

"Great, can you cross-patch it to us?" a pause, then, "Fine, use our number three line, OK?"

Glen announced, "We have a monitor now, all we have to do is listen. Bill patch number three to a speaker, that way there is no chance of them accidentally hearing us, but we can hear everything they say," He continued, "They only have a single line, activated yesterday, unfortunately what we hear will probably be Russian and we can't ask Nat to sit here and translate for us."

Walt chimed in, "The monitor is for us as much as it is for you, she can do it for a short while, can't you find a translator somewhere?"

"Of course, Bill will you call the language section and see how soon they can get a group of translators here?" Glen asked.

Bill jokingly replied, "All I need is to be two or three people to do my work around here," and then spoke seriously, "I called them earlier while Nat was translating the last word, they ought to arrive in about an hour or less."

"You are always one step ahead of me, next thing I know headquarters will promote you to Senior Agent and take you away from me," Glen spoke in an appreciative manner.

Walt spoke in an authoritative tone, "I think we need to sit down and map out a plan right now," then to Glen, "Will you be able to work with us in developing something?"

"All you need to do is say what you want and we'll do it, and that includes participation in any attack," was his reply.

There was a ring from the front door chime, Glen said, "That's the translators, I suspect, give me a minute to get them settled in and we can start on your plan of operation."

A large pot of coffee was set on the table and all of the Fixit Team joined with the three FBI men around the table. Glen provided a recorder and animated discussion started. Nat obligingly made note of salient points and gradually an outline was developed. The FBI men were to act as drivers and backup to the Fixit Team. A foray to the buildings behind their target was deemed a first step in order to seek vulnerability points. The two FBI men surveilling from across the street would drop to the ground floor and stand-by near their front door to exit if needed. Glen and Bill would enter the alley and be ready to force entry from the rear. Nat would drive the Fixit SUV and carry Walt and Kim and crash through the large front door, where the four of them would make a frontal assault, ready to deal with any guard personnel inside. Jack and Joe would hit the personnel door at the same time.

The plan carried a high degree of risk for the frontal assault group, but the Fixit Team had performed such tactics successfully several times in the past. They instinctively knew they could back one another up with a high level of confidence.

"We must be careful to avoid hitting the spacecraft firing our guns, if at all possible," Walt concluded.

Joe volunteered to make a check drive through the alley, but suggested a small car would be more suitable for this task. An FBI car was made ready and Joe was ready to start whenever it was determined the time was right. Since it was already approaching dark it was decided to send Joe immediately Joe returned within twenty five minutes and reported the alley was quiet and clear all the way through.

Before any further action could be initiated the FBI translator called out saying," hold everything for a minute, the man inside your target just called for assistance, he was concerned because a car just drove through the alley."

Nat confirmed this message by reporting the wall-mounted speaker monitoring the phone line carried the same message. She reminded them she spoke Russian.

There was hurried discussion around the table, trying to determine how this information might affect the plan. Before the discussion was complete, the translator reported more distressing news. Two more Russian guards had entered the target and were discussing whether the car driving through the alley was significant. The three guards were obviously alert and would be an added danger.

It was decided the plan developed was reasonably effective and midnight was selected as the best time for the attack.

CHAPTER 14

EACH FIXIT TEAM MEMBER DONNED body armor and harnesses for attaching special equipment and weapons. Each had holstered a Glock 9mm pistol with its 15 round clip and two spare pouches, each with two spare clips. Each of them carefully chambered a round, and added one bullet to the clip, then assured the pistol was on safe. On one side of the harness was hung a short barreled Kalishnikov sub-machine gun with its 30 round clip, in the back of the harness were 4 more 30 round clips. Each member hung 4 anti-personnel grenades to the vertical straps of the harness. Strapped to their legs were sheathed bayonets on one leg and throwing stilettos on the other. They had changed from their bright yellow coveralls to camouflage suits, less conspicuous in the night. The Team appearance was frightening in their array of deadly armament.

The two FBI men, Glen and Bill were not equipped to perform as was the Fixit Team, but they did arm themselves with pistols and sub-machine guns, and wore body armor similar to that of the Team

Finally they added communication gear, the Fixit Team with throat microphones and earpieces for their miniaturized radios carried in a breast pocket. The FBI men were equipped with standard, hand-held portable units. Each person conducted a communication check with the base unit in the FBI office manned by the third FBI agent. The Team strapped on Kevlar helmets and produced a heavy, hand-held battering ram as a back-up in case of need to force entry in the small personnel door of the garage. Together the assembled eight person task force was a formidable appearing group, displaying an outward show of confidence that was well warranted. A medical emergency kit was present in the SUV as standard equipment It had been decided that the FBI group would approach via the alley while the Fixit Team would make the forced entry. One Team in one SUV would attempt to crash the garage door while Jack and Joe forced entry via the personnel door. The SUV crashing the garage door would have to be halted immediately inside to avoid possibly hitting the spacecraft. It was not known how close to the door the spacecraft was located, but a risk that had to be taken. The other door would be forced just seconds after the SUV crashed in, logic being the second entry would also serve as a diversion, surprise was a paramount concern.

Walt was to drive the crash SUV, with Nat in the passenger seat and Kim in the rear seat, while Jack and Joe would stop their SUV some distance from the place and silently approach the other door. The FBI vehicle with Glen and Bill would enter the alley and approach to within one hundred feet and wait for the crash, then attack the rear entrance. They were cautioned to also wear their body armor, and to avoid firing toward the frontal assault group. Similarly Walt cautioned his Team to only shoot when they had a target.

As midnight approached they boarded their vehicles and headed toward the target area. Fortunately the streets were empty, and they would not have to keep people out of the danger area. Jack and Joe started their walk toward the target, when they were about twenty feet from their goal, Walt put the SUV in gear and silently idled toward the door, swinging wide to afford a straight-on assault. Just before stamping on the accelerator he whispered so his throat mike could pick up his words, "Attack on the count of three."

He spoke, "One, two, three, NOW." He jammed the accelerator to the floor and poised his left foot over the brake, the SUV leaped forward crashing into the garage door which gave with surprising ease, and he quickly applied the brakes as the SUV burst through the door. Jack and Joe slammed their battering ram into the smaller door, and dropped it as the door gave way, both shouldering their way into the room. The SUV had the garage door draped over its hood as Walt and Nat scrambled to exit the vehicle, Kim was trapped in the back seat, unable to open the rear door of the SUV and scrambled over the front seat to exit out Nat's door, weapon in hand ready to fire.

The Russian guards were alert and quickly reached for their weapons. Jack had swung his machine gun up and fired a burst at the nearest guard who already had his gun in hand nearly ready to shoot. He screamed and clutched his chest, a mass of spreading blood from Jack's blast of gunfire. Nat was out of the right side of the SUV and neatly fired three quick shots from her pistol, the first shot hitting the second guard in the neck and the second and third shots causing his head to nearly split open. The third guard had retrieved his weapon and loosed a burst of machine gun fire at Jack and Joe as they catapulted into the room. Jack caught two slugs in his upper arm as he twisted away, while Joe received two or three rounds full in the chest. He went down with a grunt and was still. Before the third guard could re-aim, Walt was able cut him down with several rounds from his Kalishnikov. The man dropped his gun and fell to the floor, still alive and cursing in Russian. Nat spoke to him in Russian telling him to shut up or die. He made no further effort to reach for his gun, speaking in Russian to Nat, asking why had they been attacked. He had caught several rounds from Walt's gun in his thigh and was losing blood rapidly.

Nat fashioned a tourniquet around his leg and temporarily stopped his bleeding. It was apparent he needed immediate medical care.

Walt turned toward Joe, concern in his eyes as he knelt next to where he lay. He looked for signs of blood, seeing none his spirits rose immediately as he began to loosen Joe's flak jacket, he then opened his shirt and saw what he had hoped for, ugly red welts had appeared on Joe's chest where his body armor had stopped the bullets fired at him. The bruises were already turning blue. He was breathing with difficulty and he started to cough as he gradually regained consciousness.

Joe spoke with difficulty, "Boy do I hurt, those damn bullets might as well have gone through my armor the way I feel." But as the minutes passed he began to feel better and was thankful he was not dead.

The rest of the Team took stock of themselves and found that Jack was quietly trying to clean the wounds to his arm. It appeared no other injuries had been sustained. Nat examined Jack's arm and discovered the slugs had both gone through without striking any bone. She quickly retrieved the medical kit from the SUV and applied antiseptic cleanser and antibiotic medication to both entry and exit wounds and bound his arm with an admonition to see a doctor promptly.

After assessing their personal condition Walt started to take stock of the interior of the garage. The spacecraft was partially assembled on a large work surface, apparently unharmed. Walt looked at it and said to Nat, "Can you tell by looking if it is OK?"

She replied, "I'm no expert, but let's see if any bullets hit it," and proceeded to carefully examine it from one end to the other. After a few minutes she said, "I don't see any apparent holes in it, but I think it should be checked by someone who knows it better than us."

Walt said, "I am tickled we were able to get it back, now we need to get it back into the right hands."

Glen and Bill had entered from a back room after entering from the alley and were surveying the damage when Bill said, "Good God, I thought you guys had started a war in here. I never heard so much gunfire in such a short time."

Glen chimed in, "Looks like you have everything under control in here," then looking at the spacecraft he observed, "So this is the thing that caused such a ruckus."

Walt jokingly said, "That's it, now that you've seen it you both will have to forget you ever laid eyes on it, it is classified Top Secret." He then added, "What you see represents about a billion dollars worth of government money."

Bill commented, "Maybe we should cover it up and not look at it."

Walt replied, "You are right, we do need to cover it up and get it out of here and under tight security, Glen, can you get a truck to haul this to a secure location until we can figure how to get it back where they want it?"

Glen said, "Can do," and keyed his mike, saying, "Base this is Glen, get hold of Security and tell them we need a large truck, Category A, and must meet clean room specs, for a special cargo. I'll give them more details later," and then to Walt, "Cat A means special security requirements."

"Walt, do you want to get Jack to a doctor?" Glen asked, and then continued, "We have a special medical facility with surgeons and all, on call 24/7. I can have Bill take him there now if you wish."

Walt responded, "We would appreciate that," then to Jack. "Jack, Bill is going to run you to a doctor for a check up. You stay there until he releases you, OK? Don't you leave until you're fixed up, we'll come and pick you up."

Walt then addressed Joe, "Do you want to ride along with Jack for a quick check?"

Joe replied, "I've been whacked before in a flak jacket so I know I'll be all right, it just takes a couple of hours to get over it."

By this time the Washington police had responded to the gunfire alarm and were asking for an explanation. Fortunately Glen was able to communicate with their police headquarters and advise them it was an FBI matter.

The police did cooperate and kept all sight seeing visitors away. It was over one hour later when the special truck arrived and was backed up to the smashed door. The door had to be removed before the spacecraft could be loaded into the truck. Care was exercised placing it in the truck, there was concern that it might accidentally move about while the truck was in motion. The Washington police again helped by escorting the truck to the FBI impound area at a very slow speed.

Dawn was breaking before the truck was secured inside the FBI controlled impound yard. The truck was securely locked and sentries posted with instructions no one was to be allowed near it except Walt Crawford or his personnel. It sat inside a double fenced, brilliantly lighted compound with grim-faced men carrying shot guns at the ready.

Everyone had followed the truck unwilling to rest until the spacecraft was secure. Once that had been cared for, the entire group happily scrambled into their vehicles and returned to the FBI office. Jack had already been to the medical facility for treatment and released, and had returned to the FBI office also.

Walt thanked the courageous FBI men for their invaluable assistance and said, "We really owe you men, I don't know how we can thank you enough for all you have done. When this is all over we will ask you to join us for a night on the town."

Walt then said to Glen, "I have a couple of calls I must make before I can call it a day. Can I use your phone for a bit, please?"

Glen's response was. "Of course."

Walt then called the Patrick Ops Center and after telling Connie all that had happened asked, "Is General Mayfair there?"

She replied , "He hasn't left here since you departed. He is looking at me right now, I think he knows you are on, shall I get him on this line?"

"Please do Connie."

General Mayfair came on the line and said, "Walt, I hope you have good news for me, what is going on?"

Walt briefly recounted the happenings and adding that he had not yet called Whitman Air Force Base to tell Dr. Bowman of the spacecraft's recovery. He closed by saying, "It will be a couple of days before we can get back to Patrick, Connie will have our latest and can keep you informed."

After terminating his call, he then called Dr. Bowman to tell him of the good news and to inquire as to where should the test spacecraft be sent. Walt was concerned about security where ever it would go. Once lost he did not want to have it happen again. He was acutely aware of his responsibility for not having a repeat of the first loss, he also realized the flight spacecraft would soon be shipped to Cape Canaveral for launch preparation. Having the flight article at the Cape and the test unit some where else would be disconcerting and mean a split of his Team to cover both locations. The Team composition was simply not large enough to accomplish this.

Dr. Bowman advised Walt the test spacecraft was to be kept at NASA's Huntsville facility, but that he too was concerned that if anything failed on the flight unit, the test article would be needed for spare parts. Walt reminded Dr. Bowman that NASA had a major operation at the Kennedy Space Center, adjacent to the Cape, the logical conclusion that the test unit might be kept at that Center. The conversation concluded with Dr. Bowman avowing he would turn 'heaven and earth' to assure that NASA could handle the test unit at Kennedy.

Walt terminated his call and tiredly decided he would join the rest of the FBI and his Team in a quick snack before bedding down. They all chatted for a brief time as they waited for the cook to appear, so they could eat before they retired for a well-earned rest.

The FBI men were pleased to have been part of the spacecraft recovery and delightedly joined the Fixit crew. Glen had roused the cook and had a generous breakfast served. In lieu of coffee he served a delicious warm milk concoction that went well with the eggs, ham, warmed over potatoes and toast. They all ate ravenously, realizing they had not eaten for some time. Following the meal they gratefully slept until late afternoon. They lazed around until evening mentally recouping from the violence of the recapture, realizing they had been very fortunate to not have had any fatalities among the Team.

They spent the early evening resorting their equipment and determining what replacement ammunition would be necessary. All weapons received a thorough cleaning and careful repackaging for their next use. Communication equipment were carefully checked and batteries replaced and added to the inventory of needed replacement items,

The FBI men were observant of the Team's activities and recognized the professionalism shown as the Team carefully prepared their equipment for its next use. Upon completion of necessary cleaning and storing of equipment the Team crawled into their bunks gratefully.

Walt discussed the injured Russian's capture and what to do with him. The FBI had a temporary holding facility used to house prisoners awaiting disposition which was used to care for the wounded man. It was recognized that he would ultimately be released to the Russians, obviously following interrogation.

The Team arose early and was once again given a generous breakfast by the FBI cook. Following the meal Joe hooked up their trailer and prepared for their departure.

The FBI men reluctantly bid them goodbye as the Team boarded their SUV's in the early sunshine and prepared to leave. The return trip was without incident.

Chapter 15

The two SUV's turned in to the motel parking lot and after stopping, Kim, who was driving the second SUV, asked Walt whether he should take the trailer out to the Patrick secure area for safe-keeping. Walt suggested he set the vehicle alarm system and take the trailer out after they all relaxed and had dinner. Kim was aware of the injuries sustained by Jack, and to a lesser degree to Joe, thinking it would not help their condition to unload any gear, he told Walt he could do all the unloading. It was a thoughtful gesture not un-noticed by Walt.

Walt spoke again, saying, "For right now, we are going in to the motel restaurant and have dinner. After that Kim and I will take the SUV's out to Patrick and store our equipment. Bobby is now a part of this Team and I am sure he would be delighted to help us put things away."

It sounded like an order and no one made further comment. Kim set the alarm on the trailers and verified both SUV's were locked, knowing each had a special alarm when they were locked.

They trooped into the restaurant, causing other diners to stare at their unusual camouflage dress. The motel manager was there and exhibited real 'savior-faire' by greeting them warmly and made sure that they received immediate attention. Walt thanked her and said they were glad to be 'home'. Walt's response generated an appreciative smile and assurance that they were welcome.

They were seated at a table off to one side of the restaurant, trying to not cause any more commotion than they already had. Once seated they were immediately attended to by the now familiar waiter who had taken their orders on previous occasions. Walt set the tone for the Team by ordering a cocktail as he seated himself, he addressed the waiter, "Johnny, bring me a scotch on the rocks, please".

The others quickly followed suit, ordering their desires, Johnny quickly returned setting a fresh drink in front of each of the Team members.

After each had received their drink, they ordered dinner. The restaurant was nicely appointed, and obviously well patronized by locals. In truth, the presence of the Team was not particularly out of the ordinary. Astronauts were frequent diners and had caused little disruption to the dining room. Since the Team members were residents of the motel their presence had become fairly well accepted.

They ate a leisurely dinner and chatted together amiably for several minutes after eating. Again Walt set the initiative by saying, "Well I guess we'd better finish up and give Connie a break."

That Connie had manned the Team desk for several days without relief suddenly struck home. They felt guilty for having forgotten her and Bobby.

Walt said. "Kim and I will take our stuff out to the Patrick storage and then go up to the Ops Center and I will relieve Connie. Nat, please call her and tell her we are coming up there as soon as we get unloaded. Have Bobby come down to the entrance and he can help Kim and I unload, it will be good training for him."

Walt then said, "Joe, will you check at the motel office for any messages, I had hoped to hear from the Camdens, Bobby's parents, they can only spend so long in the bush before they tire of it and return to civilization. They surely have received my letter before this past week. I told them about us taking on Bobby and that we would have to have their approval. I'm anxious to know their feelings about him joining us. Call me at the Ops Center if you learn anything."

He continued, "Nat, please look after Jack, I would like for him to see a doctor, maybe you can get him out to the Patrick Medical Facility, they have a doctor on duty twenty four hours a day." Then to Jack knowing he would not seek medical attention for himself, "You do what she tells you, OK?"

Jack meekly nodded assent.

Walt continued issuing instructions, "Joe, you get some rest. Kim as soon as we finish you come back here for some rest, and then I'd like you to come out to the Ops Center in six hours or so and relieve me on the desk until we can establish some sort of schedule. Jack you get at least a couple of days rest, I want to be sure your arm is going to be OK." After a thoughtful moment, he added,

"Nat, after you get Jack taken care of get some rest, we going to need you on some planning revisions we'll need to make. Oh, and let me know what the medics say about Jack's condition". He paused thought fully for a moment and then said, "I think that will cover things for the time being."

The Team members smiled knowingly, Walt thought first of his people.

They all pushed back from the table and each headed out to start on their assigned tasks.

Bobby was waiting at the base gate when Walt and the others arrived. He stepped forward to Walt and said, "I'm ready to become a real member of the Team. My Mom and Dad wrote me a letter from Nairobi, Kenya, they said they were proud that you thought enough of me to take me on."

Walt responded, "I'd like to see that letter if I may. I wrote to your parents at the address you gave me and I hope there is a response at the motel now." He then went on, "Bobby, would you help us unload our gear in the storage area. I think you might learn something about how we load our vehicles for special trips like the one we just finished."

"Yes sir, anything you say." he replied.

"Jump in my SUV and we'll head over to the storage area. Kim will already be there with the other SUV." Walt told him, then said, "You drive."

They checked in to the secure storage where Kim had started to open things up. Kim smiled at the arrival of Bobby and commented, "You'll see some things here that people seldom see, come on and I'll show what needs to be done."

The three of them managed to get everything unloaded and placed in its proper storage place in relatively short time. They were occasionally slowed while Walt or Kim explained the function of some of the exotic items to Bobby. It was less than two hours later when they verified that all equipment had been removed and carefully secured. The two trailers were neatly aligned with the other three after having been hosed down as a last action.

They signed out of the secure storage area and proceeded to the Base Ops Center. As they ascended to the Ops room Walt was querying Bobby about the long hours he had been with Connie and did he think it was very difficult to work like that. Bobby's affirmative response was not surprising, given the awareness developed of this young man's thirst for knowledge. The more Walt talked with him the more impressed he became. Walt thought to himself, 'Young people today are a lot more savvy than I was at that age, this kid is head and shoulders above me when I was as old as he is. He is going to be an asset to us if his parents give their OK. I hope they sent me something like what Bobby says he received.'

Kim took one SUV and headed back to the motel with Bobby where they immediately undressed and fell into bed. Walt went to the Ops Center and relieved Connie at their desk. She briefed him on all that had transpired during their absence. Walt sensed that General Mayfield was becoming impatient at the delay in Walt not presenting himself to the General first.

Walt approached the General and before anything could be said, spoke saying, "Sir, my apologies, but I know you understand that I must take care of my people first, just as you would have done."

General Mayfair smiled and said, "You got me there, all right, but now can you take time to tell me all that has happened since you left in such a hurry?"

It was Walt's turn to smile as he replied, "Basically the Whitman CID Team got the first break from their people in Washington, and the FBI joined in with us and we were able to recover the test spacecraft unharmed. Two of my people got a bit of what for, one sustained a bullet wound to his upper arm, that happened to Jack as he broke down the entry door. The other was Joe, who caught a couple of slugs on his flak jacket, he hurt for a while but is OK. Jack is seeing the medics as we speak. The bullets seem to have gone through his upper arm without bone damage, so that was lucky. But after he has been seen by a doctor we'll know his status for sure. He'll be out of action for a few days, even if the doctors give him a clean bill of health. The rest of us just need to catch up on some rest and we will be OK. That's it in a nut shell, sir, of course a more formal after-action report will be completed for you in a few days. It will contain pertinent details and timelines."

General Mayfair was pleased, but asked, "Where is the test spacecraft now and what is its outlook?".

"It is presently under FBI security care, at our request, later KSC Security will take over. I have talked to Dr, Bowman about what its role is to be, and he explained it would the back-up unit to the launch article. We were able to arrange for it to be housed right next door at Kennedy Space Center, they have a clean room available for it and it will be well-guarded there. That means if it is needed for spare parts it is nearby," Walt finished his long explanation without giving the General an opportunity to interrupt.

"Fine, sounds good, but when is this to take place?" he asked.

Walt responded, "I believe Dr. Bowman has the scheduling all worked out. He is to coordinate its transfer with us. We and the Air Force will provide armed escorts all the way, along with coordination with the Highway Patrols of each state as we pass through." He closed by asking, "Will that be all for now, sir?"

"Well done Walt, and thank you," the General responded, then added, "I do believe I shall go to my quarters tonight and get a real night's rest."

He called the senior NCO over and told him briefly what had happened and advised he could be reached at home. The sergeant called for the General's driver and bid the General goodnight.

CHAPTER 16

AFTER THE TEAM HAD RESTED and established a routine again they became impatient for the next phase of activity. All were aware of the need to transfer the back-up spacecraft from the FBI secure area in Washington to nearby Kennedy Space Center. It was evident that the move must be soon.

Walt assembled the Team in the Ops Center and invited General Mayfair to observe his Team briefing. Before beginning he asked the General if he had any opening remarks, to which he shook his head negatively.

Walt started, "I have talked to Dr. Bowman in Whitman Air Force Base and asked him when he planned to move the spacecraft from Washington to Kennedy and his response was that he needed it here as soon as I could arrange it. That means he is looking to us to handle the move 'lock, stock and barrel', so we must get started immediately."

General Mayfair stood and said, "I had planned to tell you that, after your meeting, but since you already have heard from the good doctor, I guess all you need from me is a confirmation," and looking at Walt added, "Right?"

Walt smiled and responded, "Dr. Bowman did tell me he had talked to you, I would like to have written orders though."

The General raised his hand and proffered the sheaf of papers to Walt saying, "I just had them made up."

He accepted the orders and said, "Thank you, sir, as always, one step ahead of me." Then turning back to his Team, he spoke, "As you heard, it is now official, we will manage the transfer of the back-up spacecraft from Washington down to Kennedy. We will move the entire Team to Washington for this operation. You will have to be especially cautious, unless I miss my guess, our 'friends' will attempt to steal the spacecraft again and we must be ready for it."

Walt addressed the General, "Sir, will it be possible for one of your senior NCO's to man our desk for few days? We'll need all our people for this move."

"I'll have your line transferred to our Ops Sergeant's desk, I'm sure they can handle it, 24/7," the General replied.

Walt nodded then turned to the Team, picking up where he had stopped, "Our first action will be to load our equipment. Joe, I would like you to rig the emergency release mechanisms on each SUV just in case we have to dump our trailers, or react in a hurry. They haven't been used for a while so I want to be sure they work, and let's be sure all the SUV's are checked, no glitches, OK?"

As expected, Joe nodded in affirmation.

Walt continued, "Kim will you line up the comm gear, use the broad band radios as well as the personal units and anything else you think we'll need."

Again, a nod of understanding from Kim.

Walt then turned to Bobby and said, "I am assuming your parents have given their permission for you to join us, so I'd like you to give Joe a hand, with all our vehicles, he could use some help. You inferred you were a pretty good mechanic, true?"

Bobby responded quickly, "Yes sir, I am."

Walt addressed Jack and Connie, "Will you disassemble and clean all our weapons and line up our ordnance. I think we should use the 'B' set," referring to a specific list of munitions that might be needed.

"Nat," he said, "I would like to have a response plan drawn up to react to several different scenarios. You know what I want, don't you?"

She too just nodded. It was a scene often repeated, when they had prepared for action in other situations.

Walt said, "You all know what we may be getting in to, except Bobby, and I think Joe can orient him as they check our vehicles. We will meet in the Ops Center in three hours, that will give you just about enough time to do our prep work. I'll be with General Mayfair if anybody needs me."

He planned to hold a conference call with the Washington FBI, Dr Bowman at Whitman, a Kennedy representative, and George Gregory from the Whitman AFB CID. He needed information about spacecraft vulnerability, the Kennedy Space Center facilities, security capabilities, en route vulnerabilities, and what support each could provide.

He spoke to Nat, "I think you should listen in on this conference call, you'll need to know the details as we develop them. And try to get some maps that will suit this operation."

She nodded.

"All right gang, lets get going," Walt stated, effectively initiating action. The Team was a smooth running unit and required little further instruction, relying on their broad experience. Nat stayed close to Walt in order to pick up on any potential changes, as he quickly toured through his Team activities.

As they re-entered the Ops Center Nat said, "I'll get the conference call lined up for three hours from now, OK?

"Sounds about right, I just hope you can get all of them at once on such short notice," Walt responded.

The three hours had passed quickly and the Team members returned to the Ops Center, each indicating to Walt they had completed their tasks.

In the interim Nat sat at the Team desk and started calling, she used priority privilege to expedite her calls. Surprisingly she was able to set up the call with each of the critical players and delightedly reported to Walt, "They will all be on the line as you requested, seems as though they were anticipating your request."

He invited General Mayfair to participate in the call, who accepted with alacrity.

Walt said, "Nat put the call on the speaker, we can each hear the whole story as we develop it," and added, "Log in each caller please."

Walt motioned for Nat to activate the speaker phone. "This is Walt Crawford," he announced, "I am advised that each agency is using a secure phone, I have my assistant Natalie Morse and Major General Billy Mayfair on at my end, as well as my Team members, please identify yourselves and state whether anyone else can hear this conversation. Start with Washington, please."

. "This is the Washington office of the Federal Bureau of Investigation, I have myself, John Cassidy, Bureau Chief and my assistant Peter Boyle, we also have Agents Glen Starbuck, the senior agent working this case, Bill Gleason, and Charles Harrington who both work with him."

"Washington CID, please," stated Walt.

"I am John Forrestor, Senior Agent, and Art Johnson, who has been on the case." was the quick response.

"Whitman Air Force Base, please," Walt called out.

"I am Dr John.Bowman, principle scientist for the spacecraft, plus Air Force officers Lieutenant Colonel Charles Donohue, Captain Phillip Johansen, Senior Master Sergeant Arthur Delahanty, and CID Agent George Gregory."

"Kennedy Space Center, please," Walt spoke again.

"This Mr. Jason Glover, Chief of Security for KSC, I have Mr. Ernest Hollander, who will be in charge of security for the spacecraft facility here at KSC, and Chief John Kuklinski, head of our police, who will have operational responsibility for facility security.

"Mr. Glover, have you been advised of over all security responsibility? asked Walt.

"Yes," was the immediate reply, "NASA Headquarters has confirmed that you and your Team, 'Fixit' I believe is the name, are to head up this operation." He went on, "I wish to offer any assistance we have available to support your operation."

It became apparent that each agency had received orders to respond to what ever request Walt Crawford made.

It was Walt's open challenge to the KSC Security Chief, and the man's response that made it evident to all, just who was 'in charge.' Walt laid out his plan for transfer of the spacecraft from Washington to KSC. He asked Dr. Bowman to provide a representative with full authority to speak for him. Dr. Bowman immediately offered the services of Sergeant Delahanty as his personal representative. Nat gave a 'thumbs up' signal to Walt.

"Fine," replied Walt, "have him proceed to the Washington office of Agent Starbuck and await the arrival of the rest of the Team, do you agree Mr. Cassidy?"

"Of course," was his reply.

As an after thought he said, "Dr. Bowman can you arrange for George Gregory to join our little party?"

"I am sure we can arrange that," responded Dr. Bowman.

"Thanks, maybe he can join up with Sergeant Delahanty," was Walt's quick rejoinder.

"Mr. Cassidy, can you loan us the agents who worked with us?" queried Walt, "If possible, Agents Starbuck and Gleason would be great."

There was a muted conversation, then Cassidy replied, "Starbuck it is, but with some reluctance, I shall have to fill Starbuck's function, which won't be easy, and sending Gleason too, is a further problem to us, but OK."

"Each member of this group will report to the office of Agent Starbuck in Washington," stated Walt, and added, "Try to be there by 1800 day after tomorrow, speak now if you cannot make that schedule." There was no response.

"Agent Starbuck, after this telecon will you please insure every one has the address of your office," spoke Walt.

"Will do," was the reply.

"I appreciate having your key personnel available for this operation. I am sure all of you know of the extreme sensitivity of anything having to do with this spacecraft. If you are not, please tell me now," he waited a moment and hearing no reply he continued. "We should plan on moving the 'Item' from Washington no later than three days from now, is there anyone who cannot meet that date?" he queried. "Note that from now on all calls referring to the spacecraft will use the word 'Item or Object', clear?"

"Nat, please record their answers," he added.

Nat quickly spoke to each participant and recorded their answers.

"Obviously Interstate Highway I-95 is our most expeditious route, do you all agree that is what we should use?"

Nat again obtained a response from each participant. All agreed. It became obvious that each agency was completely willing to let Walt 'call the shots.'

"It is now 1100 Eastern, Tuesday", each quickly checked their watch, "Can you meet a departure from Washington of 0800 on Saturday," asked Walt.

Again Nat queried each and recorded their affirmative answers.

"Mr. Cassidy," Walt addressed the Washington FBI official, "will we be able to use one of your better secure trucks, preferably armored?"

"Walt, you can have anything we have, you may be sure I will give you the best we have, and yes it will be armored," John Cassidy laughingly replied and added, "We ought to put our 'Item' in it immediately and get it ready for transport."

"Thanks, John, good idea, please have the 'Item' loaded now," responded Walt, warmth evident in his voice. A major concern had just been accommodated.

"Every person accompanying this move must be armed, I suggest a suitable weapon would be a Glock 9mm, or equivalent. Have several extra clips," Walt advised. He added, "If you prefer a machine gun, fine. You each should wear body armor during the transport phase."

Walt then reminded everyone that it was probable that the Russian crew will again attempt to take the 'Item', and that they would be as ruthless as they were in the last hijacking. Finally stating, "Every participant in this transfer is a possible casualty, now is the time to withdraw if you must......speak now!"

There were no replies, nothing but the gentle hissing from the speaker.

Walt spoke, "Thank you all, I will establish the order of the convoy after I arrive in Washington," then as an after thought, "Mr. Cassidy, would it be possible to have a second truck exactly like the transport vehicle?"

Again there was muted conversation before Cassidy came on the line, "It will be provided as your decoy, we assume."

Walt announced, "Yes, that is correct, and thank you, any other comments, if not, this conference call is now terminated."

There were no further inputs.

He then spoke to Nat, "We must have someone here to act as interface with General Mayfair, do you think Bobby could keep an accurate log and pass on any important info to us, and from us to General Mayfair?"

Nat responded, "I'll bring him up to speed in the next hour or so, he is a smart kid and I think he'll work out fine."

CHAPTER 17

AGENT STARBUCK HAD PREPARED HIS dormitory to house a minimum of 15, he thought, there will be at least 2 women on the Fixit Team, and planned a second small room for them, although he suspected the Team women shared the Team accommodations as a matter of course. It would be necessary to tell our Washington people to get local housing somewhere nearby. He ordered his cook to lay in supplies to feed the large number of people expected.

The chosen members of the transfer team all arrived at the office of Starbuck in advance of the required reporting time and were welcomed by him. Wisely he had emptied his garage in anticipation of Team needs, although there were a large number of vehicles to accommodate. He arranged extra parking at a nearby gas station having ample space and set up a vehicle to act as a taxi.

Walt's Team arrived as a group early Thursday and Starbuck directed them to the back of his building. There he explained to Walt that the garage and rear area was vacated for Team use. The Team had brought 5 SUV's and 2 trailers, the trailers fit nicely inside the garage with room left for a single SUV, the other 4 SUV's had sufficient room in the back yard, still leaving room for several additional vehicles to park.

Starbuck had rearranged his large open kitchen area into a fairly roomy conference room, with a large table, a blackboard and needed communications all patched in. Walt was impressed and said so to Starbuck, "Looks like you have done a pretty neat job of setting things up for this operation, thank you very much."

Walt turned and spoke to Nat, "Please see if you can get the players here in this conference room." A few minutes later they were all assembled in the makeshift conference room, the most senior ones sitting at the table, while others stood against the wall along with the rest of the Fixit Team. Nat had appropriated the seat next to Walt with handy access to the comm and recording equipment. The seat at the head of the table had been left vacant for Walt, indicating awareness that he headed this operation.

After all had taken their seats he stood, silence fell, his first words were, "Thank you for being here, it tells me you all know the importance of this operation. You must also know the dangers involved. Please be aware that casualties can be expected. Let's get down to business."

"Glen, I assume you are the representative for Mr. Cassidy, correct?"

"He is on the speaker phone, but I will be the FBI rep for the trip," he replied and went on, "I suspect you would like to know about the trucks we will use, right?" At Walt's nod, Glen continued. "Our two trucks are identical, armored in the true sense of the word, they will withstand any small arms fire, but can't withstand a rocket explosion in a critical spot. They look like commonplace delivery trucks except upon close scrutiny, I think they are just the ticket for our task. They are standing by in our secure compound."

Walt acknowledged, "Major milestone achieved."

"We have in our armory several specialized weapons you may wish to utilize, you can see them now or later, after the meeting," Glen spoke.

"Nat, Jack, let's take a look right now, it may affect our planning," said Walt, excusing himself momentarily.

Glen escorted them downstairs to a locked vault, opening it he pointed to an array of weapons, ranging from heavy machine guns, rocket launchers, personal side arms and an assortment of grenades, mines and other explosives.

Walt asked, "Glen, do you have a handy inventory of all this, so we can plan upstairs without counting it now."

"Of course," was the quick reply.

Walt apologized, "I should have known better than to ask such a stupid question, forgive me," as they returned to the conference room.

"How about a rocket launcher for the lead and tail vehicles, and heavy machine guns for the vehicles just before and after the two trucks?" Walt asked. "Maybe I'm getting the cart before the horse, let's establish the convoy makeup now," he said, then, "I would like to have one of my SUV's as lead and tail vehicles, and a small truck just before and after the object trucks, that is a total of six vehicles, any comments or suggestions?"

There was no input from anyone else.

"We can provide the two trucks you want, to be in front and behind our object trucks, Glen announced. "They are heavy duty, four passenger pickups, with a short cargo bed. How about people, and who will furnish them?"

"Good point," Walt replied, "Here is the way I would like to arrange it. Please speak up as we go along to agree or disagree with what I outline."

"We are going to need some competent people, willing to risk being shot at, plus qualified in the weapons we'll be using. I expect to act as point and be out ahead of the convoy by a quarter mile or so, and of my five people, one will drive each of the Object trucks, plus the lead and tail SUV's, that's four, and it would be good if I could have an Airman to ride with me to coordinate my commands."

"Jack, I'd like you to drive the object truck and Joe drive the decoy, Nat will drive the rearmost SUV with Connie as her co-driver, they have worked together before and are familiar with the comm setup. Kim will drive the first SUV and an Airman as co-driver, that about covers it, I think," he said.

"I have two more SUV's that can be used, perhaps one to go well ahead with someone to coordinate with local law enforcement and the other as a backup where ever needed," Walt noted. "They will each pull one trailer, I need someone to drive them and learn about their quick release and comm capabilities"

Cassidy spoke on the speaker phone, and said, "We can loan you two of our motor pool men to drive your SUV's, they are agents in training, so I'm sure they can handle that. Starbuck can you brief them?"

Glen responded, "Of course, please have them report to me here ASAP. Also, I can drive the pickup in front of the first object truck and Bill Gleason can handle the other pickup, but we need additional manpower to be in the remaining seats." He looked at Walt who in turn looked at George Gregory.

"George, will you be the co-driver for the first pickup and Sergeant Delahanty will you take co-driver for the second pickup?"

Each replied quickly, "Yes sir."

Captain Johansen any chance you could get us say, two Air Force people to occupy the seats I've described?"

"Yes sir, we have Airmen well qualified and with proper clearance who can support the operation. I will bring them with me," Captain Johansen said on the speaker phone.

Walt looked pleased at the manpower makeup, and stated, "That takes care of people, now about weapons and comm. We have radios in our trailers as well as considerable ordnance. Each person should carry a side arm, Nat will you be sure to verify each has one, or issue one of ours to them. Glen has heavy machine guns, let's have one mounted in each pickup," looking at Starbuck for confirmation.

"Roger that!" Glen said.

"I would like everyone to wear body armor and have a loaded sidearm with two spare clips. Each co-driver will also have a sub-machine gun with spare clips and the pickup drivers and co-drivers must be qualified to operate the heavy machine guns. They will be in the two vehicles preceding and following the object trucks. One of the extra Airmen from Whitman will ride one with me and the other in the lead SUV, they should be able to use submachine guns and have body armor," Walt reviewed.

"As soon as everybody is present I will go over our operation to insure each knows what others are doing. One last thing, have your radio on at all times, I want to be sure everyone knows what everybody else is doing. We must not allow the item to be lost again. I suggest weapons be checked now for readiness," Walt stated as he closed the meeting.

By 7:30 A.M. on Saturday all the transfer people had assembled at the FBI office, making a large group. Walt addressed the group telling them explicit details and asking if any had questions. He then asked Starbuck lead the way to the FBI compound where the two trucks stood in readiness, the back-up spacecraft components carefully braced in one truck. All the personnel were reassembled to hear Walt again spell out how the transfer would be accomplished. He verified each member was equipped as he had asked and then advised them of the very real dangers that might be encountered. The vehicles were lined up with the object truck behind the decoy truck. As Walt departed he asked the convoy to start at 0800, 15 minutes later. One of the two spare SUV's departed well in advance of Walt, the other was to follow the convoy thirty minutes or so after the convoy tail vehicle.

As the convoy wended its way through the early morning Washington traffic, they followed closely behind each other to preclude other cars becoming included in the convoy. Once out on I-95 they spread out slightly as their speed increased.

They drove without any problems for 4 hours and turned in to a rest stop, where they closed up with bumpers almost touching, well away from other trucks and cars stopping at the rest area. Those carrying submachine guns acted as guards while others stretched their legs and rested for a few minutes or had snacks. Within thirty minutes they were under way again in the same order.

They drove on for another four hours when Joe radioed to Walt, "Your bladder must be as full as mine, it needs emptying."

Walt responded through the Airman, "We are going to take a meal break in about 15 minutes, OK?"

"Roger," Joe replied.

Night had fallen and Walt had selected a short stretch of road parallel to I-95 that could accommodate the convoy and as the glaring headlights approached, he flagged them to the right on a dirt maintenance road. Again guards were put on watch while everyone ate fruit and light sandwiches. Coffee was plentiful and provided needed caffeine. Walt cautioned the next stop might be at night again. He intended this to be a non-stop trip to Kennedy, no stops for sleep. Co-drivers would be asked to drive for the next three hours, when the drivers would resume their task. As they dismounted Walt asked that guards be especially alert and for all personnel have their weapons handy. Weariness was evident in most of the people, Walt walked among them trying to perk them up.

———————

The commercial Jet Ranger helicopter was not ideally suited for the task Captain Skelsin intended, but military machines were not to be had. He had removed all four doors from his leased aircraft.

The six passengers, as well as he and the pilot, all dressed in black, were professionals, experienced in wet work. They flew at two thousand feet altitude above and just East of I-95, looking for the convoy. KGB intelligence had reported the forming and departure of the convoy and correctly determined it was carrying the back-up spacecraft.

The men at the open doors were heavily armed, having a pair of RPG's, Rocket Propelled Grenades, plus each carried a Kalishnikov machine gun and hand grenades. Skelsin was armed with a machine pistol and grenades. It was significant firepower.

When the convoy turned off onto the dirt road, Sgedgy Skelsin was sure it would be the right time to strike, he had a box-like truck following five to six minutes behind the convoy, unaware that an SUV would be not far behind his truck. He radioed for the truck to hold position until he told them to come forward, planning to take control of the backup spacecraft.

He turned his helicopter to approach from the rear unaware of the heavy firepower in the convoy rearmost vehicles. He ordered his pilot to drop to one hundred feet and approach to just behind the rearmost SUV and hover. The pilot did as directed and the would be thieves, leaning out of the helicopter, fired their RPG's, one at the rear-most object truck and the other at the pickup just behind it. The pickup exploded in a blast of flame while the other RPG struck the road surface just to the rear of the armored truck. Another blast of flame erupted, lifting the rear of the vehicle two feet in the air. Skelskin would have been aghast had he known the spacecraft was in the rear truck and not the foremost truck. He had wrongly assumed the second truck was the decoy. He was further dumfounded to discover heavy return firepower, as two heavy .50 caliber slugs pierced the fuel tank of his chopper, releasing two large streams of fuel spouting from the pressurized tanks.

The pilot screamed to him, "We must abort, we are losing fuel rapidly."

Skelsin pointed his pistol at the pilot and said, "Nyet, we go on!"

The pilot shouted a curse in reply and said, "We crash, we cannot return!"

Skelsin, ever mindful of his own skin, responded. "Da, land to the side of them." It was a tactical blunder, exposing the attackers to even more firepower. Walt quickly assessed the situation and directed the return of withering fire at the helicopter and its scrambling occupants. Four of the six were cut down and the remaining two prostrated themselves on the ground, throwing their weapons away from themselves. The helicopter was struck by a small rocket and its whirling blades were flung away as at the same time, the craft was caught by the withering firestorm. Skelskin was severely wounded and unconscious, laying half in and half out of the helicopter. The pilot and four of his black-clad passengers were a bloody mess, the heavy .50 caliber machine gun bullets piercing their armored vests.

Skelsin was roughly handcuffed and loaded into the bed of the remaining good pickup, still unconscious,

Nat reluctantly dressing his wounds. The remaining two attackers were handcuffed and their legs tightly bound, their mouths taped shut and loaded into the remaining pickup, with one of the wide-eyed Airmen assigned to guard them. Receiving instructions, "Don't kill them, just shoot the legs our from under 'em if they try to escape".

Nat spoke to the captured men in Russian to the effect that if they moved they would be shot.

Frightened passersby were screeching to a halt on the highway, some swerving into the median to escape the thundering noise of weapons firing., all frenzied with fear. Walt dispatched the remaining Airman to the highway to get traffic moving until police could arrive.

He then assessed damage to his own operation and was dismayed to discover the mutilated pickup truck and its dead occupants. He had Nat contact the nearest highway patrol for an ambulance and assistance in controlling the area. Not surprisingly, they were already under way from prior reports of shots fired.

He had lost two people in the pickup and Jack and his co-driver were bruised from the armored truck being slammed into the air from the back when the RPG hit. Its armor had protected the cargo, the object, but it had received severe jolting from the near miss, whether it was unscathed would not be known until Doctor Bowman's people could examine it in detail.

Walt approached Starbuck and told him of the loss of the pickup and its occupants, including Bill Gleason. Next he located Captain Johansen and told him of the loss of Sergeant Delahanty. He then gathered the entire escort group together, asking if anyone else was wounded.

Apparently the attackers had only fired the two RPG's before return fire had cut the attack short.

The trailing Fixit SUV arrived with more prisoners from Skelsin's truck, too many to put in the bed of the pickup. Walt was anxious to get his prisoners to a place they could be individually interrogated. The two not wounded had their legs bound and mouths taped shut, to preclude them from speaking with one another.

About this time a fire engine and its associated rescue vehicle arrived, followed by a highway patrol vehicle and three police cars with flashing blue lights. The civil authorities had traffic moving in quick order, and guided a handful of cars out of the median.

A well-dressed police lieutenant sought out Walt and insisted upon being briefed on the strange array of vehicles, asking, "What in Hell are you doing, I'm told it sounded like a war was starting here."

Walt politely replied, "I'm sorry Lieutenant, but if I told you, you would have to go on with us to Florida, I can tell you we are transporting a Top Secret cargo from Washington to Cape Canaveral, does that mean anything to you?"

The lieutenant shooed away several of his police officers and asked, "Do you have any orders to support what you are saying?"

Walt displayed his orders signed by Major General Mayfair, asking the police officer, "Did you see the TV a few weeks ago with an announcement?"

He was immediately aware of Walt's situation and replied, "I think I understand, if I am right, how can we help you?"

"Please stop any news media if you can, until we can get going again. We have a demolished truck, the attacker's crashed helicopter and there are a number of deceased to remove. If you can take of cleaning up this site, I will be grateful. If you tell me your city, we will arrange to retrieve the bodies in a few days. Please do not allow anyone to inspect the vehicle or the helicopter."

The lieutenant called the highway patrol men and the police sergeant to him and quickly briefed them and had his sergeant call for wreckers and two large flatbed trucks to haul the helicopter and demolished pickup. People who had gotten out of their cars were told to get back in and move or be arrested.

Walt gathered his crew together, verified the armored truck carrying the spacecraft was usable, quickly briefed them and prepared the convoy to depart, Skelsin and his two men had their mouths taped and placed in the decoy vehicle. along with an armed Airman. Within minutes they were able to pull back onto the highway and get up to speed. They were able to maintain a steady sixty five miles per hour. The crew came down from their adrenaline inspired high.

Sleepiness was no longer a problem.

"Is your vehicle behaving OK?" Walt radioed to Joe.

"Affirmative," he responded.

———————

Nat used her cell phone connected to a portable scrambler, and gave General Mayfair a short synopsis of what had transpired. She advised they should arrive at KSC during daylight hours.

The convoy turned East on State Road 528 taking them to the Kennedy Space Center, again Nat had requested an escort from the Gate to the new home for the spacecraft. Once the armored truck entered the actual facility Walt was able to verify that Kennedy Security Forces would take over security for the craft. Cape Security was tasked to pick up the prisoners and to have Skelsin tended to by a doctor.

Walt was tired and knew his people were also, he first assured the personnel accompanying the convoy were provided a place to get a meal and rest and asked all to meet him at the Astronaut Motel at 11:00 AM the following morning, giving everyone plenty of time to recover from the hard drive and lack of sleep.

The next morning when all had gathered he invited them to enter the restaurant, which had closed to all but his operational people. He offered Bloody Mary's to all who chose and a fine luncheon. He rose and rapped for attention, sharing a smile when he told them they would be appreciated by the Nation, if only the Nation knew what had transpired.

CHAPTER 18

TWO DAYS HAD PASSED AND Walt was concerned that something was bound to 'upset the apple cart' and when nothing occurred, he became suspicious and difficult to deal with. Finally Nat approached him and asked if she could speak frankly.

"Of course," he replied.

Nat began, "You are becoming unreasonable, just because all is well for the time being, you cannot accept it. Our Team has supported you without question and we will always do so. Please have a Team meeting and let everyone know what is bothering you to see if we can help in any way."

"Nat, you know I trust every person on our Team implicitly," Walt responded, and went on, "I agree it is time to have a Team discussion, please go ahead and set it up. Here in my room is OK."

She gathered all the members except Connie who was on the Team desk at the Operations Center. Bobby was included as a matter of course. She allowed Kim 20 minutes to check for electronic eavesdropping and said to

Walt, "All clear Walt, it's your meeting, but should I patch Connie in so you won't have to repeat yourself for her?"

He replied, "Please do so."

She quickly patched her in on the speaker and asked Connie to use a scrambler.

"OK Walt, all set," she said It was midmorning and a nice day outside as Walt stood and spoke, "I guess I've been a bit edgy these past few days, I want to apologize if I have jumped on anyone. Not only are you members of Fixit, but I count each and every one of you as a personal friend, and I hope that feeling is reciprocated. I must tell you that we have intelligence that says they have monitors watching every move we make, but who and from where is not known for sure. We think it is the same people who already hit us pretty hard. You realize it must be the Russians, as you know we got one of their key men on the way here from Washington. The couple who checked in here a week or so ago are probably Russian judging from the bug they planted. Kim, am I right?"

Kim replied, "You are right, it was Russian without a doubt."

Walt stopped for a moment to collect his thoughts and went on, "Captain Skelsin, their top guy, was badly wounded during our skirmish and is under guard in a military hospital, he has been a key operator for them, and they have already started diplomatic actions to recover him. Politics being what they are it is only a matter of time before he will be released. The other men we captured are being interrogated by our own intelligence agencies, that's how we became sure we are under surveillance. Not only are the Russkies digging around , we also have other foreign agents here somewhere, probably French or

Japanese, although if they are native Japanese they can easily be spotted. It means we must be very careful in what we say or do."

Walt paused again and added, "Now you understand why I've been like this," He then sat down.

Nat stood and spoke, "Thanks for letting us know what is happening, I can speak for all of us when I say, no loose chit chat on our part."

"I thank you all," he said and added, "We had better get with the Cape Security and see if we can help or get a daily briefing by them."

Jack spoke up and said, "I'm fairly well healed, if Bobby could drive me out to the Cape I will see what's new."

Bobby looked eagerly at Walt for confirmation and said, "I would be glad to do that, sir."

Walt smiled and said, "Good idea Jack, and Bobby, please stop saying 'sir or mam' every time you speak to one of us. You are a full-fledged member of Fixit now and you enjoy the same privileges and responsibilities as the others, you are an equal not a subordinate!"

Bobby looked crestfallen, but at Walt's smile, quickly recovered saying, "Yes sir, I mean OK Walt."

The others smiled and nodded.

"Any questions Connie, I assume you heard everything," Walt said concluding the meeting.

"Roger that," replied Connie, and added, "Bobby's stuff came in while we were gone, so if he will check with Nat she can get it out for him."

Bobby's eyes lit up and he turned to Nat saying, "Whenever you want Nat, I'm ready when you are."

"Come on Bobby, let's go check for a package," she replied, knowing that there would be a large box, or maybe more, shipped from Washington.

After he had opened the two boxes he was so surprised he could not speak. He found six Fixit uniform coveralls with his name and the logo on each one. He was astonished to find a Glock 9 mm pistol with several empty clips, an Army type web belt and a leather holster for the pistol, a harness for attaching other 'items', a set of body armor, boots, a helmet with strange devices attached, a bayonet, a stilleto, a pair of binoculars, various pouches and an envelope addressed to him. It contained an inventory of everything in the boxes for which he was to sign acknowledging receipt.

As he signed the document the boy suddenly realized he was part of something very special, feeling somewhat overwhelmed. He had become a man all of a sudden.

Nat said, "You understand you are not to touch that pistol until you have received live fire training."

"Roger, I understand," he responded.

She accompanied him to the motel office where she asked the manager if Bobby could be assigned a room next to the Team rooms since he could no longer be employed by the motel. The manager was surprised but did as she was asked and wished Bobby good luck in his new job. Bobby borrowed a luggage carrier and took his new 'way of life' to the room newly assigned him. He then moved what little he had from his small room furnished by the motel, to his new room. He spent the next hour examining his new items, trying to visualize how he now fit into this group of adults. He too, was now an adult. He returned to Walt's room.

"Cape Security has a small arms range, Jack commented, "Maybe we can qualify you with the pistol while we are out there."

Walt said, "Good idea, Jack, give them a call before you go to see if they will OK that." Then to Bobby, "Get your pistol, Jack do we have some ammo here?"

"Yes, I'll bring a box of 9mm," Jack replied. He called the Operations Desk of Cape Security and quickly received the expected approval.

Bobby obligingly opened the SUV passenger door for Jack then made his way around to the driver's side. He climbed in, adjusted the seat and looked at Jack awaiting orders to start the engine. Jack just looked straight ahead and said nothing. Bobby quickly took the hint, connected his seat belt and started the vehicle. He slowly backed out and turned north on the roadway, being careful to observe the speed limit. They were checked in to the Cape Main Gate and drove northward to the Industrial Area and entered the Security Office. Jack was welcomed and explained he needed to qualify Bobby with his newly issued pistol. A Cape Security lieutenant took them in tow and they drove to the small arms range where he hoisted a red flag and set up several targets.

Jack then showed Bobby how to disassemble and reassemble the pistol. After he showed he could perform that task with reasonable skill, Jack had him load a clip with 15 rounds of ammo. Bobby asked if he could shoot yet and was told to shoot 5 rounds at the target on the left. All donned ear muffs to deaden the sharp crack of the pistol. Bobby exhibited a skilled shooters position with both hands cradling the weapon and deliberately fired five rounds about three to four seconds apart, then safing the pistol he laid it down.

Jack, Bobby and the lieutenant walked to the target and were surprised to see each shot had hit the bulls eye, moreover, four of the five were in the 10 circle.

Bobby explained he was Captain of his school rifle/pistol team and everybody was expected to shoot well. Jack then made him shoot from the prone position with the same results. His pistol still had five shots remaining so Jack had him stand some twenty feet away and on his signal Bobby was to dash forward, pick up the weapon, release the safety, and as quickly as possible fire the remaining rounds at a new target. Bobby did as bid with similar results. Jack then had him fire two more clips to complete his familiarization. Jack and the lieutenant were impressed and both said so to Bobby.

They returned to the Cape Security office where Jack spoke to the senior officer on duty, asking if a daily briefing arrangement could be set up for the Team. The officer suggested they go into the operational area and talk with the desk sergeant. The desk sergeant was told to have pertinent data for each day's activities available and to pass it on to the Fixit Team. They jointly reviewed past logs to identify any items that might be of interest to the Team. Jack thanked them as he and Bobby departed.

With Bobby driving again they returned to the motel and brought the other Team members up to date on several minor items of interest. Jack told Walt of Bobby's prowess with the pistol and added he would try to qualify Bobby with other Team weapons the next time an opportunity presented itself.

The Fixit Team members all congratulated Bobby on his showing with the live firing. He blushingly accepted their words and felt as though he really belonged.

CHAPTER 19

DR. BOWMAN HAD MOVED HIS group to the Cape to coordinate the build-up of the launch spacecraft in a specially controlled area, designated as a clean room. A C-5 aircraft had transported the spacecraft to the Cape, which was then placed in the clean room. This facility was actually in a large hanger that had been extensively modified, providing various size clean rooms for the sole purpose of preparing exotic spacecraft for launch. Once the preps were finished and all pre-launch testing completed, the spacecraft was loaded on a special trailer having a clean environment and the unit transferred to another facility where it was mated to its boost motor, a special rocket engine developed for the express purpose placing the spacecraft into its final orbit high above the earth's surface. Following this mating operation it was moved to the Spin Test Facility where it was run up to 30 RPM and carefully balanced to preclude possible wobble when in orbit. It was soon ready for movement to the launch pad. During this testing Air Force guards, using multiple two man patrols, were in the immediate proximity of every access.

When the spacecraft was ready for transport to the launch complex Walt felt the Fixit Team would assume control of security. He met with the Air Force Commander of the Cape and finalized security details. Air Force personnel would continue to provide guards for access to the craft while it was within the launch tower. They would report to Major Holloway for on site control, who in turn, was to report to Walt Crawford. It seemed somewhat convoluted to Walt so he asked Major Holliday to join with Fixit to test the viability of security.

Walt assigned Jack and Bobby the task of trying to breach the security arrangements. Major Holloway was informed of Walt's intentions, who immediately concurred and offered to participate as a saboteur. His services were acknowledged and he was advised of the details of the Team efforts, but that the details were up to Jack and Bobby. It surprised him that Walt did not want to know when or what they would do as a test.

Jack and Bobby met with Major Holloway at the Launch Complex Ready Room, where Jack introduced Bobby as a new member of the Team. It was decided that Bobby would be taken to the Complex Gate area where he was see if he could actually enter the Complex and then try to make his way up any of the various levels of the Tower. Bobby noted that a lunch wagon came to the Complex Gate, where men could approach the wagon to buy their lunch. Many of them were from the various levels of the Tower.

As they reentered the Complex they were something of a gaggle of people, wearing hard hats and just raising their badges to show to the Gate guard as they passed through, munching on sandwiches or drinking from a can of soda. Bobby had left his Fixit coveralls in favor of civilian work clothes and bought a sandwich and drink from the lunch truck. With his hard hat he looked very much like the others returning to work inside the Complex.

He positioned himself among a group returning inside to work, and like the others held his badge up, partially covering his face by taking a large bite of his sandwich. He turned off from the group and headed toward the high pressure gas facility where no people appeared to be present. Once there, he came out from the back side of the facility and meandered up the grass embankment toward the north side of the Tower where he nimbly climbed up the structural members to the second level where he picked up a paint bucket and brush left by someone and boldly strode to the elevator, where he pressed the up button and entered when it arrived. Inside he put the bucket and brush down and pressed the button for the fifteenth level. When it stopped he exited and approached the second stage of the missile as though he was to check something.

About this time the Security Sergeant noted him as he walked down the Tower stairs making his rounds. Bobby did not look familiar to him so he addressed Bobby, "Hold on there, let me check your badge."

Bobby ignored him and started around the other side of the missile when the Sergeant shouted, "Stop right now or I'll shoot," drawing his revolver.

Not realizing the Sergeant would not endanger the missile by firing a shot, Bobby stopped in his tracks and raised his hands. The Sergeant approached with caution, his gun pointed at Bobby's chest saying, "Let me see your badge."

Bobby held up his badge so he could examine it and casually said, "What's the matter, officer?"

The Sergeant was nonplussed to note Bobby's badge had all the correct numbers on it, but somehow there was something wrong. He immediately radioed to the Complex Ready Room asking if a Robert Camden was supposed to be on the fifteenth level of the structure. There was consternation there as they noted Bobby was authorized access, but he had not been cleared into the Complex.

At this point Major Holloway interfered and told everybody their security had just been compromised. The Security Sergeant politely asked Bobby to accompany him to the Ready Room to straighten things out.

Lieutenant Colonel Jason Comiskey was advised of the test, who shook his head sadly and said, speaking to Major Holloway, "Bill, you really screwed me on this, how come?"

Major Holloway shamefacedly faced his boss and said, "Sir, please don't be pissed at me, I was told to comply with whatever Mr. Crawford wanted and the Team guys said I was to tell no one, I'm really sorry."

"Well, better to learn it now from our own people rather than from the bad guys, and Bill, it's still J.C. until I tell you otherwise," he replied and added, "All right let's review how this happened and fix our shortcomings."

Jack had quietly remained in the background during the revelation and now stepped forward saying, "With your permission sir, I would like to review just what we did and what we found."

"Please do," was the abrupt reply.

Jack asked for the Complex Gate guard, the Security Sergeant, the lower level guard and the roving patrol guards, as well as Major Holloway, Bobby, himself and whomever the Colonel would desire to be present. Once assembled Jack reviewed the errors made and by whom, pointing out the necessity for careful checks of badges and access lists before allowing whomever to pass that check point. He explained he deliberately compounded the test by Bobby actually being authorized to be present according to his badge, versus being on an approved access list. As a result the Cape Security Commander was tasked to review all security procedures to validate adequacy Results of the test rapidly spread to all security personnel and people were placed on notice to exercise diligence.

Jack and Bobby returned to the motel later in the day and gave Walt a detailed summary of all that had transpired. Walt was upset to learn of the shortcomings and debated whether to advise General Mayfair of the results of his little test. He finally concluded the General had enough on his mind without burdening him further. When the Team returned to the motel later in the day Walt asked Jack to review their activity with the rest of the Team. All were somber to think of what could have happened had the circumstances been real.

Walt said that for any future tests Lieutenant Colonel Comiskey must be aware of activities. He knew that J.C. would as a matter of course tell his Commander of what had happened. He knew then that he would have to brief General Mayfair on what he had implemented in the way of a security check without first telling the General. The General looked distressed but decided it had been appropriate for Walt to act independently. Walt advised his Team that any future such checks would be cleared through General Mayfair and Lieutenant Colonel Comiskey.

Doctor Bowman called Walt and told him that Item testing was complete and the boost motor installation was next on the schedule. It was decided that the move to the boost motor facility should be on a Saturday when minimum work personnel would be on the Cape.

Walt asked for and received extra Air Force personnel to provide heavy security during the short move. All Cape traffic was shut down on their route of travel and the move to the Boost Motor Facility was completed without incident.

The boost motor was a specially developed unit for the express purpose of finalizing the orbit of the spacecraft. It was of significant size, having a thrust of four thousand pounds for a period of four minutes. While the motor was squat it was of a large diameter enabling it to produce this required thrust. Its exhaust nozzle was long and tapered, adding significantly to the overall height of the spacecraft/ motor combination.

The forty foot long nose cone fairing was adequate to enclose this larger than usual spacecraft. Its twelve foot diameter barely fit around the spacecraft/motor, the fairing base tapering down to the ten foot diameter of the launch vehicle Transtage.

Without the nine strap-on SRM's the core vehicle would have difficulty lifting the payload to its orbital injection altitude at the required speed. After boost motor installation and checkout, the combination was enclosed in a temporary shroud for transport to the Launch Complex. After an uneventful trip from the Boost Motor Mating facility, the special air ride trailer carrying the most expensive spacecraft ever built, was positioned below the overhanging top of the complex tower and it was slowly hoisted to the top of the missile and mated with extreme care to the top of the third stage, or Transtage, which had been erected the evening before. Once mated the temporary shroud was removed and lowered to the ground and hauled away.

The two halves of the payload fairing had been previously positioned on the payload levels of the tower, its halves with hoisting slings, stowed safely away from the spacecraft itself. Mating of the two halves for launch would occur after all testing of the craft was completed.

Security forces were everywhere during this latter phase of operations, patrols circled outside the Cape fences, others stopped all traffic on the Cape main road during transfer of the spacecraft/motor from the mating facility. Doing this move at midnight meant nonessential observers were at a minimum, but it only allowed five hours to erect the spacecraft after arrival at the Complex before dawn. Every step was reviewed before starting and followed carefully, assuring a smooth, error free operation.

———————————

The move was carefully monitored and recorded by Major Vostov and Lieutenant Shadosevil even though there were no massive searchlights as used during core erection. Vostov cursed in Russian and complained bitterly that the spacecraft being erected was shrouded by a white covering, limiting visibility. He correctly concluded it was the flight spacecraft being placed on the missile in preparation for launch.

They had observed the Transtage being erected without incident and thought an opportunity had been missed for destroying the spacecraft launch vehicle. Colonel Dantilev would not hear of shooting a stage, correctly realizing that a stage could be readily replaced.

The countdown inexorably continued toward launch.

CHAPTER 20

MAJOR VOSTOV HAD NOTED THE increased security activity and correctly assumed it was in conjunction with spacecraft erection. The frequent patrols around the fences of the Cape made it impossible for a sharpshooter like Senior Sergeant Viktor Karamoski, to find a place suitable for firing such a shot He advised Major Vostov it appeared unlikely he could find a place from which he could shoot.

Vostov cursed himself inwardly, he had forgotten to pass the word that Colonel Dantilev had forbidden him to try such a stupid stunt. He should have known that security would become tight when the spacecraft came to the launch complex. He told Karamoski to pack his things and report back to his Washington assignment, and be damn sure he wasn't caught with that rifle. The sergeant had already disassembled the weapon into relatively small components and had removed the floor coverings of his rented vehicle, permitting well-covered storage for the various pieces of his prized weapon.

Sergeant Karamoski departed within an hour and Vostov breathed a sigh of relief.

Vostov was not privy to Colonel Dantilev's proposal to possibly attack the missile as it was launched, at a higher altitude where a high flying supersonic Russian aircraft could launch an air-to-air missile from a safe distance away. Such weapons were highly accurate and once launched, were locked on to its target with little chance of the target not being destroyed.

———

Major Vostov and Lieutenant Shadosevil were relaxed in their comfortable condo, having a delectable lunch of cold cuts, fruit and Vodka Collins when the telephone pierced the quiet with its shrill ring. Neither Vostov nor Shadosevil moved to answer the call. After eight rings the Major motioned for the Lieutenant to answer the call.

As soon as he had picked up the receiver he jerked to attention, saying, in Russian, "Yes sir, he is right here, one moment sir, he will be right with you," handing the receiver to Major Vostov, motioning with his mouth, Dantilev.

Vostov also stood erect as he also spoke in Russian, "Vostov here sir." He said little as he listened to Colonel Dantilev, he terminated with, "Yes sir."

After he hung up the receiver he turned to his assistant and spoke in Russian, "We are finished here. We are to return to Washington within the next three days, hardly time enough to pack up our equipment. Let's start getting ready and we will see how much time we have left to enjoy ourselves."

By early afternoon they completed loading their vehicle, a large Ford Expedition, an SUV with heavy duty capabilities. Vostov instructed his lieutenant to make reservations at one of the best restaurants in the city of Cocoa, a short drive from their Merritt Island condo. He was determined to exact every penny he could from this assignment, knowing the Colonel would never see his budget submission.

That evening they drove to the Black Tulip, a fine restaurant in Cocoa, but a bit pricey for some budgets. They parked and entered exactly at their reservation time and were welcomed and shown to a nice table. Vostov smiled appreciatively at the host and asked for a wine list. Lieutenant Shadosevil whispered to Vostov, "Can't we have a couple of good vodkas first?"

"But of course, we shall have a taste of their finest vodka," and turning to the host spoke pleasantly, "Do you have Grey Goose vodka." The host was nonplussed for a moment and went to check. He came back replying that, yes they did have Grey Goose, whereupon Vostov said. "Please place a bottle on ice and bring it to our table when it is chilled."

A waitress came to their table with a large menu and proceeded to tell them of the specials for the day. Vostov peremptorily waved his hand and asked if Duck a la Orange was available, specifically avoiding asking the price. The waitress immediately responded telling him the Black Tulip was renowned for that specialty, and recognizing here was a guest ready to spend some money. She was extra attentive to them.

In a few minutes the host returned to their table with a silver bucket full of ice and a bottle of the requested vodka sunk in the ice and two small but elegant liquor glasses, into which he poured the chilled vodka. The two Russians drank the fifth of vodka and then asked for a bottle of Chateau Olivia White Bordeau wine, to complement their duck. The service was gracious and pleased them completely, the bottle of wine was poured into their wine glasses, and were refilled as the wine was consumed. After dinner they enjoyed a cup of espresso and when the check came Vostov left a handsome tip, complimenting the waitress and the host as they departed, both slightly inebriated. Recognizing this, Vostov instructed his Lieutenant to drive, albeit cautiously.

He drove rather well, considering the amount of alcohol he had drunk, but as they turned on the roadway to Merritt Island he failed to keep the Expedition within the lane he had chosen, weaving back and forth slightly. The vehicle was moving rapidly, exceeding the forty five mile per hour speed limit by twenty miles an hour. Shadosevil did not see the pickup behind him approaching at a higher rate of speed in the next lane, the driver far more drunk than he. The lieutenant chose to change lanes at the instant the pickup came up to pass. The pickup slammed into the side of the Expedition, crushing the driver's door with a horrendous crash. Neither Shadosevil nor Vostov had fastened their seat belts, laughing at the persistent chime reminding them to do so. The driver of the pickup was catapulted though through his windshield, the steering wheel catching him at the abdomen, driving his intestines into his spine as he was vaulted through the windshield of his old truck.

Though the Expedition was a heavy vehicle it was lifted high in the air as it rolled over, hitting the roadway and rolling several more times. Both Vostov and Shadosevil were violently tossed about within their vehicle as it pitched about, the roof being crushed on them. When both vehicles came to rest, they were a mangled sight, no one moving within either vehicle.

A passer-by used his cell phone to call for the police and within minutes a sheriff's patrol came screaming up to the scene of carnage. The officer first checked both wrecks to see if anyone was left alive. As he was examining the wreck, an ambulance arrived silencing its wailing siren. The medics joined the deputy sheriff trying to extricate the men from their vehicles. It was impossible until the fire rescue vehicle arrived on site and used their 'jaws of life' device to pry metal away, permitting the lifeless bodies to be removed.

After examination by the medical technician, all three men were declared dead. The bodies were searched for identification, causing the deputy to call for more senior police presence. The identification of Major Vostov and Lieutenant Shadosevil, was made indicating their diplomatic status, causing the sheriff deputy realize an international situation was in the making.

As a matter of course, the Air Force Military Police at Patrick Air Force Base were notified of the accident. General Mayfair was notified that two Russian military persons had been killed in an auto accident. When he realized they were Russian officers he called Walt and told him of the accident. Walt suggested the FBI be advised and asked if they knew why Russian officers would be near Patrick. When Walt then suggested he could have Nat perform that task, the General quickly agreed.

The normal chain of command dictated that the Russian Embassy be notified of the death of their military men and Colonel Dantilev learned of the accident about the same time as did General Mayfair. Their bodies were to be sent to Washington where they would be cared for and returned to Russia. Their mangled vehicle was loaded on a flat bed and trucked to the Washington Russian Embassy after a thorough examination by the Fixit Team.

The vehicle contents were carefully scrutinized by the Fixit Team led by Connie, because of her skills in the Russian language . She and Kim removed the optical equipment and the recorder with its compact discs, allowing only the personal belongings to accompany the wreck.

Colonel Dantilev was not surprised when he was advised the wreck had been sanitized by the Americans before its return. He was chagrined at the loss of the recordings, but was stoic at the loss of his men.

CHAPTER 21

WALT WAS SHOCKED TO LEARN of the death of the two Russians, he immediately passed the news on to the rest of the Team. Neither he, nor any of the Team, was aware of the Russian monitoring operation and it came as something of a surprise to learn the enemy had been so close.

The wrecked vehicle was brought to the Base where they were able to carefully examine the debris. Connie was invaluable in deciphering some of the Russian recordings, included was the aborted plan to fire explosive bullets at the missile as it sat on the pad. This aspect of their information was shared with the Cape Security Office, causing them to review their Security Plan. They instituted regular security patrols touring the exterior Cape fencing, carefully looking for any sign of a trespasser.

Walt called the Team together to remind everyone that each member needed to be especially alert to anything that appeared to be even slightly out of norm. It was the minor items that would give a clue, possibly alerting them to a potential problem.

Walt then asked that Jack get with the Cape Security Office and request they do their patrols on a non-fixed schedule. That way those trying to enter, or plan an action according to a fixed schedule, could not know when a patrol would pass by. He asked Jack to also alert them to the fact that Fixit was operating similarly on non-repetitive schedule. Some Fixit member would be available at the Team's Patrick Ops Center desk at all times, or their line transferred to the Operations Center primary desk in their absence. Walt asked Nat to make up a schedule of Team members to man their desk at the Ops Center, Fixit members to be on call for General Mayfair's benefit.

He then established a new requirement for every member of the Team, they were to carry a cell phone at all times, even in bed. Each Team member was to have every other Team member's cell phone number on single digit code, Walt was number 1, Nat was number 2, and so on.

Walt then instructed each of them to visit the spacecraft in its position atop the missile before the payload fairing was installed around it. He wanted each of them to personally know what it looked like, and to understand how the power of the destructive beam would be contained during ground testing, necessary before flight. That alone was a major concern, if the beam could destroy a target thousands of kilometers away at low power, there was an inherent concern that it would be dangerous to test at higher power levels. Loads must be kept low enough so that the dummy load horns around the spacecraft beam antennas would contain the power emitted, and yet be able to validate it before launch.

Dr. Bowman assured Walt the dummy load device would safely divert the beam without damage to the spacecraft, nor would harm come to people or the launch facility, as a result of the test.

Nonetheless, Walt sought information to prove the dummy load horns were adequate. Dr. Bowman conducted a class explaining how it was accomplished, to which all the Fixit members were invited. In fact, it became necessary for him to hold several classes to satisfy General Mayfair's concerns. Two tests were run, the first with all personnel cleared from the launch complex, which in fact did demonstrate the viability of the dummy load horns. TV cameras monitored every possible angle during the first test and nothing appeared amiss. Power measuring devices at the work level of the spacecraft monitored a slight, very brief, surge of power at the instant the beam was triggered. Evaluation of the test resulted in a concern for the safety of personnel if they were to be necessary at the spacecraft level at the instant of triggering. The second test was run without incident.

After all involved participated in a post-test conference it was decided that it would be prudent to not have people present at the work level during any subsequent power test. The dummy load device would have to be removed before the payload fairing could be installed, so it was decided that all other spacecraft testing would be completed before the dummy load horns would be removed. Most of the other testing involved spacecraft control aspects and verification the uplink and downlink interfaces worked to perfection.

Ordnance devices that separated the spacecraft from the final stage were tested before installation and their circuitry tested again before final connection of ordnance. The separation devices were a set of explosive bolts, duplicated on both sides of the separation plane providing redundancy. This necessitated catch canisters to contain the fragments after firing. Similar ordnance devices were installed that would release the solar panels to deploy in orbit so they could produce electric power from the sun.

The spacecraft had small jet motors, called thrusters, which permitted it to be oriented in any direction so the solar panels would face the sun, and again to later position it correctly so the destructive beam could be precisely aimed.

The spacecraft propellant tanks were filled with highly purified propellants and high pressure vessels loaded with liquid helium. Much work was involved in all these preparations and corresponding time consumed. Work continued day after day as T-zero crept up more and more rapidly. Time flow charts, prepared far in advance of these operations, now proved their worth. Launch was but a week away!

Walt insisted each Team member get a certain amount of rest. It was a certainty that tired people made mistakes, and mistakes could not be tolerated for this launch.

Walt brought General Mayfair up to date on the latest information in their possession. The General expressed concern about the potential for sabotage and reminded Walt he looked to the Team for assurance that this launch would go off as scheduled without incident.

Walt asked the General for additional Airmen to work at each of the roadblocks to be established at time for launch. That meant at least six or eight additional men, plus needed supervisors, for each shift. For optimum alertness each man should not exceed four hours on and eight hours rest before going on duty again. Security clearance requirements further aggravated the situation.

The General immediately called the Base Commander, telling him of the need for manpower. His tact resulted in that officer responding to the General's request by assigning a unit of Military Police to Walt's control, an entire platoon of highly qualified people, along with their supervisors. Walt asked to whom should he go to brief the new personnel and when and where could he find them. He was advised to go to the Military Police building nearby.

As Walt approached the building housing the Military Police Unit, he noted the immaculate appearance of the surroundings. He entered the main door and was politely greeted by a sergeant asking, "Sir, may I be of assistance?"

Walt smiled and said. "I am Walter Crawford and I'm looking for Captain O'Rourke, I believe he is expecting me."

The sergeant remained impassive saying, "Please follow me sir," turning about smartly and led Walt to an open door and upon entering, stood at attention, saluting and saying, "Sir, Mr. Crawford is here."

The officer behind the desk stood and said, "Sir, Captain O'Rourke, I have been ordered to support your operation, can you please brief me as to your requirements."

Walt smiled in response and extended his hand in greeting. Captain O'Rourke grasped it in a firm grip noting that this civilian had a steady eye and a strong grip as they shook hands. Captain O'Rourke gestured toward a chair and said, "Please have a seat," then added, "May I have Sergeant Bryant remain for our discussion? He will be my senior NCO for this operation."

"Of course," was Walt's reply, and turning he shook hands with the Sergeant. "How much do you know about the payload we are preparing out on our launch complex?"

The Captain responded, "I have had a classified briefing about the special spacecraft that is to be launched, as has Senior Master Sergeant Bryant. If that is what we are talking about, in fact each of my men to be used for this operation have a Top Secret clearance."

"It is," replied Walt, and proceeded to explain why he needed help to protect the operation. As Walt talked it became apparent he was intimately familiar with the capabilities of this spacecraft. He held little back, hoping to break through the stern shell affected by the MP's. When he told of the test results destroying the small boat in the Pacific, he captured their complete attention. When he offered to show them the film of that, plus the videotapes of the carnage when the Whitman AFB men were killed, he had them ready to do whatever was required.

Walt called Nat and asked her to select the tapes he wanted and bring them over to the Military Police office. Bobby appeared in a few minutes with the tapes Walt had selected and asked if he too could watch the tapes. Captain O'Rourke used a tape player in his office and ran through each of the tapes, both he and Sergeant Bryant exclaiming or muttering in disgust at some of the scenes.

At the conclusion of the tape session the Captain asked if he could show the tapes to the Airmen he would select to work for Fixit. Walt agreed and expressed his appreciation for the upcoming help. Details were quickly worked out and he and Bobby returned to the Ops Center.

Walt once more passed the information to the General and his Team about the new additional personnel from the Military Police. He requested Jack bring the Cape Security operations up to date regarding the additional Air Force personnel to support security posts around the clock. The Air force Military Police were teamed up with the Cape Security patrols, easing the work load all around, and providing a fresh set of eyes needed for observation.

In addition to the increased security on the ground, aircraft patrolled the skies around the Cape. The countdown continued inexorably toward T-0.

CHAPTER 22

THE COUNTDOWN COVERED SEVERAL DAYS, necessary because of the many functions required to ready the vehicle for launch. Two days were allotted for propellant loading, the tanks were individually pressure tested and checked off as ready to fill with propellants.

The propellants were loaded aboard the missile, first fuel on each of the two stages and then oxidizer. This was an extremely dangerous task and conducted with utmost care. Many hundreds of meters around the Complex were cleared of all people. The pump station supplying water for launch was made operational and cleared of personnel, valves would later be actuated remotely permitting water to flood the Complex for protection from the tremendous blast of fire as the vehicle launched, now the pump station was at a ready status.

The persons actually present on the Complex as the propellants were loaded, were dressed in special protective suits, called SCAPE suits, meaning Self Contained Atmospheric Protective Ensemble, looking much like an astronaut's space suit. They carried liquefied air in backpacks permitting breathing for about an hour. It allowed men to work safely if highly toxic propellant vapors were released, or if a spill should occur.

Before propellant loading each Team member had visited the spacecraft levels of the mobile launch tower in accordance with Walt's orders. They were required to don special clean coveralls, booties over their shoes, a hair cover and a mask over their mouth. The sight of the spacecraft was astonishing, much of it was covered in gleaming gold foil, glittering in the bright lights of the clean room.

They were asked to step back as the ordnance devices were installed, firing circuits checked and devices connected. During this operation the levels below were temporarily cleared of all people.

One Team member remained at the payload level until the payload fairing was installed around the entire craft and all people were cleared from that area. No further access to the spacecraft was possible unless the fairing was removed. Access platforms were then folded back precluding any further entry at all to the spacecraft or payload fairing.

As the countdown moved forward there were numerous milestones to be met by the launch vehicle itself, extreme care was taken to insure that preparations were done exactly, and precisely documented. Every step was done and monitored with a Quality Control technician observing closely. As the step was completed it was entered on the primary procedure and signed off by the responsible engineer and the assigned Quality Assurance person, some were sharp-eyed women. As each step was completed it was called out on the communications net and recorded at the Ops Control Center. If the QA person was not satisfied, that step was redone. Technicians took extreme care to insure steps were not redone and their names reported for inattention to the task at hand.

The countdown had a number of preplanned holds built in to allow time for unanticipated problems to be resolved and records to be verified. The Countdown Director was an Air Force Colonel, noted for his ability to insure everything was done correctly. At his side was another Senior QA Engineer recording every step as it was completed. Notably vacant during the early portion of the Countdown was the seat reserved for General Mayfair. He would occupy that position during the terminal portion of the count.

Walt was in constant communication with General Mayfair keeping him aware of Team activities and being privy to the General's actions on the communications Countdown Net. All key players would switch from their operating net to the Countdown Net at a preplanned time, as called for in the Countdown Procedure.

Many activities were being done concurrently until hazardous operations were started. All persons were required to leave the Complex when such operations started, as when the explosive ordnance checks and connections were made. Each ordnance circuit was verified to function correctly and a firing pulse sent, then deactivated and checked again to verify the absence of stray voltage, permitting ordnance devices to be electrically connected. All circuits used for sending an electric pulse were then carefully checked and locked out. Those that were to be fired while in flight were also verified to be safe via the on-board computer functions and placed in the off position until launch.

Each missile launched from the Cape was required to have an onboard destruct system in the event the missile strayed from its planned trajectory.

Following functional ordnance operations the entire complex was cleared of everyone except destruct ordnance technicians, quality assurance monitors and the safety monitor. At this point the destruct ordnance circuits were checked, the Range Safety Officer sent test destruct commands via a special radio frequency, then his console was safed, the firing circuits checked for stray voltage and the destruct ordnance connected.

———————

Far away in the North Atlantic Ocean, A Russian aircraft carrier patrolled the angry seas. The officer responsible for launching aircraft nervously reviewed the latest weather conditions, concerned that it would be marginal for launching or recovering his aircraft during such difficult weather. He had received orders that allowed no margin for error. He had been told he must launch his best aircraft and pilot at a time to be determined, the aircraft armed with long range, heat seeking missiles as well as those that locked on to a radar return signal. To aid him, a high altitude tracking aircraft was already patrolling the skies over the mid Atlantic.

It was in constant touch with a ground observer in Florida, just outside the Cape gate, ostensibly a tourist. He was equipped with a long range radio set on a special frequency, the radio sending a preset slow pulsed signal, assuring reception and which would be changed to a fast pulse when the missile was launched.

The Russian aircraft was to be launched from its Navy aircraft carrier a few minutes before T-0, the countdown being monitored by the tourist. The change to the rapid pulse signal would be the key to have the fighter aircraft arm his missiles and be prepared to launch them.

The Russian long-distance, high flying monitor was prepared to pick up the Absolute" missile shortly after it left the ground, and transmit necessary radar illuminating parameters to the fighter, permitting it to lock on the launch vehicle at its maximum range.

The fighter pilot had been instructed to fire his missiles only when he was certain of good radar lock. He would be about 20 to 25 miles from the ascending missile and be at about forty thousand feet altitude in order to achieve this.

Unbeknown to the Russian planners, the American plan also had a tracking aircraft aloft to the East and high above the Cape, already aware of the Russian tracking airplane. The American AWACS aircraft personnel were monitoring the foreign aircraft with keen attention, knowing it was a tracking aircraft much like their own.

When the missile launched they would send jamming signals hoping to interfere with the foe's ability to track at this distance. It appeared obvious that the Russian plane was going to track the missile as it rose up and away from the Cape, the reason for this was misinterpreted, tracking launch vehicles leaving the Cape was common. That it was to provide information for an attack aircraft had not been considered.

Two modern fighter aircraft were scheduled leave Patrick Air Force Base a few minutes before T-0, giving them time to climb to forty thousand feet to monitor and follow the missile as it ascended toward orbit. They would be in communication with the AWACS continuously. Their mission was to chase uninformed or unsuspecting aircraft away from the launch area. They were fully armed with air-to-air and heat-seeking missiles as well as twenty millimeter cannons.

———————————

Those on the ground in the Countdown Control Room were unaware of the tense drama being played high above, with the possible exception of General Mayfair. No glitches were encountered as the countdown doggedly moved forward. The built-in holds were unnecessary, as problems simply did not appear. Keyed up personnel breathed a sigh of relief each time a hold was passed without a countdown delay.

Each activity operated like a well-oiled machine, all charged with some aspect of the complicated countdown. T-0 would be met on time.

As the missile would lift skyward a thrill of anticipation would go through each person associated with the launch. Perhaps General Mayfair said it best as the countdown neared T-0, saying, "This is more like a Countdown to Hell, God help us do the right thing!"

———————————

At the prescribed time everyone was cleared from the launch danger area by the Security and Safety organizations. No further access to the missile could be had unless a hold was called. Personal thoughts ran amok, imagining every conceivable problem that could arise and contrary to expectations, nothing went amiss. T-0 was scheduled for 6:45 A.M., only fifteen minutes away when the Air Force AWACS airplane alerted ground controllers of the suspicious actions of their Russian counterpart and that a Russian fighter aircraft was orbiting some 40 miles east of the Cape.

Two additional Air Force fighter aircraft were sortied from Patrick Air Force Base and rapidly climbed, with after burners roaring, to thirty five thousand feet, climbing eastward toward the Russian fighter.

The countdown clock approached T-3 minutes and the missile destruct system was armed, producing green "go" lights on the Safety Console allowing the Safety Monitor to depress his OK to Launch switch, the last deterrent to launch. The Test Director activated his Launch Enable switch, causing the Launch computer to take over the terminal countdown activities occurring too fast for them to done by human actions.

Walt had positioned himself at the Impact Convoy position, embodying specially trained people and equipment to take action in the dreaded event that the missile fell back to earth shortly after launch, or if the Range Safety Officer sent the destruct signal, if the missile veered off course, creating a volatile situation on the Cape.

Walt was in communication with Jack, stationed at Patrick Air Force Base and received a radio transmission about the dispatch of the two fighters toward the east. The Cape Superintendent of Range Operations, known as the SRO, was also in contact with the Impact Convoy Commander and he was able to apprise Walt of the Air Force actions as they occurred.

It was hard to believe there were so many different activities under way simultaneously, as lift-off of the missile occurred. A monstrous blast of fire erupted at he base of the vehicle at ignition, the core engines ignited and three of the strap on rockets, SRM's also ignited, the stupendous gout of flame shot through the flame bucket with a huge roar, smoke and fire streaking past the base of the launch pedestal and down the spillway. Tons of water deluged the area in and around the pedestal and umbilical tower. Similarly the various facilities within the complex were sprayed with water, precluding them erupting in fire as the missile left the complex. Visibility at the complex was temporarily obliterated by smoke and fire, water continuing to pour over everything for several minutes before being shut down.

The launch was a thing of beauty, the huge missile, well over one hundred twenty feet tall, gracefully arcing upward and away from its earthbound confines, toward the early morning blue sky, its noise deafening, even discernable miles away in nearby communities.

Shortly after the missile left the complex a spotter in the AWACS plane screamed out in alarm, "Missile launch, missile from MIG Fighter." The crew reacted immediately by sending jamming signals on the same frequency as the Russian monitor aircraft had used to illuminate the launched American vehicle as it rose in the morning air.

The air-to-air missile launched by the Russian fighter lost track and pitched forward slightly, as its propellant drove it onward toward the Cape. It unerringly seemed to target the precise location of the Safety Impact Convoy, unknown to those on the ground. Its high speed traverse was quickly picked up by the AWACS plane, whose controller immediately alerted the SRO of the incoming missile headed to the Cape. There was no way of determining precisely where the Russian rocket would land. It was headed directly for the Cape. The SRO passed the incoming message to the Impact Convoy Commander, who in turn called out on his bullhorn, "Alert, alert, all personnel immediately take cover under a vehicle, incoming missile."

There was mad scramble as people dove to get under cover, Walt looked to the Pad Safety Impact Convoy Commander to see what he was going to do. The shrill scream of the small rocket could be heard as it sliced earthward, directly at he Convoy Commander's vehicle. The Commander was just too slow to get under his vehicle, Walt noted as he tried to scramble under the passenger side of the truck. The rocket struck the driver's side of the truck exploding with a huge blast as it hit. The Impact Convoy Safety man was torn apart by the explosion. Walt was struck with several fragments and knocked unconscious, sustaining severe wounds. His bright yellow coveralls were turned a brilliant crimson in several places from blood spouting from his mangled body.

The Safety man was killed instantly and it looked as though Walt was near death. The Impact Convoy had in its makeup, medical technicians, who rushed to the Command Vehicle and seeing he could do nothing for the Safety man, turned to Walt with a shocked expression. "Jesus Christ," he exclaimed, then shouting to his crew, "Bring the ambulance and my kit. Hurry, hurry it up."

The Convoy Commander's assistant took charge and ordered Security police, also a part of the Convoy, to set up a perimeter and keep non-essential people away. Fortunately most were still so frightened at the explosion they were in a state of shock. Only by training and experience were the Safety and Medical men quick to respond.

The Medical Tech was able to staunch the flow of blood from most of Walt's wounds, but he was still unconscious and his breathing was very shallow. The Impact Convoy Assistant Commander quickly organized the area, calling for Explosive Ordnance Disposal to verify whether the small rocket presented any further hazard. Once it exploded there was no further danger, except in handling the residue. The EOD men picked up what debris they could, knowing it would be needed for the after-action report. The Senior Master Sergeant in charge noted the Russian markings on the bent casing and placed all the remaining debris in a box.

Walt was placed on a stretcher, loaded into the ambulance, which immediately departed for the Cape Canaveral Hospital in Cocoa Beach, the nearest hospital. The hospital was advised by cell phone of the incoming injured patient and was ready to react when the ambulance arrived. The hospital Trauma Team did their best to save Walt, but were unsure of whether their ministrations would be enough to keep him alive.

General Mayfair had been made aware of the terrible accident, but concerned as he was, there was a greater concern over what was happening to his precious spacecraft. The AWACS plane tracked the Russian fighter as it turned toward the Cape, and which was able to launch a heat-seeking missile at the now fast-rising launch vehicle as it thundered toward space. The immense trailing flame a very good target for the heat-seeker.

Both American fighter jets were now in close proximity to the Russian jet as it released its heat-seeking bird at the thundering launch vehicle. The strap-on SRM's had done their job and had fallen away from the core. The missile was about to stage, the first stage would separate form the second stage and it would immediately ignite. The resultant diminishing of the first stage trailing flame and ignition of stage two apparently created a hesitation in the computer of the heat-seeker long enough for a slight deviation in its track and allowing the American fighter to launch hits own heat-seeking rocket at the Russian rocket. The second U.S. fighter also fired another similar heat-seeker toward the Russian rocket almost simultaneously. The two American rockets converged on the little Russian rocket which exploded in a bright glow, destroying it one short mile before it could hit the launch vehicle. The number one Air Force fighter pilot reported, "Patrick Base, target missile destroyed, our bird is flying high, returning to Base."

Of the four American aircraft, one had fired a rocket at the Russian fighter as he launched his heat seeker, he quickly turned east, acquiring lock on the Russian fighter and fired its second rocket at it. Chaff could been as it sprayed from the fighter to no avail, the American rocket struck the Russian fighter, as it desperately tried to escape, creating a large fireball. Ground stations expressed concern whether the Absolute missile was under attack again. Their fears were allayed as they became aware of staging, as the second stage finished its task. The Transtage would now carry it on into its elliptical orbit and separate. After its coast period the spacecraft boost motor would perform its function and complete the spacecraft's final circular orbit.

Though there was some jubilation at the successful launch, it would be several hours before the spacecraft would be in final orbit.

Once orbital altitude was reached, the Transtage would separate and the long coast period would follow until the exact instant the payload boost motor would fire, placing the spacecraft in final circular orbit.

Doctor Bowman and General Mayfair waited for word that the final function had occurred. There was nervous jocularity between them as they waited.

Several hours passed when the speaker at the Launch Directors console crackled and a clear voice announced, "The bird is now in orbit. Doctor Bowman, please advise of your test requirements to validate operational capability. Spacecraft monitor standing by."

"Please monitor the spacecraft and perform the preliminary function tests," replied Doctor Bowman, "Upon completion we will allow it to remain in nominal orbit for 24 hours before we do the system test," referring to actual firing of the destructor beam.

Turning to General Mayfair he said, "Billy, let's go take a break until tomorrow!"

CHAPTER 23

JACK AND NAT ARRIVED AT the hospital parking area at the same time, both rushing in to the reception desk to inquire about Walt.

The receptionist inquired of them, "Are you family members?"

Jack looked as though he was about to tear the desk apart, replied in a nearly civilized tone, "No, we're not family, he has no family here. He is the head of the group responsible for the launching of the missile that you probably saw on TV a few minutes ago, and we are the closest thing to family he has. If you decide we cannot be told how he is doing, or be near him you'd better go find the chief of this hospital .....!"

At that moment a tall gray haired man came up and inquired, "What's the trouble, Emily?'

She merely pointed to Jack and replied, "Doctor Jones, these people are inquiring about the trauma case just brought in from the Cape."

The doctor faced Jack and asked, "What is your relationship to our patient?"

"We are the closest thing to family he has here, we work for him. He is the man responsible for that spacecraft just launched."

"Can you tell us his name and what happened. Oh I'm sorry, I am Doctor Ed Jones, Chief of Surgery for the hospital. We have nothing on him for identification, other than the name on what's left of the coveralls he was wearing, 'Crawford'. Can you tell us more?"

"Certainly," said Nat, "His name is Walter Crawford, he is forty years old and is in peak health, he is working for Major General Billy Mayfair at Patrick Air Force Base, he has family in Arkansas, I shall communicate with them when I get back to Patrick. Now can somebody please tell us how he is, he was unconscious the last word we had. Is he going to die?" tears welling up and streaming down her cheeks.

Doctor Jones told them, "He is in surgery now and in very serious condition, he has lost a lot of blood, he sustained multiple fragment wounds and it is much too early to say if he will survive, but we will do everything we can to bring him through this."

Jack stepped forward and asked, "Can we stand by when he goes to recovery?"

"I'll arrange for you to be near the nurse's station and if the situation permits, we will let you see him through the window to his bed after we stabilize him," Doctor Jones advised them, then added, "If we can stabilize him."

Jack asked, "Where can we wait? We will have a person here around the clock, if possible."

The doctor led them to an elevator and they rose to the surgical level. He took them to the nurse's station, and advised the Chief Nurse of the circumstances surrounding

Walt's injuries. She looked at them with concern and commented, "Are you aware how seriously he was hurt?"

Doctor Jones told her, "Karen, they represent family, they will have a person here continuously. Please arrange some sort of accommodation for them and see to it they are kept informed of any changes. This is Jack Johnson and Natalie Morse, they are his employees, consider them and the people they send to relieve them as family." Then turning to Jack and Nat he introduced them to Karen Meisner, Surgical Chief Nurse, saying, "Karen will try to keep you informed, but please bear in mind we do have other patients here, she's a busy person."

Nat stepped forward, her cheeks still showing the tears she had shed and said, "We will be grateful for whatever you can do. We will try to stay out of your way."

Karen softened her demeanor, recognizing Nat's concern and said, "Come with me and I'll fix you a spot in our nurse's office."

The office was not large, but did have two spare chairs that Jack and Nat sank in to appreciatively.

"I'll see if there is anything I can pass on to you about his present condition. I'll be back in few minutes, but you must realize Mr. Crawford has suffered very severe lacerations, wounds that are critical." She left, her crisp white uniform leaving a soft swishing sound as she exited She was gone for nearly twenty minutes when she suddenly swept in to the nursing office. She sat at her desk, trying to gather herself to tell these people of the poor outlook for Walt. Finally she turned, looking back and forth between them, and spoke, "Your man's condition is very serious. The surgical team has removed a number of fragments from him. He has lost a lot of blood, luckily we were

261

able to match his blood type and have given him a blood transfusion, which helped significantly. Unfortunately, he still has a major wound in his abdominal area, a piece of fragment is still in there and must come out if he is to survive. The fragments taken out were contaminated with burned explosive residue, as is the remaining piece inside him. "

"Oh God, Jack, what will we do if we lose him?" Nat almost wailed.

"Come on Nat, get a hold of yourself, he is strong as an ox, he is going to make it," Jack replied without conviction.

A half hour later the nurse came to the office and spoke to Jack and Nat saying. "I just checked, the surgeon told me Mr. Crawford is barely holding his own. It will be a good twenty four hours before we will know if he is going to make it, but the surgery is complete and the best we can do now is to wait." Under her breath she thought, 'and pray for him.'

Some twenty minutes later the nurse's phone chimed softly and she promptly picked it up saying, "Meisner here". She turned to Nat and Jack and said, "If you would like to see him come with me."

They stood and followed her to a glass walled room a short distance from the Nurse's Station. She motioned for them to stand at the window as she entered and opened the curtain.

Walt was lying on a white bed with ceiling lights brightly illuminating his prone figure. He had several tubes coming from his body as well as one from his mouth. An oxygen tube was fitted to his nostrils, his face was pallid, his eyes closed. There was an IV attached to his arm, its box emitting gentle beeps. A TV camera was aimed at him transmitting a picture to the nurse's station where a row of monitors recorded data about his condition.

Jack clenched his fists muttering, "Come on Walt, hang in there, you've got to make it!"

Nat was shocked at his appearance, saying, "Oh my God," Then, "Lord, please don't take him, we all need him, please......," Once again tears streaming down her face.

Jack put his arms around her as she buried her face in his shoulder. He awkwardly patted her back, giving her a hug and saying softly, "He's strong, he will get through this. We need to talk to the rest of the Team, I'm sure they are all wondering about him."

"Jack will you please call them, I don't think I can handle it right now."

"Sure, I'll go down stairs and bring them up to date." He told the nurse he would be back after he called Patrick AF Base. In the lobby he called the Team number at the Ops Center, with Connie answering on the first ring. He quickly told her the situation and promised he would let them know if anything changed.

When he returned to the recovery area Nurse Karen suggested he make up a list of people who would be coming to stand by, saying it would be helpful to have just one at a time. Recognizing that having more than one at a time was an imposition, he sat down with Nat to prepare a roster of Team members and hours they would be on station. Nat indicated she would take the first shift and suggested Jack get some rest before he scheduled himself to be there. Recognizing her logic he completed the list giving it to Karen, the nurse, and tucked a copy in his pocket.

The entire Team was assembled in the Ops Center at the Team desk awaiting Jack's arrival. After he had told them of what details he had, he then set up the schedule showing the time each member was to be at the hospital recovery room. It was a somber group that briefed General Mayfair. He thanked them and told them the spacecraft was now 'on orbit' and would perform a test firing after assurance that it was 'healthy'. He expressed his concern and asked to be kept informed of any change in Walt's condition.

Once launched, control of the Spacecraft was transferred to a special facility set up for that express purpose in one of the hangers at the Industrial Area of Cape Canaveral Air Force Station. General Mayfair sat at a special seat next to Dr. Bowman observing the deliberate tests being performed on the spacecraft.

He spoke to Dr. Bowman, "With your permission sir, may we have a member of Walt's Team present to observe these tests?"

"Of course," was the quick reply.

Jack had returned from the hospital and had told each member of the Team when to be at the hospital. He told each person individually of Walt's condition and poor prognosis, all were shaken. They were told that Nat would act as interim chief, pending Walt's recovery. In the meantime Nat had been relieved at the hospital and dozed fitfully on the cot near the Team desk at the Patrick Ops Center.

General Mayfair reluctantly awakened her with his call to tell her he was going to the hospital to see whether any assistance was needed that the Air Force could provide.

Upon arrival he sought out the Surgical Chief and advised Dr. Jones whatever was needed could be gotten within hours of the request, no matter what the request. The doctor told him the surgery was complete and the recovery was dependent upon Walt. He cautioned against too much optimism, and that there was little to be done, except to wait.

Aware that the Team would keep him apprised of Walt's status, the General reluctantly left Dr. Jones to resume his function as responsible person for the Spacecraft. He instructed his driver to return to the Cape Industrial Area to park in the reserved place for him at the Hangar Control Room.

Upon entering he gave no indication of his concern for Walt, rather he greeted the Spacecraft Controller with, "Well how's our bird doing so far?"

"Right on schedule," the Lieutenant Colonel replied. "We still have quite a few checks to complete, but so far she checks out fine," then adding, "Sir it's going to be a bit before we can do the firing test, probably several hours at least. Would you like me to call you when it gets a little closer?"

"How many hours?" queried the General.

"Best guess, sir, would be five or six at least. It might be a good time for your order to notify all agencies to stay clear of our bird."

"I do know the time line Colonel, but thank you for the reminder," responded General Mayfair. He turned to leave saying, "Call me immediately if anything unusual crops up."

"My apologies, sir, I will do as you expect," the blushing Colonel replied as he stood.

The General entered his sedan and picked up his radio transmitter microphone. As he headed south he entered a special code and when his speaker crackled to life he spoke, "Transmit message number one, please."

"Roger, Willco," was the quick rejoinder."

The message was cryptic and sent to every nation having a spacecraft in orbit. It read, "The United States of America has launched a spacecraft into a variable orbit above the earth with a capability for destroying anything coming near it. You may track it, but should you cause anything to approach it, that device will be summarily destroyed. All questions may be referred to our State Department. End of message".

General Mayfair thought to himself, 'Perhaps a bit premature, but every nation involved has now been put on notice'.

Upon arriving at the Ops Center he looked to the Fixit Desk inquiringly, Joe, who was on duty, shook his head, understanding that the General was inquiring about Walt. Joe spoke aloud saying, "Kim is at the hospital now sir, he'll pass any news to us as quickly as he gets it".

"You have my quarters number, don't you?" he queried, then, "No matter what the hour call me if anything changes."

"Yes sir."

At that moment the General's phone jangled and he snatched up the receiver before the ring had faded away, "Mayfair here, he said, then "Roger, understand."

He spoke to Joe, "Please have a Team member on station at the Spacecraft Control Facility for the oncoming hours to monitor its activities. You have my authority to discharge the beam at anything that comes within 1000 miles of it. That decision will be a joint one between you and the Air Force officer on duty, unless I am present. A target craft has been released in the mid-Atlantic which will serve for test firing. I expect to be present at that time. However, if I am not present the test will be fired on schedule, understood?"

A chorus of, "Yes sir," was the prompt reply.

The harried General departed to his quarters for a brief respite.

After the General had left Jack said, "We are going to have a helluva time making that schedule, we just don't have enough bodies."

Bobby reluctantly spoke, "I am not qualified to be on that assignment so why can't I just stay at the hospital and keep track of Walt's condition? That way there would be enough of you guys to do as the General says."

As one they turned to Bobby with the realization that this was no ordinary kid, he had grasped the situation and had a viable solution.

Joe spoke first saying, "Bobby you are really something else, here we are trying to figure out how to do the job, and you already have a good answer." Joe went on, "Since I just came on, why don't I take the first shift at the Spacecraft Control Center and we can get the Ops Center here to cover our desk."

"Good," said Jack, "We'll use the same schedule that Nat set up for the hospital, everybody knows when they are on, all we need are a list of phone numbers for Bobby and we're set."

Then to Bobby, "You do know where the hospital is, don't you?"

Laughingly Bobby replied, "Sure do, been there a few times since I was born there."

Jack grimaced, saying, "You got me! How about heading there now and seeing if they will let you be our rep for the next day or so."

"I know lots of the people there and if they accept me as a Fixit member, I should be OK," he replied.

"I'll let that Chief Nurse know you are one of us and you should have no problem, " Jack said. Bobby departed using one of the Fixit SUV's.

Bobby relieved Kim at the hospital, passing on that Joe would take the first shift at the hanger and that Kim would relieve him per the schedule at the Hanger Control Facility at the Cape.

After Bobby checked in at the hospital he was recognized by the Chief Nurse who gave him a hug upon his arrival at the surgical nurse's station. "They called me and said you would be coming, but I sure didn't know you had grown up so much. Jack said you were part of their group and spoke very highly of you."

"Thanks," he replied, "I've only been with them for a few days, but I hope it becomes permanent."

Karen took him to the recovery room where he saw Walt's still figure and returned him to the her office where he could wait.

Bobby asked in a subdued tone, "Will he be OK?"

Karen told him it was too soon to know, but that as soon as she knew anything she would tell him.

He sat back to wait.

CHAPTER 24

AFTER COMPLETION OF WALT'S SURGERY, the doctor said, "He has suffered terrible trauma, there is little hope he will survive."

Seven small fragments had been removed, two of which were quite serious, another major fragment removed from his lower abdomen presented the gravest concern, it had grazed his colon, leaving several marks of near penetration, albeit no actual puncture. The cuts caused by the fragment could rupture without warning, causing massive hemorrhaging and probable loss of his life. However, Walt had been carefully sedated to a level that would limit his movement, precluding strain on his colon.

Bobby kept a careful log of actions taken in the care of Walt and kept the Team informed of the small amount of progress he made.

As was done for the test firing in the Pacific, a cryptic message was broadcast by the Sate Department announcing that a test firing was to be performed in the open waters of the Atlantic on 14 June. All questions were summarily turned away.

The Hanger Control Room was a beehive of activity, large screens depicted the status of the spacecraft and a row of consoles facing the monitors were manned by both uniformed and civilian scientists and engineers.

Test after test identified the high flying spacecraft was functioning perfectly. One console was dedicated to tracking foreign spacecraft. Its primary mission was to determine if anything approached within 1330 kilometers, about 1000 miles. One of the large screen monitors depicted the spacecraft location with red circle around it showing a line which nothing was to penetrate.

There were many other orbiting spacecraft and bits of space junk that required tracking by various agencies. Even the Multinational Space Station was tracked, though it was in an entirely different orbit, well away from the track of Absolute. The Hanger Control Room kept tabs on various orbiting craft on a similar path to that of Absolute by receiving inputs from these other agencies.

In order to maintain maximum efficiency and alertness the officers watching the screens were changed every two hours. In addition the senior Officer in Charge periodically observed the Absolute screen as well as the other screens. Known missile launch sites were displayed on a screen with another officer watching it carefully.

The entire room was tense awaiting some foreign action, hoping it would not happen but fearing it would.

As General Mayfair sat down at his console he perused each of the screens and asked, "Anything unusual?" of the concerned senior officer seated next to him.

"Yes sir, a ground station in Japan is showing activity that looks like launch preps," he responded, adding, "We are watching it pretty closely", then, "Damn, launch away from Japan," he called out loudly.

Doctor Bowman spoke, "Quickly now, check the trajectory."

The tracking officer immediately replied, "On an easterly azimuth, it's homing on our bird."

"This may be our test firing", said the General, "Lock on and fire if it comes within a thousand miles".

A few minutes later the tracking officer reported, "It's on course to hit us", and added, "We have lock on their craft."

The General ordered, "Set max power to fire!"

The officer, a young Air Force Captain responded, "Roger sir, max power set, ready to fire."

Immediately the General said, "Fire, Fire, Fire!"

The absolute spacecraft floated serenely along its path when suddenly a brief flash of light emanated from it, flashing down the beam the ascending missile used to lock on the craft, seconds later there was a stupendous explosion as the Japanese missile was blasted to pieces, albeit the missile was well beyond one thousand miles away.

The Japanese Envoy called the U. S. State Department from their Embassy and in sputtering English complained that a test firing of theirs had been aborted by the Americans shooting it down. The State Department responded in calculated terms saying no American missile had been launched anywhere and that the Japanese Envoy must be in error.

As a matter of course the State Department advised the Air Force Chief of Staff of the call the Japanese had made and that response was passed on to General Mayfair.

General Mayfair smiled in satisfaction, saying, "Well done," adding, "I do believe we should proceed with our test firing on the Atlantic, let's see if we get a rise out of anyone."

That test was carried out with deliberation with the same kind of results seen in the Pacific. This caused a chorus of inquiries as to what happened, when will more information be made available.

———————

The Secretary of Defense called the Joint Chiefs of Staff together and prepared a briefing for presentation to the President. It was a carefully worded document touching upon the design background, the many tests, the B-52 test and recounted the various problems associated with program development. Included was a suggested announcement to the world, stating in the strongest possible words, that the United States of America would no longer tolerate terrorism or warlike actions by any nation or entity. Violation would result in destruction of the offender. There would be no excuses accepted. Should any nation or group attempt to destroy the United

States satellite, retaliation would be swift and sure. The Joint Chiefs accompanied the Secretary of Defense as the briefing was presented to the President. Only the President and his Staff were present.

Following the briefing some members of the President's Staff were concerned over the political ramifications of playing this 'God Father' role for America. After much discussion the primary problem arose as to whom would order these retaliatory strikes.

It was determined that the Secretary of Defense would authorize only specially trained senior officers to order retaliatory strikes against an enemy. A group of ten Colonels were selected from the various services, who had combat experience, and were ordered to be trained and certified by Major General B. Mayfair. These ten would permit continuous monitoring around the clock and would be under the direction of General Mayfair.

There were officers from the Air Force, the Army, the Navy, the Coast Guard and the Marine Corps, they were assigned a tour of duty for one year They would be permitted to volunteer to serve beyond the one year tour of duty, otherwise ten officers, or however many were required would be assigned this duty. The system worked well, allowing six officers to perform shifts of fours each, adding one permitted them to be on a different shift each day. Three more officers were available to relieve others as needed.

General Mayfair called upon the Fixit Team to assist in training these officers. Nat, Jack, Joe and Kim were utilized in this role as well as his senior staff. Connie and Bobby kept their focus on Fixit matters and tracked Walt's slow recovery progress.

CHAPTER 25

DOCTOR JONES WAS FINISHING UP his rounds when he chose to see Walt. He listened to Walt's shallow breathing and shook his head, thinking 'I doubt he will last another twenty four hours.' As he left the Intensive Care room he saw Bobby watching closely.

"You won't let him die will you doctor?" Bobby was close to tears as he spoke to the doctor.

"Bobby, you know we are doing everything we can for him," the doctor replied, "He is in God's hands now."

Bobby morosely walked to the viewing window to Walt's room and stood silently staring at Walt's motionless body. He gasped and shouted loudly, "He moved, he moved!"

Doctor Jones quickly turned around to reexamine Walt. His breathing was still shallow, but perceptibly better. He shone a light into Walt's eyes and noted the constriction of the pupil and expansion as he removed the light. Walt offered slight resistance as he moved Walt's head and arms.

"I'll be damned, he's made a slight turn for the better," he exclaimed, and called for the nurse.

Karen Meisner jumped from her chair and ran to the cubicle to respond. Doctor Jones told her to check and verify his findings. She listened to his heart with her stethoscope and smiled, turning to Bobby's face at the window and nodded. She repeated the doctor's checks with the same results. She then verified each of the tubes from his body were securely in place and came out of the room.

"Looks like he might make it after all," the doctor said to the nurse as he departed. She logged hers and the doctor's findings on a log, feeling pleased.

"Bobby you must not get too excited that he moved, he is a long way from being out of the woods yet. His breathing is not quite so labored and his heart sounds a little better," she told him. It might be OK to tell the rest of the folks that he is slightly improved, but he still has a long way to go."

Bobby called Connie at the Team desk and told her, "Connie he moved, Karen says he is slightly improved, but not out of the woods. She said I could tell you, but I know he is going to make it now!"

Walt slowly improved from day to day and awoke on the fourth day to see Bobby's grinning face at the window. He had turned his head a little and smiled slightly in return. Bobby spent most of his waking hours at the hospital, keeping tabs on Walt. It was a happy day when he was moved to a recovery room, a step upward from the glassed cubicle he had occupied. After a week he was again moved, this time to a regular patient room.

At this point he was started on rehabilitation, a slow process to regain his ability to walk. He labored through the exercises designed to teach him to walk again. When he reached the point of using a walker for a few minutes at a time, he told the doctor, "I think I am about ready to leave."

"Not just yet," Doctor Jones told him. You will be transferred to a rehabilitation hospital to complete your recovery," and then added, "You may not ever be able to do as you did in the past."

"Just watch," was Walt's rejoinder.

———————————

Lieutenant General Mayfair, he had been promoted as a consequence of his stewardship of the Absolute Program, reluctantly told Nat that the support of the Fixit Team would terminate at the end of the week, allowing time for them to prepare for their departure. Nat wrote the final check for the motel bill and bid the staff a fond farewell, Marie sobbed at their leaving.

The entire Team trooped into Walt's room at the rehab hospital finding him in the process of packing his meager possessions into a plastic bag.

"Walt, have you been released from here? Are you sure you can handle this?"

"They balked a bit but, I am going to leave this lovely place and get back with my Team!" He showed them a sheaf of papers adding, "I've got to say goodbye to General Mayfair before we leave." At Walt's insistence they assembled at the Base Ops Center, congratulating the General and bidding each of the Center men a fond goodbye.

The convoy of Fixit vehicles and trailers headed North on I-95 on their way to Washington. The Team members were quiet, each involved in their memories of the task just completed, wondering what lay ahead.

END

ABOUT THE AUTHOR

THE AUTHOR IS AN 84 year old man (born in April 1922) with a broad spectrum of experiences seldom seen, regardless of age. George Meyer was the product of a service family, his father spent most of his adult life in the Coast Guard and the Navy. As a consequence Meyer was often left to his own devices, he sometimes was not what people would refer to as a model young man.

He claims to have lost his virginity at the tender age of 14, the girl a neighborhood friend. He seldom speaks of subsequent conquests except to say he truly enjoyed female company, until he met his wife to be in 1946. Marge was the love of his life, they were married for 55 years, 3 months, and 2 days, but she is now deceased.

He bought his first car at the age of 14, unrelated to his loss of virginity, a 1927 Buick. The left rear wheel was missing, but presented no problem, he discovered one that would fit, and "borrowed" it, on a permanent basis. The car was not registered, nor was there a license plate or driver license.

Surprisingly when he attended a New York Vocational high school, he turned out to be quite talented as an artist. He was skilled in the use of an air brush, unfortunately once removing a girl's bathing suit from a photograph with the air brush and printed several copies. He actually graduated after his father had been transferred to a new city and he returned to New York City to take the state

Regents exams. He graduated in the upper 20% of his class.

At age twenty he enlisted in the Army and was again something of a problem, repairing equipment which he should not have touched. Once, he shot at the Sergeant of the Guard, who was just testing alertness of the guards on post. He was promoted to Corporal and sent to Officer Candidate School. Again he excelled, graduating in the top 10% of his class and was commissioned a second lieutenant. Overseas duty followed, where he became a parachutist and then participated in the assault on Normandy on D+2 ½. He distinguished himself a number of times, earning the Silver Star, the Bronze Star, three Purple Hearts and numerous other awards. WWII was a shocking experience.

After the war, he completed varied tours of service, during which he attended the University of Maryland overseas branch in Okinawa, earning a bachelor's degree in Military Science. He served overseas more than 11 years, both Europe, Korea and the Far East and many places in the U.S., even learning Hungarian at the Army Language School, with subsequent classified assignments and finally retiring with 20 years of service as a Lieutenant Colonel, his last duty station Fort Wadsworth, in New York City.

He worked at Cape Canaveral for 13 years in the launch business, retiring from Pan Am World Services Division, then going on to serve in Air Force Civil Service for another 13 years still launching missiles at the Cape. He retired again as a GS-14 and then worked for Research Triangle Institute as a Senior Research Engineer until he had a major stroke and was forced to retire again. He also did quite a bit of consulting work over the years.

He now lives in a senior retirement community in Melbourne, Florida, where he served as Association President for 2 ½ years. His most recent endeavor has been to write his fourth book, the first 2 for the military, a special manual for RTI and another effort, a work of fiction regarding our Nations space efforts.

His last endeavor was to write his autobiography, a surprisingly different look at life and quite entertaining.

Printed in the United States
91046LV00001B/40-48/A